Bear and Girl

A Story of Hope,
Friendship,
and Strength

James Peter Behr

This book is dedicated to Emmy, whose strength, resilience, intelligence, and compassion inspired me, and whose friendship brings me joy.

Contents

Foreword: Girl is Real

These stories were written for a real person, whom I call "Girl." She was an abused woman who has since left her ex-husband and is now creating the life she was cheated out of for so many years. These stories were written to help her sleep at night.

I am publishing them in hopes that they might help you as well. They are very much bedtime stories, and are even better read aloud.

I first met Girl online on a writer's website. We started chatting, and to my horror I realized that she was being abused by her husband. After consulting a friend of mine who had been in an abusive relationship, I did what I could to support her quest to break free and live a safe, happy life, mostly by being a supportive listener. As I had no idea who she was or where she lived, and only communicated with her online, there seemed little I could do. And yet, over time, she confided in me, and our relationship grew.

She would often go to bed frightened, crying, and in pain after being abused. To try to divert her and in an attempt to soothe her and help her sleep, I started making up stories about a talking polar bear who came to the aid of an abused woman. This entire series of stories grew from there. I shared some of them with other people, including my formerly-abused friend who had advised me on how to help. My other friends liked the stories and encouraged me to finish the story arc, which is how this book came to be.

Much of the abuse that happened to the Girl in the story happened to the real Girl. I've used those details with her permission. My hope is that these stories may be of some comfort to others who are in distress, and need a Bear to help get them through the night. May they find the strength and determination to find their way into a happier, safer, more peaceful life.

– James Peter Behr

Chapter 1: The Bear and the Girl

Bear yawned, stretched on the rag rug, then walked out onto the porch and into the sunlight. He decided it was about time to patrol his territory, marking it out and making sure other carnivores weren't taking liberties. That Mama brown bear seemed to be trying to nudge her boundaries over onto his, but he guessed that was because she had two littlies to look after now.

So Bear started ambling along, enjoying the day, checking that his markings were still fresh, and that the local fauna were suitably deferential. It was a lovely day, and he was relishing it – except for the usual pit, the loneliness that he carried with him always. That.

He sighed, then turned his mind back to the present.

After some time, which included some hunting for food, he came to the human road and stopped, as he usually did, to look up and down it. He did that partially to see if there was any traffic to worry about – even a ten-foot-tall, 1500-pound polar bear would get beat up if he was hit by an SUV – but also on the off-chance that he might recognize someone driving by.

Yet, as was usually the case, the road was devoid of traffic. And even when he had seen a vehicle driving by, he had never recognized anyone in them. Somehow, hope was harder to take than despair. He had lived solely with despair at first, and that had been hard. But now, for no accountable reason, he found himself living with hope, and sometimes it almost broke him.

Sighing again because there were no vehicles in sight nor any sound of one, he started to amble across the road, aiming to climb the ridge to one of his favorite lookouts.

He was halfway across when he heard a low groan. He stopped, trying to locate it, but was unable to do so. He swiveled his head back and forth, trying to find the source. It had been a human voice, a woman's. Although he stood still, he heard nothing.

He was sure he hadn't imagined it. He did imagine things sometimes, but not sounds, not moans like that. He turned and paced slowly up one side of the road for thirty or forty feet, heading north, looking off the road into the steep ditch on the side, but saw nothing.

He turned about, walked to the other side, and paced back southwards, looking in the other ditch, planning on going as far the other way.

He smelled her before he saw her and eventually found her far off the highway, in the ditch, and hidden by grasses that had grown up since the Spring mowing. Being careful of the slippery, sloping verge, he stalked, pace by pace, to where he smelled her, and finally caught sight of her.

She was lying as if thrown from a great height, arms and legs akimbo, head tossed to one side. Her eyes were closed.

He padded quickly to her side and pressed his ear to her torso, listening to her heartbeat. It was fast, but steady. She was dressed warmly – but not warmly enough for overnight in the Canadian Rockies.

He sat, and pulled her gently towards him, then gathered her in his arms and lifted her up, clambering back up the verge onto the road. He could walk upright if necessary, but walking on four legs in this body was far more efficient. He shifted her onto his back and dropped his forepaws down, settled her weight carefully across his shoulders, then started to walk slowly back towards his cabin on four paws.

He had gone about fifty feet into the woods when he heard a vehicle approaching. Whoever it was, they were driving slowly north along the road. He wondered if they were looking for her and almost went back to see if they were there to help her.

Yet, the thought of interacting with humans made him feel tired. He had tried it, and it almost never worked out well. It raised too many questions, some of which he couldn't answer, and some of which he didn't want to answer. Worse, sometimes the humans came back and tried to capture him. He imagined they wanted to sell him to some kind of freak show as a talking bear.

So, although he paused and considered going back, he decided not to. At least, not yet. He could always contrive to get the girl back to her people through Riley, his only human contact. But later.

For now, he turned and headed back to the cabin.

When he got there, he opened the door, walked in, and gently set the Girl down on the rag rug in front of the fireplace. Now, for the first time, he took a good look at her.

She was older, perhaps in her 50s or 60s, but still trim and attractive. She had bruises on her face and neck, her clothing was torn in places, and her expression looked as if she was...terrified.

Bear huffed, as if thinking, then shrugged, removed her boots, then gently lifted her in his arms, carried her into the bedroom, and laid her on the bed, drawing the sheet and blanket over her. He sat back on his haunches, shook his head, and said, "Poor kid. I wonder what happened to you?"

He returned to the great room, built up the fire, then settled down in front of it and watched the flames leap until his eyes closed and his breathing was smooth and even.

Sometime later, the Girl woke, sat up, and carefully shook her head. It hurt, which didn't surprise her. Confused as to where she was, she got gingerly out of bed, left the bedroom, and limped around, looking for a bathroom. She found it in the expected place – at the end of the hall – finished up, then started to hobble slowly back to the bedroom.

She got partway there, then stopped when she was passing the great room. She stood staring into the room, still partially lit by the remnants of the fire. There, on the floor, was an enormous polar bear, sleeping. Its chest rose and fell as it breathed.

She stood there for a long time, mouth open, until finally, the Bear, sensing something, opened its eyes and looked at her without moving its head from the rug. She knew she should be scared. Polar bears are apex predators and have no qualms about eating humans when they can catch them, but for some reason, she was not afraid.

The Bear lifted his huge head, looked at her with startlingly blue eyes, then said, in a deep voice, "Get some rest, Girl. You look like you could use it. We'll talk in the morning." He lowered his head back to the rug, regarded her for a while, then closed his eyes and restarted his deep breathing.

The Girl was not sure whether she was dreaming or not, but searched her heart and felt no fear. Quite the contrary, she felt safe for the first time in as long as she could remember.

She limped back to the bedroom, climbed cautiously back to bed, pulled the covers up, and slept peacefully for the first time in years.

The next morning, when she woke, she lay in bed unmoving for a moment, wondering where she was and how she had gotten there. She sat up, gingerly, and felt the familiar bruises that would make her day painful, then looked around.

She was in a small bedroom of a rustic log cabin. There was a window with wavy glass, beyond which was an astonishing view of up-thrust craggy mountains, the Canadian Rockies, she guessed.

She turned back to the room. The floor was wood, apparently polished by long-use, and a single, simple, wooden chair. There was a painting in the room, brownish, with a small farmhouse off to the left, a river meandering by it, and the sun setting behind the barn. It seemed somehow sad.

Gingerly, she turned to get out of bed and winced. It seemed as if everything hurt, starting with her head. She slid her feet to the floor and cautiously stood up. At least the bottom of her feet didn't hurt!

She stood, then had to put one hand down to steady herself. Finally, she was able to stand and tried walking. She found as long as she didn't think about it too much, she could hobble her way forward.

She retraced the steps to the bathroom, made use of its facilities, including a clean towel hanging on the rail, then replaced it, opened the door, and with some trepidation, hobbled back to the entry of the great room.

It was empty, and the fire banked.

She noticed that the front door was open, so she walked very carefully over and looked outside.

There, seated on the porch floor, looking up at the mountains, was an enormous polar bear. She swallowed hard, then said, feeling foolish, "Goo...good morning, Bear."

His massive head swiveled towards her, and his mouth split in what she could only interpret as a grin. "Well, there you are! I was wondering if I'd picked up Sleeping Beauty! Good morning!"

She blinked and said, "So...I wasn't dreaming. You talk."

He nodded. "And so do you."

"Ho...how do you...I mean, why...uh..."

He nodded again. "It is a puzzle, isn't it? Now, how are you feeling this morning?"

She stared at him, then said, "Uh...I'm...I'm fine. Well, not really. I ache all over, especially my head."

"I'm not surprised. There's some aspirin in the medicine cabinet if I remember properly. Why don't you see if that helps?"

She looked at him, staring into those impossibly blue eyes, then said, apropos of nothing, "Don't polar bears have *brown* eyes?"

He nodded again. "Yes, they do." And fell silent.

She stood for a moment, waiting for an answer that didn't come, then shrugged, turned, and slowly hobbled back to the bathroom. She found the aspirin, took three with water from the cup that sat there, then hobbled back to the front door.

"Have a seat, pilgrim." The Bear nodded at a big, wooden rocking chair that looked as if it were left over, not from the last century, but from the century before that.

She gingerly lowered herself onto the rocking chair and found it surprisingly comfortable – which would account for why it had been preserved for so long. Without realizing it, she started rocking gently back and forth, her body finding comfort in the motion.

They sat silently for quite some time. The Bear seemed content to let the time flow around them, and the Girl was unsure what to say, or how to say it.

Finally, she said, "I...I owe you my thanks. You saved my life."

The Bear nodded again, "You're welcome."

She had been hoping he would say something more – anything – but when he didn't continue, she said, "Where did you find me? I don't remember anything about it."

He sighed, moved slightly, then settled down, and said, "I found you by the human road. You were well off the side, down almost into the ditch. You looked like a broken doll. I brought you back here and put you to bed. You didn't seem to be bleeding, and nothing appeared to be broken, so I thought sleep was the best thing for you."

The Bear hesitated, then said, "Shortly after I picked you up, a vehicle came cruising slowly north along the road, as if they were looking for something. I almost walked back to ask if you were theirs."

The Girl looked shocked, "No! I'm not! I'm trying to get away from him...from them!' She gulped, "Oh, thank God you didn't let them know where I was!"

The Bear gazed at her for some time. She found his gaze disconcerting, and turned away from it but said nothing more.

"If I were the prying kind, I'd guess you were trying to escape from an abusive husband. Fortunately, I'm not that kind of bear." And he chuckled deep in his chest.

She looked at him in astonishment. "How...do you know about these things? If it comes to that, how are you even talking?"

The Bear shrugged, then said, "Just naturally talented, I guess."

The Girl decided that if Bear didn't want to talk about it – which he clearly didn't – then she would be impolite at best, and more likely foolish to pursue the matter. She turned and looked out over the mountains.

"It's a gorgeous view."

"Thank you."

She looked at him, surprised.

He gave that deep chuckle again. "Family heirloom. The cabin, that is, not the mountains."

The Girl continued to rock back and forth, and found it easing her mind as well as her body. "Your family?" She made it more of an almost-question than a question-proper, as if not wanting to push it if he didn't wish to answer.

"Yes, you know those people who have to take you in, whether they want to or not? Them." He chuckled again.

"Oh."

After a while of contemplating the mountains, she cleared her throat and said, "Uh...I'm sorry to ask, but do you have any food? I didn't get to eat much yesterday." She looked down. "And I'm not sure when or how I'll be able to pay you back."

The Bear looked at her and gave her what she would later interpret as a gentle smile. "You already have, my dear lady, you already have."

He got up and ambled into the cabin. "Follow me."

He led her into the kitchen area of the great room, and hooked open the refrigerator. "Mostly fish and fruit in here, I'm afraid, but up there..." and he tossed his head towards a series of cupboards, "...you'll find canned and packaged goods. All kinds of things, including, I think, some oatmeal. And there's some brown sugar in an old peanut butter jar that's probably still good. Help yourself. I've already eaten."

And he padded slowly back to the porch.

She rummaged around and made herself a large bowl of oatmeal with brown sugar and canned peaches, some instant coffee lightened with some tinned evaporated milk. She flaked some of the fish – trout? – onto some slices of tinned bread, and put everything on a tray, then carried it out to the porch, setting it down carefully on the small table there.

"Can I get or make anything for you, Bear?" she asked. "I should have asked before, but I was so hungry I didn't think of it. Sorry."

Bear sniffed the coffee wistfully, then shook his head, "No, I'm good – but thank you for asking." He chuckled. "It's a nice thought, but the normal way that a human would feed a polar bear is...well, kind of final. For the human."

She had a big mouthful of oatmeal in her mouth, and almost spit-laughed it out but put her hand to her mouth, choking it down. "Don't *do* that!" she laughed, wiping the edges of her mouth and nose with the back of her hand after she had swallowed.

He sat, smiling at her for a time, then said, "You have a nice laugh."

She smiled back at him, "So do you – even if you have a nasty sense of humor!"

He got up, and said, "I'm going for a walk. Would you like to come?"

She consulted her body, then shook her head. "No, alas, I'm too beat up. I'll just stay here and enjoy your – your family heirloom."

He nodded acknowledgement, then loped across the meadow in front of the cabin and disappeared into the woods.

The Girl finished eating, put the tray aside, rocked steadily for a while, then gradually slowed, stopped, and was still. Her head lolled to one side. She slept.

When she woke up again, she was lying on an old, red leather sofa in the great room of the cabin with a soft, woolen blanket over her. She stretched, then winced, and saw the Bear snoring on the rug.

She lay there and watched him – and as before, he must have felt something, for he opened his eyes and looked at her.

"May I ask you a question?" she said.

"You just did."

She grimaced, "Okay, may I ask you two questions?"

"And...you have...again."

This time she snorted. "God! Would you believe it? A smart-ass Bear! Okay, may I ask you *four* questions?"

Bear shook his head, "No, that would be pushing things, don't you think?"

"But..." she started to say, then heard his deep chuckle. "*OH!* You can be so infuriating!"

The chuckle deepened into a laugh. "Go ahead. Ask."

"How is it you can talk, Bear?"

He stared at her for some time, then turned away and said, "Magic."

She snorted. "I don't believe in magic."

"Oh, good, but you believe in talking bears?"

She stopped. "I don't know...what to believe."

Bear sat up, and shifted his weight to his rear haunches. "Do you believe your own senses?"

"Yeesss..." she said cautiously.

"Then perhaps you have an explanation for how you are talking to a Bear that doesn't involve magic, or you being crazy?"

She flopped over onto her back, looked up at the rafters way above, and tried to think. She felt as if she might still be slightly concussed, but tried to focus. "Well..." she began.

"Uh-huh?" the Bear encouraged.

"Uh...genetic modification?"

"Okay."

"...enhanced cortical activity...vocal-chord replacement...um..." she trailed off.

"Have you ever heard of Clarke's Laws?" the Bear asked after she'd been silent for a while.

She turned to look at him. "No. You mean, like Clark Kent?"

The Bear shook his head, "No, like Arthur C. Clarke. *Sir* Arthur C. Clarke, in fact. Knighted by Queen Elizabeth for contributions to literature and science. Famous science and science fiction writer. Invented the concept of the communications satellite, among other things."

"Okay, I think I've heard of him."

The Bear shook his head, "Kids today." He sighed. "Well, Clarke is given credit for coining three laws, all of which are self-evidently true."

"Okay...", she said, waiting for the punchline.

"Clarke's Third Law is: 'A sufficiently advanced technology is indistinguishable from magic.'"

She looked up at the ceiling and repeated, "A sufficiently advanced...technology..."

She looked back at him, "Right. Right! Of course, it has to be! A telephone would be considered magic to, oh, I dunno, a Roman legionnaire, and a smartphone would be considered magic to the, um, the Wright Brothers! A sufficiently advanced..."

"Not sure about that last one. The Wright Brothers were pretty savvy dudes...as was their sister, by the way."

"Okay, I was just using that as an example, so pick whomever you want. I don't care."

"So...you would agree that magic exists?"

That stopped her, and she thought for a while. "No...not quite the way you mean it. Or I mean it. Or...whatever. When you say 'magic', I think you mean 'supernatural', or outside the laws of physics as we know them."

The Bear considered for a moment, then said, "Show me a law of physics. Point to it."

The Girl sat up, looked around, then picked up the pillow her head had been resting on, held it up over the floor, and dropped it.

The Bear quirked an eyebrow at her, but said nothing.

"There!" the Girl said, "The Law of Gravity!"

The Bear shook his head. "No, that's a pillow...that's now getting dirty on the floor. Where's this 'Law of Gravity'? Show it to me."

The Girl waved her hand, "I just showed you! The pillow fell because of the Law of Gravity!"

"Are you sure? Perhaps the pillow just liked the floor enough to want to be close to it."

She gawked at him. "But..." She shook her head.

"Your 'Law of Gravity' is actually just a bunch of observations grouped together. Since you let go of a pillow yesterday and it fell, you expect that if you let go of a pillow today, it will fall again, right?"

The Girl nodded, "Right."

"But what you label a law might just be a coincidence, mightn't it?"

She thought for a minute, then shook her head, "No. I mean, we have explanations for why the pillow falls, so...it's science, not magic."

"So, if you have explanations for why things happen, then they're science, not magic, is that it?"

She paused for a minute, then nodded slowly, "Yes...I guess."

"Then talking bears are magic?"

"Right! No, wait..." she shook her head, then regretted it. "Ow!" She put her hand to her head. "No fair! You...cheated!"

He huffed, which she interpreted as a laugh. "Right. So, you just lost an argument with a talking bear, and it was only because he cheated."

She opened her mouth, and couldn't think of a thing to say, so closed it.

She sat up and looked at him again. "You...you're really a man, aren't you?"

Bear looked away, then turned back. "Is your head still bothering you?"

She stared at him and realized he didn't want to talk about this. "Uh...yes, it is. But only when I shake it like a maraca." She giggled. "Then you can hear my brains rattling around!"

Bear huffed again. "Yeah, I can hear them from here!"

"Oh! Not nice, Bear, not nice!" But she giggled again.

"So, you should have some lunch. Sorry – you know what's in the pantry, so help yourself, okay?"

She threw back the blanket, and swung her legs over the side of the sofa. "Okay." She stood up, then flopped back down. "OH! Not as steady as I thought."

Bear chuckled. "Take it slow, Girl, take it slow." He stood up. "I'm going out to rustle up some lunch. Probably some fish. Wanna come?"

She shook her head. "I think I'd better stay here until I'm...better."

Bear nodded his head. "Yes, I think so. Have some lunch, then a nap. I'll be back presently. Go gently." And he turned and walked off toward the woods.

Chapter 2: The Bearable Lightness of Being

When Bear returned from getting his lunch and marking the boundaries of his territory, Girl was again asleep in the rocking chair. One hand was trailing down the side, her head lolled against her shoulder, and she was drooling slightly. He stopped to look at her and again shook his head.

"Poor kid."

He gently picked her up and carried her into the great room. She stirred, smiled, leaned her head against his chest, and put her arms around his neck – or at least as far as she could reach – but didn't open her eyes. He carefully deposited her on the old leather sofa in the great room, once again laid the old, soft blanket over her, ambled back out to the porch, and sat down.

When Girl awoke, the sun was getting low, and light was reflecting off the mountains through the front window. She stretched and gingerly got up, noting that although she still ached, it wasn't quite as bad, her head didn't feel anywhere nearly as muzzy as before, but there was still pain, especially in her face.

She thought for a moment, then carefully stood up, waiting to see how steady she was on her feet, then slowly walked out to the porch, once again finding the Bear sitting up and gazing at the mountains.

His head swiveled, and he turned to face her. "Hello, there. Feeling better?"

She nodded, then winced, and placed her hand on the top of her head. "I...I think so." She didn't realize that her face looked worse, with deep purple splotches around her eyes. All she knew was that she felt a little bit better.

She looked at the Bear, then back at the mountains, and then smiled, saying, "Enjoying your family heirloom?"

"Always. And it's always there." He turned back to look at the view.

The Girl gingerly sat on the rocking chair and, without realizing it, started rocking back and forth. It was almost as if the chair caused its inhabitants to perform this ritual.

The two of them sat for a while, looking at the mountains, and the mountains sat patiently to let them. Finally, Girl said, "Are you waiting for something?"

The Bear turned to her and said, "Such as?"

The Girl stopped rocking, nonplussed. "I...I don't know. What...what do Bears do?"

The Bear chuckled, "Well, for one thing, they shit in the woods."

The Girl, caught entirely by surprise, threw back her head and laughed aloud.

"Ow! That *hurts!* You caught me off-guard, Bear!" She covered her mouth and giggled. "You're a bad influence!"

"My mother always told me so."

The Girl sobered up and almost asked where he had grown up – then decided it wouldn't be polite. She thought for a moment and looked at the Bear, who looked back at her, grinning.

"Uh...I mean, you've been sitting here for...how long?"

The Bear shrugged. "A while."

"What...what do you do while you're sitting?"

The Bear smiled at her, "Forgive me, but I thought 'to sit' was a verb."

The Girl shifted slightly in her chair, then said, "Well, yeah, it is but...you're not really *doing* anything when you're just sitting!"

The Bear thought for a moment, then said, "You know, I think the Buddha, as well as the entire body of Zen practitioners, past, present, and future, might just disagree with you."

Just then, the Bear's head went up, as if alerted to something.

He held up his paw and listened, then got up and turned towards her.

"Humans. They're coming this way. Get into the cabin, and for God's sake, be absolutely quiet." He herded her into the cabin, then softly closed the door and locked it.

"Come with me." He led her into an internal storeroom that had no windows, carefully shut the door, and indicated to her that she should sit.

He leaned forward and whispered, "Be completely quiet. They won't be able to see the cabin but can hear us as if we were out in the open."

She looked at him and opened her mouth...at which point, he put a claw up to his mouth, as if making a shushing noise.

They waited for a while, and nothing seemed to be happening. Then she heard the sounds of shoes on grass and gravel. It was almost as if she was hearing someone not far from her, out in the open. She looked quizzically at Bear, but he just shook his head.

The footsteps stopped, then they heard a male voice that sounded close by. "Geez, Trev, how much farther do you wanna go? I mean, we didn't see any trace of her by the road, and if the wild animals got her, then that's good, right?"

Another voice replied, sounding annoyed. "So how come there wasn't any blood? If an animal got her, there would be blood and other signs. No, she's around here somewhere, and I've got to make sure she doesn't get away. She could start squealing to the authorities. Can't allow that to happen. Not *gonna* allow that to happen. So, we keep looking."

"Look, Trev, I understand you want to find her, but...well the only thing we've found so far were those bear tracks back by the highway." There was a pause. "I mean, hell, look at this place. How the *hell* are we ever going to find someone lost in these mountains?"

There was a pause, and then the second voice spoke, sounding more subdued. "I have no freakin' idea, but we've got to try." Another pause, then the sound of a belt clinking, as if he were hitching up his pants. "Okay, let's keep going. It'll be sundown in another couple of hours, and we can't be out here after that. Too dangerous, even with shotguns."

The sounds of footsteps moved away.

Bear held up his paw, urging her to stay still and be quiet for what seemed like a long time.

"Stay here," he finally whispered.

He quietly opened the storeroom door and disappeared, returning about two minutes later. He exhaled, then said, "I think it's okay. They've gone down by the lake. I don't think they'll be coming back this way – it's a long uphill hike, and there's an easier route back to the highway. You can come out now – but don't make any loud noises, okay?"

Girl nodded, then stood up cautiously and stretched. She was feeling stiff and, now, sore from her extended stillness. In a much-subdued manner, she walked out to the porch and sat down slowly on the rocking chair again, looking down and deliberately *not* looking at him.

Bear returned to his porch perch. His head swiveled towards her. "Friends of yours?"

She shook her head. "No."

"You don't want to talk about it, do you."

She shook her head again. "I think...I think I'd better leave you." And she got up from the rocking chair.

Bear stood up to his ten feet in height. "No."

She looked startled.

"If you leave now, you could well lead them straight back to me. I need you to stay here, at least for tonight, okay?"

She looked startled again, then sat slowly back down. "Oh, right. Well, tomorrow then."

"What's your hurry, Girl?"

She bit her lip and looked away. "I'm...I'm endangering you."

Bear slumped back onto his haunches, then chuckled. "Actually, reports to the contrary, polar bears are not yet endangered, although their habitats are becoming so."

He looked out at the mountains, then back at her. "Girl, where do you think you're going to go?"

"I...I don't know, but I can't put you in danger. It's not fair. You've done enough for me already."

The Bear turned and stared at her for a long time. She glanced up at him, then down again, and fidgeted.

"You don't realize it, Girl, but you may be saving my life."

She looked up, shocked. "H...how? I mean, what do you mean?"

Bear looked at her and then spoke, looking down. "Who is there for me to talk to, Girl?"

She looked at him. "I...I don't know."

"Neither do I," and he looked back at the mountain peaks in the distance.

Bear stalked off a while later, ostensibly to find some food but also to check on the humans who had gone off down to the lake. Meanwhile, he told Girl to make herself some supper.

He came back a couple of hours later to find Girl waiting for him in the rocking chair, looking out over the mountains. He stopped just inside the clearing to look at her, a warm feeling in his heart for the first time in he couldn't remember how long. Shaking his head, he padded up to the cabin.

"Evening, Girl."

She started, as if awoken from a dream. "Oh, hi Bear! You startled me."

He seated himself at the end of the porch in his usual spot, and she resumed rocking. After some time, she said, "I think I understand now."

"Oh?"

She rocked some more, then said, "I understand what you are doing when you are 'just sitting'. This..." She waved her hand at the scene before them, "...seems, well, magical. I could sit here for hours, doing nothing."

Bear ducked his head. "I know. I have. I do." He turned back to face the reddening peaks with the sunset line creeping up from below.

When the last light vanished from the highest peak, Girl sighed.

"It's hypnotic, isn't it?"

"It is that."

"But Bear..."

"Yes, Girl?"

"Wait...why do you keep calling me 'Girl'?" She sat up straight, and tension returned to her body.

"Because you *are* a girl."

"Bear, I'm sixty-three years old. I'm not a girl."

His head swiveled to look at her, his mouth open in what she interpreted as a grin. "So? 'Girl' is easier and, in my mind, better than 'Old Woman.'"

"But I'm not...Oh! Why do you keep doing that?"

"Moi?" he put a paw to his chest and managed to look insincerely innocent.

"Yes, you! You're infuriating!"

"I try."

She stopped, then threw her head back and laughed.

"So, why do you call me Bear?"

She stopped laughing. "Because..."

She stopped and looked puzzled. "Well, you *present* as a bear."

She looked at the mountains for a moment, then said, "Besides, I don't know what else to call you. What would you like me to call you?"

Now, it was Bear's turn to look out to the fading mountains. He heaved a heavy sigh, "I like Bear. Call me that. Please."

She nodded. "Do...do you have another name you'd rather I called you?"

He shook his head. "Not anymore."

She sat quietly for some time, thinking. "Bear..."

"Yes?"

"When you're ready, I'd like to hear...you know."

He nodded, although it was getting dark enough that she could hardly see him by this time. "Thank you."

She grabbed her shoulders suddenly. "Brrr! It gets cold here quickly, doesn't it?"

Bear stood up, "Yes, it does. Let me get you the blanket."

He padded back into the cabin and returned with the blanket in his mouth, dropping it on her lap. She picked it up and wrapped it around herself. "Why don't we just go back inside?" she asked.

"Because you're about to see the opening of the greatest show in the known universe: the night sky." He swiveled his head to look at her, "I'll bet you haven't seen it in years, have you?"

She considered for a moment, then shook her head, "No, not really. I mean, you can see maybe five stars in the city at night."

"And some of those are planets, not stars," Bear added.

The two friends sat together, watching the stars emerge in their crystalline thousands. Finally, Bear got up. "Follow me," and walked off the porch.

Girl followed him but put her hand on his back to guide herself, walking carefully to avoid tripping. It was very dark.

He walked for a few minutes, then sat and waved his paw at the sky. "Look," was all he said.

She looked up, then turned in a circle and gasped. "Oh, my God!"

"Probably," Bear said.

Chapter 3: Of God and Bear

"Probably what?" Girl said.

"Probably the stars are there because of God."

She blinked. "Um...why 'probably'? And how would you know?"

Bear got up and said, "Why don't we go back into the cabin? I don't think there are any short answers to either of those questions, and you're going to get cold if we stand out here for long."

Girl put her hand on his fur and followed him back to the cabin over the uneven meadow floor.

When they were once again safely inside, with the door closed and bolted, Bear built up the fire, then slumped down in front of it on the rag rug, cradling his head on his front paws. "Now, which question did you want me to attempt to answer first?"

Girl thought for a moment, then said, "Why do you think the stars are probably there because of God?"

Bear lifted his head, then nodded. "Right. Well, first, can we agree that there is no way to prove the existence of God?"

Girl thought and said, "I'd have to think about that, but let's say you're right...for now."

Bear chuckled, a deep gurgling sound in his chest. "Well, I actually asked God about it once, and that's what He told me. But that's a different..."

"Wait! What do you mean you asked God? Do you mean in prayer, or...in person?"

"In person."

"But...how?"

"Okay, I can see this is going to be an even longer conversation than I expected. Why don't you get yourself some food, then bring it back here, and we'll start there, okay?"

Girl thought for a moment, then shrugged, got up from the sofa, and disappeared into the kitchen, returning several minutes later with a tinned meat and mustard sandwich.

Bear looked at her plate, and said, "I've made arrangements to get some fresher food for you. It should get here tomorrow morning."

Girl, who had a mouth full of sandwich, looked at him, and tried to speak, but stopped to chew and swallow, then finally said, "How...?"

"Look, which question do you want answered? We're going to be here all night at this rate!"

Girl took another bite, then mumbled around it, "Okay, I'll come back to that one, too. So, how did you meet God."

"Actually, an incarnation of God. Have you ever heard of a guy by the name of Ram Dass?"

She cocked her head and said, "It sounds familiar, but..." She shook her head, "Not sure. Tell me."

"Ram Dass was born Richard Alpert, son of the president of the New Haven Railroad, and raised with a silver spoon in his mouth. He was a classic overachiever, eventually becoming a professor of clinical psychology, with simultaneous appointments, I think, at Stanford, Michigan, and Harvard. That's kind of the textbook definition of the classic overachiever.

"But he became famous for being Timothy Leary's sidekick at Harvard, turning on and dropping out on acid – LSD. But when Leary was framed and busted for the possession of marijuana, he and Alpert were bounced from Harvard.

"Alpert didn't go to jail but instead went to India, looking for the purpose of life – which I know about, by the way – and..."

"Stop! You can't just slide that by! What is the purpose of life?"

"Wrong question, and if we keep getting side-tracked, we'll never get anywhere. So, back to God, right?"

Girl scowled, shook her head, then begrudgingly said, "Oh, okay...God."

"Alpert literally fetched up at the feet of an Indian guru named Neem Karoli Baba, hoping for a miracle to transform his life – and got it."

"Wait, what?"

"A miracle."

Girl just stared at him, then shrugged. "Okay, go on.... No, wait. What miracle?"

Bear heaved a deep sigh. "So, Alpert didn't believe in this holy man crap, but couldn't shake the feeling that there was something there. Finally, he wanted to get away from all the people surrounding the supposedly great guru and went for a walk around a lake at a park far away.

"Just totally confused about his life and what the hell he was doing, he finally gave up and said, 'Okay, God, I haven't got any faith. Send me a miracle.'"

"Wait...that's, uh...Matthew, isn't it? 'Had you faith, you would not need miracles' or something like that?"

Bear nodded, "Matthew 21 somewhere. I think."

Girl stopped, thinking, then nodded, "Go on."

"When Alpert got back to the ashram, Maharaj-ji walked over to him and said, 'Were you at the lake?'

"Alpert's chest got very tight, and he said brusquely, 'Yes.'"

"Maharaj-ji said, 'While you were there, were you *talking to God?*'

"Alpert just looked at him, unable to breathe, but nodded.

"Maharaj-ji leaned forward and said, 'And did you...*ask*...for something?'"

"Alpert fell apart, collapsed, and started to cry, and all his tension disappeared."

"Wait...that's not a miracle!"

Bear looked at her. "Isn't it?"

Girl opened her mouth to say something, then closed it and finally said, "But that's only a story."

Bear nodded. "Yes. Look – I don't care if you believe it or not. But you asked, remember?"

Girl started to pout, then shrugged, "Okay, go ahead."

"Well, don't be too long-suffering about it on my account." Bear chuckled deep in his chest again.

"So, Alpert studied with Maharaj-ji – who has had several other Western disciples, by the way, including Steve Jobs – later he took the name 'Ram Dass,' meaning 'Servant of God.' Maharaj-ji sent him back to the West to work because spiritual work is done in the marketplace, not on the mountain top..."

Girl held up a hand, "What do you mean?"

Bear sat back and grinned. "Okay, grasshopper. If you're building a house, for example, you don't work in bed, do you? You go to where the work is, right?"

She nodded.

"Likewise, you do spiritual work where the work needs to be done. There's a lovely Jewish parable about that, but that would be yet another diversion, so let's save that for another time, shall we?"

"Uh...I guess."

"May I continue?"

She nodded.

"So, Ram Dass, among many other things, started lecturing here in the West. I first heard of him when a friend of mine gave me a cassette tape of one of his lectures, and I really liked it. It spoke to me and seemed much more accessible than most spiritual stuff I'd read or heard, including the Bible. Which I've read cover-to-cover, by the way."

Girl giggled at the image of a polar bear holding the Bible in his paws, then coughed and sobered up. "Sorry. Go on."

Bear glared at her, then went on. "Then I read that before he starts a lecture, Ram Dass goes out into the audience and chats with people. And I heard he would be in my hometown for a lecture, so I got an idea."

Bear shifted and dropped down onto his front haunches, lying on the floor, cradling his head. "So, here's this person, who claims to be an incarnation of God...which is part of Hindu mysticism, by the way...and if I went to his lecture, I might be able to ask him a question. I thought: how could I pass up an opportunity to ask God a question?"

"Wait...this is all very entertaining, but the son of the former president of the New Haven Railroad as God? I have a problem with that. He can't be God!"

Bear looked at her and grinned. "You're sure about that, are you? Maybe a carpenter's son would be a better candidate?"

Girl started to sputter, "But...well, yes! It's in the Bible!"

"So it is. But is that the only way God can manifest on Earth?"

She thought for a while, started to speak several times, then finally said, "I'd...have to think about it. So, what question did you ask Ram Dass?"

"Well, I had an advantage over you. I thought about that question for several weeks before the night of Ram Dass' speech, and discarded most of them.

"So, here's my question: Is there any physical evidence of spiritual existence?"

She looked off into the distance, "Physical evidence of...Okay, why that question?"

"Because it told me where I needed to go next. If there is physical evidence of spiritual existence, I could go look at it and evaluate it for myself. If the answer is no, then I could stop looking and just accept that spiritual matters are beyond science and evidence."

"So, what did Ram Dass say?"

"I was surprised. He closed his eyes, turned his head up, and took quite some time thinking about his answer while people clustered around him, wanting to speak with him. Then, finally, he looked back at me and said, 'No. It's almost like asking if there is objective evidence of subjective experience. The two domains are mutually exclusive.'

"Then he turned to the next person."

Girl sat for a moment. "You must have been disappointed in his answer."

"No! I was delighted! It meant that I could stop looking for proof of God's existence and start thinking about what I chose to believe and accept. Faith is faith, not evidence. Thomas Merton said something very much like that."

"Thomas who?"

"A Trappist monk and essayist. Not important, let's move on, okay?"

Girl looked at him and almost asked Bear who he was, then decided not to, so she simply nodded. "So, how does that get us to where you can say that the stars are probably God's work?"

"Well, that's where William of Occam comes in."

"Wait, I know about him! Some kind of...monk of the, what, thirteen century?"

"Franciscan friar, not a monk, but you're close. Born in the thirteenth, died in the fourteenth. You get a gold star! So, what's Occam's Razor?"

"Something about the number of theories, I think."

"Sort of. There are a variety of phrasings, but my favorite is: Whenever a phenomenon permits of more than one explanation, the simplest is the most likely."

She looked up again and started mumbling, "...the simplest is the most likely...Okay, right. Got it."

"It's not a law, like your so-called Law of Gravity..."

"Hey!"

"...but it is a very useful rule of thumb for sorting out explanations. Now, let's keep things simple and assume there are only two hypotheses. First, that God created the universe – whoever or whatever 'God' is. Right?"

Girl nodded.

"Or second, that the universe just happened, as the atheists say."

She nodded again.

Bear smiled at her, "So, which explanation do *you* favor?"

Girl looked uncomfortable. "Well, both, kinda. I mean, I believe in God, but I also believe in science. So much of our lives has been improved and affected by science that it's kind of stupid to say it's not true, right?"

Bear nodded, "Yup. 'The proof of the pudding' and all that. But now, let's examine this...scientific...hypothesis that the universe 'just happened.'

"There's a wonderful book, *Just Six Numbers: The Deep Forces that Shape the Universe*, by the British Astronomer Royal, Martin Rees, that crushes, in my opinion, the 'scientific' hypothesis. The six numbers are the universal constants of physics, including things like the strength of gravity; the strength of the strong and weak nuclear forces; the relationship between those two; the index that measures the amount of material in the universe; and the number of dimensions in our reality, which is, of course, three: height, length, and depth.

"Think of these six numbers as the dials to be tuned to define what kind of universe we have. Now, here's the kicker – if these dials were tuned even the *tiniest* bit differently, the universe as we know it *would not exist!* Then we would not be here, discussing it. And that's on *any one* of the six dials.

"What are the chances that all six dials just happen to be set so *precisely* right that we can exist and be here talking to each other? The probability is so small that it would be ridiculous even to suggest it – except it happened.

"So, that being the case, let me ask you a question, one that the Astronomer Royal almost posed, but then chickened out on: *Who* set those dials with such infinite care? Or did this infinitesimally, ridiculously outrageous possibility *just happen* by chance?"

Bear laid back, rested his head on his paws, and went quiet, watching her and waiting.

Girl sat back, then said, "So – you're saying God *does* exist?"

"No. I'm saying Occam's Razor would argue strongly that He does. But we don't know God exists any more than we know that there is anyone or anything outside of our own heads. Or rather our own consciousness."

Girl sat staring at Bear for a long time, then stirred and said, "You're a very strange...um...individual, Bear, do you know that?"

Bear chuckled deep in his chest, "I think most people would agree with you. They certainly did before...well, before."

She thought he might have been about to say something about his past, then stopped. Once again, she thought about asking him...then decided to try to be patient.

Finally, she nodded. "I can accept that God...probably...created the stars and the heavens. It's what I was taught as a child anyway, and you make it seem so...reasonable. But your way of arguing it is so unusual. Do you believe in science?"

Bear snorted, "You weren't paying attention. Of course I believe in science – to the extent that science needs my belief. It is self-enforcing. People who don't believe in science – in the evidence of science – are fools or have accepted the word of fools or knaves. The acceptance of science applies as much to questions of creation, evolution, vaccinations, and climate change as it does to why your TV goes on when you hit the 'ON' button.

"But I'm not a scientist. My father was. I'm a mathematician, and we're a different breed of cat – or bear, as it were." Bear lifted his head and gave what seemed to be a silent laugh.

"But...I thought mathematics *was* science," Girl said.

"Another mistake fostered by our education system. Mathematics is more like art or philosophy than science. And it is the *only* area of human thought that is provable. You can prove whether any mathematical idea is right or wrong – or at least correct or incorrect – mathematically. There are no grey areas. And it is totally value-free. It doesn't make a particle of difference whether you're a communist, conservative, liberal, libertarian, anarchist, or anything in between."

"So, how come people confuse math with science, as with STEM – Science, Engineering, Technology, and Mathematics?"

"Because science uses math, but math doesn't use science – except in applied mathematics, where we are deliberately using it for science and technology."

Girl looked far-off again, "So, science uses math, but math doesn't use science?"

"Right."

"Why not?"

"Because mathematics doesn't need science. It's a mental discipline that is divorced from the real world. It resides in the mind of mathematicians and nowhere else. It's actually rather spooky if you think about it. Indeed, if you need proof of the existence of God, mathematics might just be it."

Now Girl was thoroughly confused. "I don't...get that."

"So, mathematics is something that exists only in the mind of mathematicians, does not exist in the real world, yet turns out to be the only mental discipline that is completely provable – right or wrong, with no uncertainties except for unsolved problems – and has immense applications to science and technology in the real world. How could that happen? By accident?" Bear snorted. "I doubt William of Occam would buy that."

"Oh-kay...so has being a mathematician helped you in your...your quest for God?"

Bear looked at her and nodded. "Oddly enough, it has. I was raised a devout atheist. I told you my Dad was a research scientist. To him, God was a ludicrous fairy tale suitable for gullible children, and that was the church I was raised in. That was my faith.

"I remained an atheist until I started thinking for myself. I knew nothing about religion – unless you count Santa Claus and the Easter Bunny – but was finally exposed to people who *did* believe in various religions – mostly Jews and Christians – when I was in university.

"And, like a good little scientist – I started as a physics major before I switched to mathematics – I listened to various testimonies and evidences, including those relating to cosmology, with an open mind. I finally decided that I wasn't smart enough to be able to decide the ultimate questions of life, so I started describing myself as a lapsed atheist, which I thought was amusing.

"I kept encountering fine, intelligent people who believed in God in some way or other, and it made an impression on me. By this time, I had graduated university with a degree in mathematics and thought like a mathematician."

Girl stirred, "So, how did that affect your thinking on God?"

Bear sat up, "Well, when a scientist encounters a brick wall, a problem for which he has no solution, he has no choice but to keep beating his head against it until something gives. After all, it's reality, right?

"But a mathematician doesn't have to do that. He – or she – will beat her head against that wall for a while, then simply change their assumptions and define themselves to be on the other side of the wall, thus creating a different kind of mathematics."

"But that's cheating!"

"Nope, that's mathematics. A mathematician has a different way of looking at the world than a scientist. Now, let's consider the brick wall presented by the question of the existence of God.

"We've already agreed that you can't prove your way to God, so what can a scientist do when faced with that particular brick wall? They *should* give up and admit that they don't know. Only many scientists don't do that. They *start* by assuming that God *doesn't* exist, which is a logical fallacy.

"Instead, as a mathematician, I looked at the problem and said, 'I've spent all these years assuming that God *doesn't* exist. What happens if I assume God *does* exist?' And that made an enormous difference."

"How so?"

Bear thought for a while, "Well, to start, it made me look at people differently. Instead of being merely evolutionary competitors, they became children of a common Father – or Mother, if you prefer. My attitude towards people became much more positive, and I started giving people the benefit of the doubt more often and taking myself less seriously. And that made my life sweeter in exchange.

"I found death easier to deal with than before. It was still distressing, but I felt I would see these people again, so it wasn't as sad. Likewise, I found life easier to deal with, that I wasn't alone in my own skull."

"So, since science tells us that the best answer is the one that produces the best result, and since believing in God produces the best result for me, therefore, as far as I'm concerned, God exists. Probably."

Bear paused for a long time then, looking out the window at something only he could see, and Girl waited, sensing something profound was disturbing him.

Finally, when he showed no sign of saying anything further, she said, "Bear, you must be terribly lonely here. I can't imagine that talking with...chipmunks, for example...is very fulfilling. And you don't seem to interact with humans much."

His head swiveled to look at her, then down at the floor. He shook himself, then said, "I'm sorry, I've been prattling on about metaphysics and stuff. You should go off to bed. With your injuries, your body needs the sleep."

"Please, Bear – you've been so good to me. Let me help?"

Bear turned and looked at her, staring for a long time, then said, "I'm sorry, Girl. I'm...I'm not ready. Yet. Maybe never."

She looked at him and swore he had tears in his eyes – and asked herself: Do polar bears cry?

Chapter 4: Recovery

Girl was exhausted by their deep discussion on the nature of God, the universe, and reality. She was also recovering from what looked like a significant beating, which showed on her face, and the parts of her arms and legs that were visible.

Bear was very much aware of how tired she would be, so that night he encouraged her to lie on the couch when she had begged not to be left alone, to stay in the great room with him.

He also suspected that she was in a great deal of emotional distress, which was part of the reason he had distracted her with his long diatribe on the probability of God's existence. Besides, it had been a long time since he had had a chance to talk about anything with anyone. He found that it also soothed his soul, which seemed appropriate to the subject.

He covered her with the old, red, woolen blanket that had been scratchy at one time but was now worn smooth. He watched her for a few minutes, then lay down on the rag rug nearby.

Girl lay on the sofa, with a pillow under her head, facing the fire, watching it leap and dance before her. Normally, Bear watched the fire until he slept, but tonight, he was turned sideways so he could keep his eyes on her. He did not stare at her, but mostly watched her through his peripheral vision, glancing over from time to time, until it was clear she was asleep.

He waited further until she turned. One hand fell from the sofa towards the floor, and her face turned towards the ceiling. Knowing that this would leave her stiff and aching the next morning, he got up, went into the bedroom, drew back the covers, and then padded back into the great room.

He gently lifted her from the sofa and carried her into the bedroom. She collapsed like a rag doll, boneless, which was probably better anyway, but he was careful to cradle her head so it didn't droop.

He placed her softly on the bed, head on the pillow, then pulled the blanket up over her. She stirred, moving stiffly, with pain showing on her face, then anxiety.

Bear lay on the floor, opposite the head of the bed, next to the chest of drawers. From there, he could watch her, and she could see him if she woke, but she wouldn't step on him if she got out of bed...which seemed likely at some point in the night.

Seeing that the expression on her sleeping face betrayed fear, he started humming a lullaby his father had sung to him when he was little. He didn't even know the name of the song but called it "Skeeters am a hummin'..." from the first line of the song. He had always found it soothing while his pappy...as Bear thought of him in the context of this song...held and rocked him when he was little.

Girl's face gradually smoothed out, and she settled into what looked like a peaceful sleep. Bear watched her for a while, then shut his eyes and slept in his turn.

He heard her get up in the middle of the night, listening to be sure she didn't fall. He didn't let her know he was awake but listened to her walk to the bathroom and back, then collapse back into bed. She turned for a bit, apparently trying to find a position that invoked the least amount of pain from her bruises, until finally, her breathing became smooth and regular. He listened for a while, then returned to his own dreams.

And for once, they were not lonely dreams, full of yearning for times and people now gone from his life. Instead, they involved a mysterious Girl who appeared out of nowhere and kept him company. They were comfortable dreams, unlike the painful ones that usually afflicted his sleep. He smiled in his dreams and slept more soundly and comfortably than he usually did.

When the sun started to limn the sky through the window, Bear opened his eyes, and listened to Girl's breathing, smooth and even.

After a while, Bear got up cautiously and padded quietly into the great room, leaving the door to the bedroom open so Girl could see where she was.

He would normally have gone out foraging for food, but today he wanted to be there when she awoke. He suspected she would be disoriented and did not want her to panic on finding herself alone in a cabin in the middle of nowhere in the mountains. He was also aware that the man who was hunting her might come back, and she did not yet understand about the Charm. So, he stayed, eating the remaining trout out of the fridge and letting that soothe his stomach.

He checked with his friend, the hawk, and found that the arrangements he had made had been carried out. Later, he would go down and collect the things he had ordered, but now he needed to stay close to the cabin.

He made what arrangements he could for her breakfast, padded back to check that she was still asleep, then went out to his favorite spot on the porch and made himself comfortable.

Sometime later – neither Girl nor Bear would have been able to tell how long – Girl stirred, opened her eyes, looking confused, then fearful, then, remembering, puzzled.

She sat up carefully, swung her feet to the floor, and looked around, the puzzled look on her face persisting. Finally, her face smoothed out, and a sense of wonder overtook her.

She gingerly got up and carefully walked, barefoot, into the great room. Bear heard her, but decided to let her find him, rather than risk startling her. Eventually, she walked out onto the porch, using one hand to steady herself on the door frame. She looked at Bear, sitting at the end of the porch, staring off into the mountains.

"You're...you're real! You're not a dream!"

Bear continued looking out towards the mountains. "Well, that might be a matter of conjecture, but for argument's sake, let's assume you're right, okay?"

Girl looked blank for a time, then put her hand to her mouth and giggled. "And you're just as much of a smart ass as I remembered!"

Bear's head swiveled towards her. "Guilty as charged. How are you this morning, Girl?"

She stopped to take stock, then said, "Painful, I fear...but I can tell it's getting better. Bruises are usually worst on the third day, and then they start feeling better."

Bear looked at her for a moment. "One would almost think you had some...experience...with this." He shook his head. "Never mind. There's not a lot we can do about that now except let Nature take Her course. Hungry?"

She looked relieved that he hadn't pursued the subject, then said, "Yes. What taste sensations do you have for our delectation this morning?"

"Ooohh! Aren't we all imperial all of a sudden? Well, I'm afraid it will probably be oatmeal again this morning. But I'm picking up some supplies in a bit, so you'll have some more choice later."

Girl moved over to the rocking chair, eased herself into it gingerly, then said, "Bear, how on Earth do you...order stuff?"

He grinned at her, "We Bears have our ways. If you ask nicely, I'll tell you more about it...later. Now, I need to go get my breakfast, then pick up the supplies. But before I go, let me explain a couple of things you need to know, okay?"

Girl nodded, "Sure. Go ahead. I'm all ears!"

Bear rocked back on his haunches, looking uncomfortable for the first time Girl could remember. "This may be hard to believe..."

Girl snorted. "Harder than talking Bear, who discusses philosophy, metaphysics, and cosmology? Okay, now I'm *really* all ears!"

Bear swung his head to look at her. "Are you going to listen, or snark at me?"

Girl spluttered a laugh, then covered her mouth with her hand, pretending to cough. "Um...yes, well...I'm, uh, listening." She straightened up, trying to force her face to be serious, but failing.

Bear shifted his shoulders. "This cabin is...Charmed."

Girl looked at him. "Charmed? As in...a spell?"

"Well, I don't mean that it's merely charming. Yes, as in a spell." He looked away from her.

She shrugged. "Okay."

Bear looked back at her, surprised. "Okay? That's it?"

She shrugged again. "Compared to the other impossible things I've already had to believe before breakfast, that one's easy. Okay, it's Charmed. What does that mean?"

Bear shifted again. "It means that no one can find it...unless I lead them to it. Or allow them to see it."

He turned to her. "Remember when those two...men... came hunting for you?"

She nodded, solemn now.

"They didn't see the cabin, but I made sure you kept quiet, remember?"

She nodded again.

"Yet we could hear them very clearly."

"Right. I *thought* that was strange!"

"That's the Charm. If we had made enough noise, they could have found the cabin...and us. Any outcome after that would not have been good for either of us."

Girl thought for a moment, then nodded, "No, I can see that. You might have overpowered them...but then, a search party would eventually have come looking for them. Not good, even if you had clobbered them. And they had guns, so..."

Bear cleared his throat. "What I'm trying to say, Girl, is that if you think anything is amiss, then quickly but quietly go hide in the storage closet and stay there until I return, okay?"

Girl nodded soberly. Then giggled.

"What?" Bear asked crossly.

She giggled again, then said, "Maybe I'll be part of your *provisions*." Then wondered if that was such a smart suggestion.

Bear, caught off guard, opened his mouth and then laughed. "Well, it *has* been a while since I had any fresh Girl – and you certainly are fresh! – so it would make a nice change from fish."

He sobered up. "Seriously, though, Girl. If you think there is any kind of threat, from man or beast, hide there and wait until I return. Can I trust you to do that?" He looked at her steadily, no hint of a smile on his face.

She nodded, then stepped towards him and put her hand to his face. "Thank you, Bear, for keeping me safe." She stretched up and kissed his muzzle.

He put his paw lightly on her head. "Good girl. I'll be back soon. Now, can you help me with these panniers?" He nodded towards a pair lying on the floor next to Bear. "It makes it easier to carry things any distance."

She helped him on with the apparently custom-made rig that stretched across his shoulders, then watched him lope off into the brush, heading towards the road. After he was well gone, she seated herself on the rocking chair, sighed deeply, and turned to watch the mountains.

She let her mind wander where it wished...then pulled it back to the much happier present. After a while, she found she was wiping tears of relief and joy from her eyes.

For the first time in a long while, she felt safe. More than that, she felt *grateful* that someone had finally *seen* her, and paid attention to what they saw. It was a lovely feeling.

Chapter 5: A Story of Days

The days that followed passed in lazy friendship, while Girl's bruises and aches slowly started to heal. Finally came the day when she was tired of behaving sensibly and hanging around the cabin all the time. No matter how entertaining – or infuriating, or amusing – Bear could be, she was aware that the world around them was beautiful, and she was seeing only the part she could witness from the cabin's porch.

First, Bear and Girl had an almost full day of hiking. Bear was enjoying having someone to show the Canadian Rockies to, and so had stopped several times for breathtaking views as they walked. Girl was blown away by the splendor of it all – as was Bear, even though he had seen these views countless times.

Now the two friends were back at the cabin, with Girl having had a lovely supper of fresh trout, caught in a stream, pan-fried in butter, wrapped in bacon, and with a splash of Chardonnay at the end. She wondered how it had all gotten here but avoided asking.

They had chatted during supper, and now, dishes done, had moved over towards the fire, Girl to the sofa, Bear to the rag rug. Gradually, the conversation had slowed, then stopped.

The fire burned steadily, giving off heat, a sense of well-being, and the glow of friendship, appreciated on both sides. Girl moved from the sofa to lean against Bear on the rug, watching the glow and flicker of the fire before them.

The two friends curled up together on the rag rug, Girl in front, leaning back on Bear, stroking the fur on his enormous head. Bear was humming a lullaby his mother used to hum to him as a child.

Outside, the stars were bright overhead, and Bear and Girl eventually got up and went out on the porch to watch them sparkle. Girl wrapped in the blanket, sitting on the rocking chair that seemed like home to her now. After a time, she started to droop, and finally went limp, asleep, head on one shoulder, drooling.

Bear finally picked her up and carried her to her bed, placing her gently in it and pulling the covers up to her neck.

She stirred, smiled, and murmured, "Night, Bear."

He kissed her on the top of her head, chuckled, then said, "Good night Girl. Nothing but good dreams."

He padded back outside to have one final look at the stars, then took a deep breath, turned back into the cabin, closed the door, curled up on the rug...and went to sleep.

It wasn't quite as nice the next day. When the two friends woke, it was to the sound of rain on the roof of the cabin.

Girl was grumpy and didn't want to get up, so Bear built up the fire, then rustled up some breakfast for her – granola and trail mix, plus some coffee, and some leftover bacon from the night before. Then he went and rousted her from bed...although the smell of coffee probably had more to do with her willingness to get up.

Once she had some food in her, Girl felt a bit more cheerful, so Bear told her to get the rain poncho from the storeroom, because they were going out.

"In the rain?" she squeaked.

"In the rain," he confirmed.

So, they did.

"Won't I need boots?" Girl asked.

Bear replied, "I believe you wore something on your hind paws when I picked you up, yes? Now stop stalling and get ready!"

The two friends walked along the stream by the cabin, uphill to make the return easier, then stood by a place where the stream widened out, and the water was rushing downhill, making a kind of natural music.

The rain kept falling steadily. It wasn't a cold rain, actually kind of pleasant, and the sound...well, combined with the sound of the stream rushing over the rocks, the beauty of the mountain, and the absence of other sounds, it was enchanting.

They stood there for what seemed like forever, just listening and watching. It was...hypnotic, majestic, even magical. It silenced them both; they just stood, listened, and waited with the world.

Its breath was their breath.

Its light was their light.

Its peace was their peace.

Finally, when Girl's feet were getting cold, so they walked back to the cabin in contemplative silence.

Bear got her to go in and change into dry clothes while he built up the fire again.

Then he wrapped a blanket around her shoulders, and they sat, gazing into the fire and talking about everything and nothing, laughing back and forth at jokes and puns and letting the rest of the day pass in peace.

Girl fixed a light supper for herself: chicken with green beans from the supplies Bear had sent up from the valley, plus sugar cookies for dessert. And Bear found a container of hot chocolate mix in the storeroom, so Girl used some of the powdered milk to make herself a rich, hot drink against the cool weather outside.

The two friends sat, dreaming into the fire, while the day faded, yet remained in their minds and memories.

It had been a nothing day.

Except it hadn't been nothing. It had been filled with the joy of living, the pleasure of being together, and the comfort of friendship.

As darkness fell, and Girl's eyes got heavy, Bear lifted her up, placed her in her bed, pulled the covers over her, ruffled her hair, and said, "Good night, my friend. Nothing but good dreams, always."

Then he went back and made himself comfortable by the fire.

The fire flickered for a while. Owl called...and answered...from outside. Silence filled the cabin.

And they slept.

The next day had been mixed. The morning dawned cool and grey, with low scudding clouds and hints of rain.

The two friends huddled indoors, chatting and doing nothing important.

After lunch, the sky cleared, the sun emerged, and the day became fine, so the friends decided they'd go for a walk and get some air.

Along the way, they noticed there were a lot more wildflowers out than there had been before, so they picked some – making a small bouquet.

They brought them back to the cabin, put them in a water glass, and set them in the middle of the table to brighten the cabin.

Then they sat together in companionable silence on the front porch, waiting for the setting sun to paint the mountains opposite.

And when the sunset line finally worked its way up past the highest peaks, then extinguished the orange glow of the topmost peak, they went in and made supper.

After Girl had finished eating, she cleaned up the cabin, folding the dish towels so they would dry. Bear built up the fire, and the friends sat together on the rug before it.

The light danced on the ceiling, and they talked quietly, so as not to disturb the gathering, solemn peace.

And when night had properly fallen, and the fire was burning low, Bear picked up Girl, carried her gently to her bed, tucked her in, kissed the top of her head, and then went back to bed down in front of the fireplace.

But before he lay down on the rag rug in the great room, he walked out to the porch to look up at the night sky. He smiled up at it and said, "Thank you, Mother. I was lonely."

He returned to the great room, slumped down onto the rug, closed his eyes...and slept.

Chapter 6: Monarchs

The day dawned clear and cool, giving the two friends a break from the hotter weather than they had lived there for the last few days – and reminding them that winter wasn't that far away. It never is, in the mountains.

So, when she arose from her night's sleep – dreamy and sensuous – she felt refreshed by the air and the sun and a sense of gratitude and joy, the wonder of being alive. It was the first time she could remember in many, many years when she hadn't woken up with an overhanging feeling of dread, and she was luxuriating in it.

She dressed, then stepped out into the great room, looking for Bear. And, as usual, he was already gone. The rug where he slept was clear, and the door outside was open, so she stepped through it, looking for him.

And was surprised to see him, sitting a ways off in the meadow, looking up. At first, she couldn't tell what he was looking at. His head seemed to be tracking something moving very quickly in the distance, for his muzzle kept moving up and down, and from side-to-side, erratically.

But then, looking more carefully, she noticed that there were butterflies dancing about his head. Monarchs, to be precise, with their black and gold wings, dancing in the air.

And not just two or three, but seemingly dozens. Nor were they just flitting by. They seemed to be flying as close to him as they could, veering off, flying up, and repeating as if being near him was important to them.

He saw her and raised a paw in greeting her. "Good morning! Come and meet my friends!"

Girl thought she had ceased to be surprised by Bear, but still felt a sense of wonder at this...person...about whom she knew so little, yet to whom she owed so much.

She smiled, stepped off the porch, and walked towards him.

As she neared, the butterflies began to fly towards, then around her, as if including her in their dance. Delighted, she raised her arms as if they were wings and started to dart and dance with them through the meadow, veering, swooping by Bear, running a hand through his fur, listening to him give that deep laugh from down in his chest. She would swoop up again and flit off, then circle around, and return, again and again.

Finally, she collapsed, laughing and breathless, by Bear's side, leaning her head against his side, panting and happy.

When she had recovered somewhat, she looked up at him, noticing that the butterflies had dispersed a bit, flitting off to the milkweed plants growing in the meadow, but always returning to hover close by him, or even, occasionally, landing on his head or his fur, waxing and waning their wings, then flying off again.

Bear sat through it all, a big grin on his face.

"How do you get them to do that?" Girl asked.

Bear swiveled his head towards her. "I don't. They're my friends, and they're as happy to see me as I am them. They've come all the way from Mexico to visit me – or rather, my friends' grandchildren or great-grandchildren have come back to visit me. It's quite marvelous, really, and one of my happiest times of the year! I woke up this morning, and somehow knew it would be today – and I am so happy you're here to share it with me!"

Bear looked at her with a face that she now interpreted as happy and said, "You looked quite transported yourself. I could easily have mistaken you for a butterfly!"

Girl leaned up and rubbed the fur around his ear, and smiled. "I felt like one. It was like nothing I've ever experienced before! I felt free, as if I could actually fly! And joyous..."

Her eyes filled with tears. "Oh, Bear! How do you bring me such joy? Why do I feel so...so much *me* when I'm with you? I feel more at home here than I have anywhere for decades."

She sighed and leaned more heavily against him, stroking the fur of his shoulder.

He turned to her, and smoothed his paw down her head. "Because, dear Girl, here you are free."

He sighed in his turn, "And I'm not alone..."

He looked up at the Monarchs. "Begging your pardons, of course, my friends!" And he chuckled.

Later that evening, after a day with the butterflies, the two friends slouched against each other, eyes on the fire. Finally, Girl spoke.

"Bear...you are a marvel. Do you know that?"

There was a rumbling in his chest. "Yes."

She grimaced and swatted him, which only increased the rumble.

She lay back against him, and found herself in a strange place.

Happy.

Chapter 7: Breath-less

The afternoon was drawing in. Girl had spent a lazy day rocking on the front porch and looking at the mountains, feeling very much as if they were looking back at her. Later, she had discovered some jigsaw puzzles in a closet, and pulled one out with a happy cry. She spilled it out on the dining table and started sorting the pieces, looking for the edges.

Bear wandered over after a while to see what she was up to, then started pointing out pieces she'd overlooked – until she got sore and told him to knock it off. He chuckled, then wandered out to his favorite spot on the porch and settled down, seemingly waiting for the mountains. Or something...

She eventually finished the edge, creating the outline of the puzzle, and decided to stop. She wandered back out to the porch, rocked for a bit, then said, "Bear?"

His head swung to look at her, "Girl?"

"I'm sorry I shouted at you."

He laughed his deep, throaty laugh. "Perfectly okay, Girl. I hate backseat drivers myself. And I know I'm a bad one!"

They sat in silence for a while, then he got up and said, "Come with me... please." And loped off the porch, wandering towards the woods.

Puzzled at first, Girl got up, stretched a bit, then hurried to catch up, finally placing her hand on his back, both to help her keep pace, but also to let him know she was there. He turned his head and grinned – she was starting to understand his expressions – then looked forward.

They were following a trail that seemed familiar, although she couldn't quite place it. Then he veered suddenly, down a path she would have completely missed if he had not shown it to her. They had to push their way through undergrowth, but eventually found themselves on a ledge, overlooking the lake, which gave a view she hadn't seen before.

Bear said nothing, but just sat, so Girl set herself down on the ground, sitting tailor-fashion, and waited.

While she waited, she looked out at the view. It was stunningly beautiful, like so many views here in the mountains.

But the more she looked, the more something profound seemed to happen to her. She tried to figure out what was happening but finally gave up.

And gradually, she found it. The scene before her seemed...perfect. It was almost as if it had been composed as a painting. Everything ahead of her – the dead tree, the overhanging branches, the mountains off to her left, the dappled reflections on the water far below – it all seemed in harmony.

And it inspired quietness.

The two friends sat there in silence. Not doing anything, not saying anything, hardly moving.

Eventually, Girl found she was barely breathing, and her breathing was even and measured. It reminded her of a weekend she had spent at a meditation retreat in university. They had been big on breathing – and had made a big deal about it.

Here, she found herself just...doing it, and it soothed her.

Finally, when the sun started to go down, Bear stirred himself, got up, looked at her, and said, "Come. Let's be getting home."

She slowly rose from her cross-legged seat, looked around, took a deep breath and said, "Thank you, Bear."

And they wandered home.

It had been a good day.

Chapter 8: Thunderstorm

Girl was rudely awakened by a massive **BLAM** and an incredibly bright flash of light. She jerked upright, hand to her mouth, quivering and afraid. She was confused as to where she was, having been ripped from a sound sleep. Her head whipped around, quartering the room, looking for something familiar and not finding it, her heart beating furiously.

Another blinding flash and crash of thunder shook the cabin, and she shrieked, completely disoriented and frightened.

Then, a dark shape loomed in the door to her room, huge and moving quickly towards her. She screamed and crawled up the wall.

"GIRL! It's me... It's Bear! It's okay, it's just a thunderstorm!"

The shape backed off, then settled, seated in the doorway. Another flash and crash illuminated the white form of a huge animal, regarding her with large, liquid eyes.

As soon as she remembered and recognized Bear, she leaped across the room and fastened herself around his neck. "Oh, God, Bear! I was so frightened. I didn't know where I was, I didn't know..."

"It's okay Girl, I'm here. You're safe. No one will harm you."

He felt tears on his neck. "And that's what happened, isn't it? Someone...hurt you...didn't they?"

She didn't answer but nodded her head into his neck.

"That's not going to happen anymore. You're safe here. I promise."

She clung to him even more tightly, then said in a muffled voice, "Why?"

Bear drew back, "I'm sorry – why what?"

She slowly drew back from him, keeping a hold of his neck. "Why would you do that for me? I'm...nothing."

Now Bear drew back farther so he could focus on her. "Girl? There is no way on God's green Earth that you are nothing. And anyone who would tell you that is...well, less than human."

She shook her head no.

"Girl, please, look at me. Please."

Slowly, she eased back and looked down, not meeting his eyes.

"You are not nothing. Someone has been telling you that for, I'm guessing, a very long time, trying to beat you down, grind you into submission. But it's not true." He shook her gently.

"In the short time that we've known each other, it is clear to me that you are bright, even brilliant. You are educated, articulate, feisty, funny...and fun. You are someone I have come to respect very quickly – and that doesn't...I mean, didn't happen – very often."

Bear heaved a deep sigh, "And Girl? You have already made an incredible difference in my life. You have no idea how...lonely...I was. I told you that you might have saved my life. I was not exaggerating. I was truly getting desperate.

"You saved me, Girl. Thank you."

She looked up at Bear in wonder.

Bear hugged her close. "You are a wonder, Girl. A marvel, and no joke."

She leaned back and looked at him, tears in her eyes. "Bear...that's...that's the kindest thing anyone has said to me in...in...I don't know how long. I just wish it were true." And she looked down at the floor again.

Bear thought about repeating himself but decided it would take time and patience to clear up some of the damage that had been done to his friend. "Grab your blanket and pillow, and come out into the great room with me, okay?"

Still looking at the floor, Girl nodded, turned, grabbed the bedclothes, and pulled them out onto the rag rug before the fire.

"There's probably not much point trying to get back to sleep until this storm front passes. Would you like to watch the fireworks?"

Girl looked at him, "What do you mean?"

Bear padded over to the door and swung it wide. The view outside, where lightning still crackled, although farther away now, was quite remarkable.

"Aren't you afraid of letting the rain in?" Girl asked.

"Nope. Nothing comes in without my approval...especially rain! That's part of the Charm I told you about."

Girl nodded, then stopped. "But...then those...men couldn't have come in anyway, could they?"

Bear shook his head. "No – but then what, after they'd seen a cabin and found they couldn't enter it?"

"Ohhhh...right. They would have kept trying and eventually brought other people up here to try...yes, I see. It can protect you from immediate harm, but, long-term?" She shook her head.

"Right. The best way to deal with some problems is not to let them arise in the first place. Anyway, snuggle close and enjoy the show."

Girl wrapped the blanket around her and sat beside Bear in the doorway. A warm breeze blew in – air, after all, was something Bear wanted to allow in the cabin – and it caused her blanket to flap, but the rain stayed out.

Girl leaned against Bear and watched Nature's pyrotechnic display, the two of them watching well into the night until the storm front finally moved away. And although Girl flinched every time there was a flash of lightning or a crash of thunder, she managed to avoid panicking. She did, however, cling tightly to Bear's fur, sometimes pulling it painfully. Bear made no comment.

By the time the storm passed, Girl was more than drowsy but she made a cranky fuss when Bear tried to move her back to her bedroom. Sighing, he curled up on the rug in front of the dying fire, then had her curl up, leaning against him.

They slept, both of them in separate dreams, but both with a strange but wondrous, feeling of coziness that neither had felt in a long time.

Girl woke in her bed the next morning. Looking at the window, she saw a beautiful day outside, and so carefully swung her legs around, and stood. Feeling better, although still achy, she started to walk out of the room, then stopped and looked at the chest of drawers.

She pulled the wooden nobs on the top drawer and saw several pairs of women's cotton underwear inside. She checked the other drawers and found other women's clothing. She held some of the items up to herself and found that they were close enough to her size that she could probably use them – at least as a stop-gap. The bras, unfortunately, were too small to be helpful.

She carefully returned everything to the drawers from which she had found them, then walked into the great room.

She was unsurprised to find it empty and walked out to the porch. Now she was surprised because Bear was not in his usual place. She sat on the rocking chair and let the magic of the mountains soothe her as she remembered the dramatic scenes from the night before.

After a while – she couldn't really tell how long – Bear came walking back into the meadow with what seemed like a jaunty swing to his gait. Finally seeing her, he sped up somewhat, then said, when he was close, "Well, good morning!"

She smiled back at him. "Good morning to you, too, Mr. Bear. You are well?"

"Yup, fine as rain, full of breakfast, and looking forward to spending time with my current favorite human!"

She giggled. "Are there a lot of competitors for the role?"

Bear's face split into a grin, "Well...now that you mention it...no. You win by acclamation! Congratulations, Girl!"

She giggled again, "It's nice to win something! I *never* win contests, not even the ones that offer '10% off your next purchase!' as a consolation prize!"

She shifted slightly, then said, "Bear, there are women's clothes in the chest of drawers in the room where I'm sleeping. Would it be okay if I borrowed some? My underwear, in particular, could use a change of scenery!"

Bear's good mood suddenly seemed to vanish, and he looked down. He walked past her into the cabin and said, on the way past, "Sure. Go ahead."

Girl realized that something was wrong, so she followed him in. "Bear? I...I'm sorry if I said something wrong or poked into something I shouldn't have. Forgive me?"

Bear looked off to the far end of the room for a time, then swung his head back to face her. "You did nothing wrong. Of course, you should use those clothes if you can. I didn't even stop to think about clothes for you. My apologies."

Girl walked slowly towards him. "She...she was important to you, wasn't she..."

Bear abruptly got up and left the cabin, brushing past her, then loping off back into the woods until he vanished from sight.

Chapter 9: Girl's Story

Girl watched Bear disappear into the woods and felt terrible about hurting him. Clearly, she had touched a nerve. She waited for him to return, perched on the edge of the rocking chair.

Finally, she sighed and went back into the cabin, fixing some breakfast for herself. Once done, she returned to the porch, settled on the rocking chair, and waited some more, knowing that there was nothing else she could do.

It was quite some time before Bear reappeared at the edge of the clearing, walking slowly, head swinging from side to side with his gait. When he got close, Girl jumped off the porch, ran over to him, and threw her hands around his neck. "Bear, I..."

"Girl, I'm..."

They both stopped, waiting for the other to start speaking again, then both started again at once.

"Girl, I shouldn't..."

"Oh, Bear, I never..."

They both stopped again, looked at each other, and burst out laughing.

Bear nodded, "After you."

"Oh, Bear. I'm so sorry. I should never have asked about the clothes. And I'm sorry about whatever happened to you – and her – whoever she is. It's none of my business, and I..."

Bear held up his paw. "It's okay, Girl. I shouldn't have been so sensitive. It was some time ago, and...well, I've never been able to talk about it to anyone, so it kinda never went away." He heaved a deep sigh.

Girl smoothed her hand down his head and over his shoulder, then repeated the gesture. "Bear – I know you don't know me, but if you want to talk, I'd like to listen."

The two friends turned and walked slowly back towards the porch. "Have you eaten yet?" Bear asked.

She nodded. "Yes, while you were away. At least I don't feel hollow as well as wretched. How about you?"

Bear nodded, "I figured that as long as I was out there, I'd help myself to some brunch." He licked his lips, and Girl got a glimpse of sharp teeth and a surprisingly dark tongue. "Lovely!"

They settled into their accustomed places and watched the light play with the shadows on the mountains for a time. Eventually, Bear looked at her and said, "You seem much better today. Your bruises are disappearing. You almost look human!"

She snorted, "Which is more than I can say for you!

Her hand flew to her mouth, "Oh shit! I'm sorry, Bear... I didn't..."

But Bear was laughing. When he had stopped, he said, "Well, it's true enough. I *don't* look very human!" He stopped and sighed, then was silent for a long time.

Finally, he swung his head towards her. "It was her or me."

Girl looked startled. "I'm sorry?"

Bear dropped his head, "I said it was either her or me,"

"You...killed her?"

Bear's head came up quickly, and he showed his teeth. It was the first time she had ever seen him angry. She drew back. An angry polar bear is a scary sight!

He breathed hard, then dropped his head again, "No, I mean I had to choose whether she lived or I did. I chose her."

Girl was silent in her turn, turning what he said over in her mind. "You...sacrificed yourself for her."

"Or tried to. She survived at least."

There were a thousand questions Girl wanted to ask. She asked none of them, just kept quiet, and started rocking again, staring out at the mountains, trying to be patient and listen to what he would say in his time, not hers.

When he didn't say anything more, and his head stayed down, obviously distressed, she sighed. Finally, she said, "You were right about me. I was escaping from my...husband." She spoke the last word with loathing. "He beat, abused, and belittled me for more than thirty years. When I finally realized that if I stayed, I would die, at emotionally and possibly physically as well, I got up my nerve and made a plan to escape.

"And I almost made it. Almost..." She stopped and looked away. Bear saw tears in her eyes.

"Somehow, you got up here from...wherever, but he found you." Bear made it a statement, not a question.

She nodded, and pain crossed her face. "It was...horrible. I thought he was going to kill me, right then and there. But he had other ideas. He was going to take me back, he said, and teach me a *real* lesson. And I would never be able to run on him again. Or walk. Crawling would be more my speed, he said." And she shivered. "I think he was planning on maiming me permanently."

She paused, "Then he literally tossed me in the back of his pick-up, snapped the lid closed, and started driving back towards the border. I have no idea how he planned to get me through the border crossing...but we didn't get that far before I escaped. Again.

"I was being tossed around in the back and was already in great pain without all the extra bruises that I got from the ride. But I knew if he got me home..."

She stopped and swallowed hard, unable to continue.

"Somehow I managed to push up the cover that was keeping me in the pickup's bed and jumped out as he was driving. I figured I'd rather die that way than...whatever he had in store for me.

"I guess he didn't notice. But I must have been knocked unconscious when I landed."

She looked up. "The next thing I knew, I was here...and safe."

She got up and slowly walked over to him, stopping just short. Then she leaned forward and put her forehead against his. "You. You saved me. You saved me from dying, but more than that, you saved me from...him." she stretched up and kissed him on the side of the head.

"Thank you," she leaned her forehead against his again and closed her eyes as tears ran down her cheeks.

Bear reached his paw around and pulled her closer to him in a very gentle bear hug. "It was perhaps the second-best thing I've ever done. And I'm very glad to know that I helped."

Bear sat quietly for a time, then pushed her gently away and got up. "What we need is a rainbow. Come on!"

She scrambled up, then said, "Do I need to take anything?"

Bear stopped, "Right. I'm not used to thinking about human needs anymore. There's an old canteen hanging in the store room. Rinse it out and fill it. We'll be back before you need any lunch, but bring something to snack on."

Girl hurried to the store room, found a round canteen with a cloth cover, shoulder strap, and screw top, took it into the kitchen, rinsed it out, filled it, then slung it over her shoulder. She grabbed a bag and shoveled in some nuts and raisins for an impromptu trail mix, which she stuffed in her pocket and then hurried outside.

"Okay, let's go!" And Bear loped off towards the wood, away from the lake.

"Bear, not so fast! I only have two legs, not four!" She was laughing as she said it.

Bear reared up on his hind legs and said, "I could beat you on two feet. C'mon!" And the two friends ran laughing into the woods.

There was barely a trail...or "bearly" a trail, as Girl laughingly said...but Bear knew where he was going, so it didn't matter. Eventually, they pushed through a final set of branches and emerged into a clearing leading to a waterfall.

There was a constant background hissing noise from the water hitting the rocks below. The spray from the fall made the glade seem foggy, with clouds of mist constantly rolling through. It made the air cool and the glade refreshing, and,...yes!...off to one side was a rainbow.

"There's nearly always a rainbow somewhere here, as long as the sun's shining," said Bear. "I often come here when I want to think. Or when I'm feeling particularly lonely."

He smiled at Girl, "Or when I have company I want to impress. Like now."

Girl walked over and ruffled his fur. "Thank you, Bear."

She found a convenient rock and sat down, contemplating the glade, the mist, the rainbow...and her newest, but perhaps most important, friend.

Chapter 10: The Fall

The next day was warm, so Bear and Girl hiked up the ravine again as Girl wanted to revisit the waterfall. Bear didn't mind, as it was one of his favorite spots.

The two friends sat in companionable silence, neither one feeling the need to talk when they had nothing that needed saying. They eventually were covered in spray, and both wiped their faces from time to time, smiling at each other when they did so.

Finally, Bear got up, walked over next to her, and shook himself like a dog coming out of the water.

"Bear! You're getting me all wet! *Bad* Bear!"

She shoved his shoulder. He pretended she was much stronger than she was and rolled over, groaning.

She jumped on his stomach. "Aha! Gotcha! What are you going to do now, hunh?" she asked.

"Oh...help, help! The ferocious hunter's got me! What can I do...except...THIS!" And he rolled over, pushing her underneath him but being careful not to let his almost 1500-pound weight crush her.

She started hitting his chest, not hard, but with purpose. "Get...off...of...me...you...big...overgrown...*rug!*"

He rolled off her, laughing so hard that he couldn't stand.

She leaned up on one arm, saw him rolling around laughing, and then she started laughing. Soon, they were rolling around helplessly, until finally, neither could breathe properly and started gasping.

Eventually, they both stopped, and lay, one by the other, breathing hard and staring at the sky.

"Wow!" Bear said, "I haven't done anything like that since...before..." and fell silent.

"Me, too!" Girl said. "At least that long!"

That started them off laughing again.

When they finally stopped, they were both exhausted but happy.

Girl sat up, tailor fashion, and took the cloth bag of trail mix out of her pocket, only to find that it had been partially squashed with the raisins crushed and many of the nuts in pieces. She chuckled, then scooped some of the mess out of the bag and stuffed it in her mouth. She looked at Bear, who was lying on his back, watching her, grinning. She took some squashed raisins and dabbed them on the end of his nose.

"Hey!" He licked them off. "Mmmm...good. More?" And he opened his mouth wide.

"Uck! Bear! Your breath stinks!" She fanned the air with her hand.

"Well, *you* try living on a diet of fish and game and see how *your* breath smells. Besides, I don't think the supermarkets stock 'Breath Mints for Pristine Polar Bears'!"

Girl burst out with a surprised laugh. "No, I guess not." She looked over at him, then stroked his head. "Bear?"

He looked at her, still on his back. "Girl?"

He saw tears form in her eyes, "Thank you. I haven't laughed...or had anything to laugh about...in, I don't know how many years! You are a true friend...even if you are an overgrown rug!"

With a laugh, she smacked his side, then jumped up and raced off into the underbrush, following the edge of the river gorge uphill.

Bear scrambled up and lumbered after her, impeded by his own laughter. He was able to easily track her movements by what seemed like the incredible racket she made, although he probably would have barely heard it if he were in a human body.

Then, suddenly, it stopped, and he heard a man's voice shout, "*Gotcha!* And there's no way in the world you're going to get away *this* time, you sneaky little *bitch!* I'm going to fix you so you never can even *walk* again, let alone run. And we're going to start right...*now!*

Bear heard her scream in pain.

He ran as quietly as he could, edging off to the right in order to come at them from the side rather than head-on.

He burst into a small clearing, and saw a heavy-set man roughly six feet in height, twisting Girl's arm well up her back, hurting her, and the other hand tangled in her hair, yanking her head back. A shotgun lay at his feet, closed, and probably loaded.

The man's eyes opened wide when he saw Bear. He shoved Girl away from him, reached down, and had just grabbed the shotgun when Bear barreled into him, bowling him over.

The man slipped towards the gorge behind him but grabbed a low-lying tree root at the last second, checking his fall, but only just hanging over the edge of the precipice. Looking back at Bear and Girl, he lunged up for his shotgun, and just managed to grab the stock.

Bear moved towards the man, growling deep in his chest, then stepped hard on the wrist of the hand holding the shotgun. Bear heard bones snapping as he let his full weight press down.

The man screamed, and his hand opened. Bear removed his paw, and the man fell back, tumbling into the gorge, where he crashed off several rocks before landing with his head in the water, body in a mangled position, one foot trapped between two rocks. The shotgun followed him, clanging on rock outcroppings along the way, then splashing into the water.

Girl got up and groggily walked over to look. "We...we need to go down and get him! He'll drown!"

Bear shoved her away from the ledge so she sat, then placed one paw on her leg, pinning her to the ground. "No. First, there is no way I would lift a finger – or a paw – to help that scum. And second, there is no way to get to him in time – unless you want to dive into the water and hope you don't smash your brains out on the rocks."

Bear looked at her, baring his teeth. "He's dead, either now, or before anyone, *including us*, could do anything about it. And...isn't it better that way?" Bear paused, "I take it that...*thing*...was your husband?"

Girl's face showed nothing but shock as she stared at the rim of the gorge, then nodded. "Yes...it is...it was..."

And she crumpled to the ground, collapsing onto Bear's paw and crying hysterically.

Bear released her but was prepared to prevent her from moving towards the ledge. When he saw that she was overcome with emotion and wouldn't be moving any time soon, he nudged her.

"Girl," he said urgently, "We need to leave. *Now*. We don't know if he had anyone with him.... *Girl!*"

When she continued to weep, he stood, then scooped her up in his paws, and started walking on his hind legs, awkwardly, but still with appreciable speed.

After a few moments of being jolted by Bear's progress, she said, "Bear, put me down, please. I can walk...I think."

He laid her gently down but watchfully for fear that she might run back and attempt some kind of foolish rescue.

She looked at him, then shook her head as if clearing it. "Yes, right. Which way home?" She wiped her face with the palms of her hands, eyes red, and shock still showing in her features.

"That way," Bear pointed. She turned in the direction he had indicated and started to jog, picking her way with care, apparently focused on her footing as if afraid to think of anything else.

Bear loped along behind her. Then, when he was sure she wasn't going to do anything stupid, he went slightly ahead of her to show her the way.

After a few minutes, she started to flag, the combination of fear, the ebbing of the adrenaline, and exertion sapping her energy.

"Get on my back and hold on!" Bear said, coming to a stop.

She looked at him, then nodded, jumping up, throwing one leg over his back and clambering aboard, moving her weight onto him and clinging to his fur. Bear started moving off at a steady, ground-eating lope, and the scene of the conflict was soon far behind them.

Bear slowed slightly after a few minutes but kept up a steady pace until they finally burst into the cabin's meadow. Bear loped up to the cabin stairs, then stopped and said, "Okay, get off and into the store room. Now!"

Girl slid off his back and ran unsteadily into the cabin and thence to the store room, collapsing on the floor. Bear walked into the cabin, pushed the door closed, bolted it, and then followed her into the storeroom, closing and barring the door.

Girl was slumped in tailor pose on the floor, head in her hands. Bear collapsed onto his stomach, breathing hard, head towards her. She looked up at him, then launched herself at him, clinging to him and sobbing.

"Steady now," he whispered. "Cry all you want, but *quietly*, okay? We don't know if he was alone or if he had others with him. Shh, shh, shh..."

Girl clutched his fur, weeping into it to muffle the sound, her body racked with sobs. Bear sat up, put one paw on her back, and gently stroked her.

She eventually cried herself out and stopped. A while later, her breathing became deep and regular. She had fallen asleep on the shoulder of a 1500-pound polar bear, which most people would have found more than a little scary.

Yet she felt safer there than anywhere else in the world.

Bear blinked when he thought about the paradox of the situation, heaved a deep sigh, and settled down to listen to the outside world and guard Girl.

Eventually, he fell asleep as well.

The two friends had found safety in each other's arms.

Later, after they'd woken up and had supper, Bear had settled back down by the fire, and was starting to drift off to sleep, his ears perked up. Girl walked softly into the great room, her blanket around her shoulders.

She walked quietly over to his side, then slid her sock-covered feet across the rag rug as she slithered down with her back against Bear's side. Finally, she settled into his stomach, between his fore and back paws. She turned her head forward and almost lost herself in his wide, blue, liquid eyes. "Bear?"

He blinked slowly, then she heard, as well as felt his voice rumble, "Girl?"

"I'm sorry I woke you. I...I think I owe you an explanation."

Bear's head moved from side to side. "Uh-uh. No you don't."

She bit her lip, "Bear, I'd like to."

Bear heaved a big sigh. "Okay, but you don't need to."

Girl turned away. "My marriage was not a happy one."

Bear raised his head quickly, as if surprised, and said, "No kidding? Gee, it was when he threatened you that I got an inkling? Or was it when I saw the bruises? Or..."

Girl turned and swatted his shoulder. "Okay, okay. I get it!"

She turned back towards the fire, away from him. "But sometimes I get flashbacks of...the...things he did to me. And it hurts."

Bear heaved a great sigh. "I know, Girl. And I truly wish there were something I could do about that. I had a wonderful life and a lovely wife..."

His voice trailed off,, then he shook himself after a moment and continued, "I wish I could give you some of my memories, Girl. They are...beautiful."

Girl was silent for a moment, then scrambled up, walked around to Bear's head, and knelt before him.

She had a big smile on her face, then closed her eyes, took his head in both of her hands and leaned forward until her forehead touched his.

The two friends kept their eyes closed with their foreheads against each other for a long while. Then Girl slowly got up, let one hand linger on Bear's muzzle before she walked back to his side, settled in, snuggled up to him, pulled her blanket over herself, and said, "Good night, Bear."

A deep chuckle rumbled in his abdomen, "Good night, Girl."

And the two friends slept.

Chapter 11: Hot Stuff!

When Girl awoke, she stretched, then quickly got up.

"Are you okay, kid?" Bear asked.

Girl stopped, looked at him, and said, "Yes, but I really need to pee!" and hustled out of the great room.

Bear gave his deep, rumbling laugh, then got up, unbolted the front door, and strolled away into the woods.

Shortly after that, both friends were reunited, refreshed and ready for the morning. Girl made some breakfast for herself...plus some bacon she cooked up for Bear, which he really enjoyed and hardly ever got...and the two friends chatted companionably about nothing important. It was as if they had used up all the heavy subjects earlier...or were postponing them, at least...and just wanted to enjoy each other's company for a while.

When Girl had finished breakfast, washed and cleaned up, and hung the dish towel on its appointed rail, she turned to Bear and said, "We need to do something fun today, something to wash away the memories of yesterday's events. Any ideas in that vast trove of treasurers trapped in that tête?"

"OOhhh...alliteration! I like it. Lemme see..." and he turned his head up and to the left for a few moments, thinking. "Okay, I've got it. Get your boots on, mate; we're goin' adventuring."

She smiled at him, skipped into the bedroom to get socks and her boots, and returned quickly. By this time, she was mostly wearing clothes from the dresser and closet in the bedroom – all except for the bras, which were too small. But she decided that today she would skip wearing her only bra and let the girls bounce free for a change. She smiled at herself. She *never* did things like that...until now.

She returned to the great room, then went to the storeroom, picked up the day pack hanging there, the canteen, plus some ad hoc trail mix, and returned to Bear, skipping the last few paces to stop, quivering, before him.

She saluted smartly. "Adventure Girl reporting for fun, Captain Bear!"

Bear dropped his head, laughing, then raised his right paw to his eyebrow and saluted back. "Excellent work, Adventure Girl. Now, quick march...ho!"

He pivoted and walked smartly through the door, down the porch steps, and off to the left side of the meadow. Adventure Girl followed, pausing only to close the door behind her, then hurried to catch up.

The two friends started singing through the woods after about a whole ten paces, with Girl leading with "I love to go a-wandering..." and Bear joining in with a deep baritone. Girl was a bit surprised that he knew the lyrics, but raised her voice even louder in celebration.

The two crashed through the woods, scattering birds, squirrels, chipmunks, and a family of deer, who stood transfixed for a moment by the sight of a polar bear and girl singing together before dashing off into the woods, fleeing from their most feared predator and the bear accompanying it.

Song led to song, and soon they arrived at their destination. "Well, here we are!" Bear commented.

Girl looked around. There was a smallish waterfall, not as dramatic or anywhere near as big as the one they had visited the day before, plus a series of pools off to one side. Two of the pools had what seemed to be mist hovering over them.

"Now, you need to be careful here. These are hot pools fed by hot springs from underground. Those two over there..." he nodded towards the two steaming pools, "...will parboil you in seconds, but the three closer to the waterfall are a tad more comfortable, and you can pick your temperature. The one closest to the waterfall is coolish, the one next to it is warmer, and the third is pleasantly hot. And, of course, the waterfall is rather cold – glacier-fed. And don't say I didn't warn you, okay?"

Girl looked at the pools and waterfall, then back at Bear with distinctly mixed feelings.

"Uh, Bear?"

He swiveled his head to look at her, "Uh, Girl?" he mimicked.

"I...I don't have a swimsuit."

He looked at her and smiled, "Oh my goodness!" He put a paw to his cheek, "I totally forgot!"

He shook his head. "Look, Girl, the air is warm, the water is lovely, and...well...if it bothers you to have a naked Bear look at a naked Girl, then I will turn my back. I'll even promise not to peek...too much!" And he chuckled.

She stood, uncertain, for a moment, then swatted him on his back. "You sneaky critter! This was your dastardly plan all along, wasn't it?

"Okay, then; turn your back!" And she eagerly started unbuttoning her plaid shirt, dropping it on a nearby rock, then awkwardly unlacing her boots and hauling them off, then her socks, and finally pushing her jeans and panties down to her ankles before pushing them off, one leg at a time.

Meanwhile, Bear studiously turned away, facing the nearby mountains and humming loudly and deliberately off-key. Every once in a while, he chuckled to himself, then returned to humming.

When she was done undressing, she picked her way carefully over the rocks to the coolest pool. She dipped her toe in it, shivered, and then moved to the second pool, repeating the process. Finally, she dipped her toe in the third, hot pool, then slowly and carefully walked into it, finally sliding down into the water until it was up to her neck, resting on a convenient ledge.

"Okay, you can look now!" she called.

Bear turned back, then padded over to the pool, looking at her bare form through the water. She smiled coquettishly at him, then splashed him to make ripples in the water, distorting his view. "Pervert."

"Ecdysiast!" he chuckled back at her. "Move over, I'm a-comin' in!" And he waded slowly into the pool, which was easily large enough for the two of them, plus five or ten more as well. Finally, he settled into the deeper part of the pool, with just his head out of the water, and gave a deep sigh of contentment, closing his eyes and turning his head up. After a while, he tilted his head back to get the top of his head wet, then slid under the surface, making a bit of a splash.

Girl smiled at the circle of ripples spreading from where his head had vanished. "Silly Bear."

Shortly thereafter, he re-emerged and started to walk back out of the pool. "Much as I love the heat, this body can't take it for long. I'm going to cool off." And he padded out of the hot pool, water streaming from his fur onto the rocks.

Girl lay back, eyes closed, and let the warmth bake into her bones, feeling herself relax and her muscles unkink in the heat.

Bear trotted over to the waterfall and stood under it, moving to cool different parts of his body under the gentle splatter of water from above. Finally, he stood with his head bowed, letting the water fall gently onto his head, and lapped at it occasionally, drinking.

When he had done, he walked slowly up to a wide, flat rock overlooking the scene and settled down, watching Girl but also keeping an eye out for any potential dangers. He doubted any other predators would come near his scent, but he wanted to make sure.

Eventually, Girl opened her eyes, looked around, and started to emerge from the pool.

"I'm not looking!" Bear called out.

Girl dropped back into the water. "You...you sneak! I didn't see you up there! I need to cool off in one of the other pools. Avert your eyes!" she said imperiously.

Bear ostentatiously covered his eyes, peeking just below his left paw. "You're *absolutely safe*. Come on out!"

Girl looked at him for a moment, snorted, then said, "Fine!" and marched out of the water, sloshing through the shallows as she emerged. When she was completely out of the water, she stopped, hands on hips, facing him, and said, "If you're going to cheat, then go ahead and take a good look – pervert!"

Bear slowly removed his paws from his eyes and looked at her, first into her eyes, which were blazing with defiance, then letting his gaze travel slowly down her body. "You are a beautiful woman, Girl. Truly."

She stared at him. "I'm sixty-frickin'-three years old, Bear. I'm *not* beautiful!"

Bear looked her in the eyes and quietly said, "Yes...you are. Now, go cool off," and nodded toward the waterfall.

Pausing, made uncertain by his remark, she looked at him, then turned and strode unselfconsciously towards the waterfall. She cautiously stuck her hand in the water, pulled it back quickly, then stepped into the water flow.

She screamed but stayed there for several seconds before jumping out of the flow. She wrapped her hands around her shoulders and gingerly picked her way over to the cool pool, slipping into its waters, then sighed deeply.

"Oh, my. That feels *so* good! The hot, then the cold, now this...it feels almost hot, but it's really barely warm." She lifted her head and looked at Bear. "You were right, this is lovely. Thank you...again...Bear."

Bear rested his head on his crossed paws and said, "I had hoped you would like it. You're welcome, Girl." And he gave a deep, contented sigh as he watched her lolling in the pool.

72

The two friends eventually agreed it was time to head home. Girl slowly pulled herself up and out of the cool pool, shook herself to get the excess water off, wrung out her hair, then used her shirt to partially dry herself before putting all of her clothes back on.

Bear kept watch, not to ogle, but merely to ensure they were safe from other critters – or humans. When she was finally dressed, he heaved himself up, lumbered down to where she stood by the path, and said, "Hop on. I'll give you a ride home."

Girl patted his back, then grabbed a handful of fur and hauled herself aboard. This time, she sat up as if she were riding a horse.

After a few steps, Bear began to chuckle.

"What's so funny, you perverted furball?"

Bear continued to chuckle, then said, "Can you imagine if someone saw us? It would start a whole new, Loch Ness monster-type of thing. You know: if someone saw a naked girl riding a polar bear in the Canadian Rockies."

"Hey!" she smacked him, "I'm not naked, okay?"

Bear continued to chuckle, "I know...but it makes for a better myth that way, don't you think?"

Girl thought for a moment, then laughed. "It almost makes me wish there were someone around. Almost."

And the two friends continued to chuckle and talk as they rode along.

After a while, Girl fell silent. She was feeling good from the hot springs, the cold waterfall...and, if she were to admit it, from the close contact with her friend. Her grip tightened on his fur, and he swung his head back to look at her. "What's up, buttercup?"

She smiled but just shook her head. "Just feeling...uh, *good*...is all." And she shifted around on her legs, clasping him with her knees, leaning forward slightly, and settling closer into his back.

Bear sniffed deeply, smiled to himself, and started into a slow trot that jostled her up and down more vigorously.

By the time they arrived back at the cabin, both were sweating slightly, although for different reasons. Girl slid off his back and moved quickly into the cabin, then the bathroom, closing the door quietly but firmly.

Bear settled into his favorite perch on the porch, still panting slightly from the exertion but chuckling to himself.

He'd enjoyed that!

Chapter 12: Nightmares and the Hawk

Bear had settled onto the rag rug in the great room and was starting to drift off to sleep when he thought he heard something, so his ears perked up.

There it was again.

He lifted his head and turned it towards Girl's room; this time, he heard it clearly. He lumbered up and padded quietly down the hall to her door, then stood and listened.

The sounds were intermittent. It almost sounded as if she were talking to someone. Then her voice got louder and more strained.

Bear pushed the door open softly with his nose and padded into the gloom. He could see that her bedclothes were twisted, and her covers were only partially over her.

She turned her head away and mumbled something that sounded anguished.

Her head turned back towards him, and he could see her eyes were closed – but her face was twisted up and almost frightened.

She started speaking more loudly. "No. NO. I didn't. I wouldn't! NOO! Please don't! *Please!*"

Bear moved to her shoulder and started to speak into her ear.

"It's okay, Girl. Bear is here. No one can touch you now. No one can hurt you."

Her head turned towards his voice. "Bear?" she said, almost puzzled. "You're *here?*"

"Yes, Girl. I'm here. No one can hurt you when I'm here. You know that."

"Yes, Bear. I know that."

Her face started to smooth, and her body moved to a more comfortable position.

Her breathing started to even out and gradually slowed.

Bear stayed where he was, then lowered his muzzle onto her stomach.

Her left hand rose and landed gently on his head, stroking his fur.

Her eyes opened, just a slit. "Bear?"

"Shhh...it's okay, Girl. I'm here."

Her mouth moved into a smile, "Bear's here. No one can hurt me now."

And she fell back asleep, quiet and calm.

Bear stayed there for a long time, and then, when her hand slid down to her side, he lifted his muzzle, curled up on the floor next to her bed, and finally went to sleep.

Bear didn't say anything the next morning, and Girl didn't seem to remember what had happened. She merely seemed surprised when she woke up to find Bear asleep next to her bed. She shrugged and thought no more about it.

Later that day, the two friends were lounging around in the great room while flames leaped in the fireplace.

"What's it like being a bear?" Girl finally worked up the courage to ask.

Bear lifted his head from the rag rug to look at her. "About like you'd expect," he replied.

"Well, that doesn't tell me a lot!" Girl said indignantly.

Bear chuckled. "Maybe it wasn't supposed to."

Girl turned and put her bare feet up on his back, with her head on the floor towards the fire that was warming them against the evening's chill. It also gave her the opportunity to look Bear in the eyes, which she couldn't do when she was leaning her back against him. "You're really a man, aren't you?" She dared.

Bear opened one eye and looked at her, "No, I'm really a bear. Or didn't you notice?" He shut his eyes again.

"*Bear...*" she began, exasperated.

He heaved a sigh. "Okay, I wasn't born a bear. I had to work up to it. Think of it as a promotion." He chuckled deep in his throat.

Girl looked at him, but he kept his eyes resolutely closed. "Bear...?"

He opened both eyes. "If you want to ask something, ask it, okay? But stop pecking at me. It's irritating, all right?" He stared at her.

"Bear, you were born a man, but you're not one now. What happened?"

"There. Was that so hard?" he sighed. "None of your business." And he closed his eyes again.

She wriggled on the ground, digging her heels into his back.

His eyes flew open, *"WHAT?"*

She giggled. "I'm sorry, Bear, but I'm incurably curious. I didn't mean to...*irritate*...you."

"Well, you know what they say about curiosity and cats?"

"Yes, but I'm not a cat!"

Bear snorted. "And a good thing, too. Cats are barely worth the effort to catch and eat! Mountain lions, I mean, not house cats."

The two were silent for a time, Girl wondering if he was kidding about eating mountain lions and Bear hoping she would stop this line of questioning.

Finally, he said, "Would you like to meet one of my friends tomorrow?"

Girl gave him a severe look. "*You*...have...*friends?* That's hard to believe."

Bear rolled over, far enough away from her that her feet fell with a *smack!* to the ground. "Ow! That was a mean trick!"

"Did I invite you to put your smelly feet on my nice, clean fur?"

She looked at him and giggled again. "Okay, yes, I'd like to meet one of your friends. Who is it?"

"She's a hawk."

"A what?"

"A hawk."

Girl sat up, "You mean, like a bird?"

Bear sighed, "Yes, I mean, like, a bird."

"Can she talk?"

Bear snorted. "Don't be ridiculous. Animals can't talk. Except for humans, of course. And whales. Porpoises, certain kinds of..."

"Okay, okay, I get it. Humans think they're different."

Bear raised his head, "Oh no, humans *are* different. *Very* different."

Girl looked surprised. "In what way? I mean, what do *you* mean when you say they're different?"

Bear looked at her for a long time. "They destroy things they don't need immediately. They kill for no good reason. They assume they have the right to take anything they want as long as they're stronger than the animal...or person...they want to take it from. They..."

"Stop!" Girl, closed her eyes. "Okay, I get it." She sighed. "I'd like to say you're wrong, but...I've been on the wrong end of that, and I know you're right."

She swallowed, then looked at Bear again. "Being a bear has given you a very different outlook on things, hasn't it? I'll bet it's unique...if we could just get someone to listen to you."

Bear snorted again, but kept his eyes closed.

"Bear?"

He lifted his head. *"Girl?"*

"Please don't be mad at me. I...I'm struggling with this stuff. I'm not used to being able to talk to animals. Or at least, *an* animal. And I can understand why you'd be mad at humans. So please, tell me about your hawk."

Bear put his head down on his paws again but kept his eyes on her this time.

"She's not my hawk. She's nobody's hawk." His mouth quirked up. "But she is my friend. I'll introduce you tomorrow."

He heaved a deep sigh. *"Now* can I get some sleep?"

Girl got up, kissed Bear on the head, ruffled his fur, and said, "Of course. Good night, Bear. And thank you for last night, as well as many, many things." Then she walked off to the bedroom but left the door open.

Bear quirked one eye and saw her outline as she changed out of her clothes and into a night dress. He heaved another deep sigh, this one seemingly sad, not mad, then went to sleep.

The next morning, after breakfast and chores were done, Girl met Bear on the front porch in her Adventure Girl outfit – hiking boots, tartan shirt, jeans, day pack with trail mix and canteen.

Bear nodded, then walked off the porch, picked up the dead carcass of some kind of furry animal, perhaps a rabbit, in his mouth, and led the way off into the woods.

Girl almost said something, then stopped herself. She knew he ate game, but wondered why he was carrying this obviously fresh-killed mammal in his mouth.

After a while, the trail led to the base of a cliff. Bear dropped the kill, then sat back and looked up at the sky.

"What are we looking for?" Girl asked.

"A red-tailed hawk named *Skrreee!*" Bear said.

Girl almost said something, then just nodded and looked up.

High overhead, she saw some kind of raptor circling lazily and pointed it out to Bear. "Is that her?" she asked.

Bear twisted his head to look, then shrugged. "Think so. Kinda hard to tell at this distance. Let me try calling."

He lifted his snout and gave forth with a loud but high-pitched yowl, startling Girl, who burst out laughing.

Immediately, the bird changed direction and started twirling toward them.

"Guess so," said Bear. He picked up the dead mammal, tossed it clear, then backed away from it.

Spying the mammal, the bird came diving in towards it, landing on it with a *thump!*

Perching possessively on the carrion, the red-tailed hawk turned its neck toward the two other animals, fluffed its feathers and wings, and readied itself as if to take off again.

"No, it's okay, *Skrreee!* She's a friend – and she's with me."

The hawk quirked its neck the other way, fixing an eye on Girl, then settled down and began to tear into the carcass, ripping up gobbets of the meat and swallowing them.

Bear and Girl sat waiting, Girl cross-legged, while Bear sat back on his rump.

Finally, when the hawk had finished feeding, it hopped off the carcass towards Bear, ruffling its feathers, then settling down, its cruel beak pointed at them, and its big eyes staring at them, blinking only every once in a while.

"*Skrreee!* this is Girl. Girl, this is my friend *Skrreee!*"

Girl ducked her head and said, "It's a pleasure to meet you, Ma'am."

The hawk quirked its neck to stare at her, then back at Bear, looking as if it were querying what the heck Bear thought he was doing.

Bear chuckled deep in his throat. "I know. I mean – a *human* right? Who would have thought it? But she's okay...for a human. And a girl."

Girl swatted him, and he chuckled, but *Skrreee!* hopped into the air, as if unsettled by the act of violence.

"No, it's okay, *Skrreee!* that's a sign of affection among some humans. And yes, they are strange, no question."

Girl looked at the two other animals, wondering what to say to a hawk, even a red-tailed one. "So, uh, how did you two meet?"

Bear turned to *Skrreee!* "Shall I?" The hawk flapped its wings once.

Bear turned to face Girl. "I was down fishing in the river, farther down from where we were yesterday, and I saw something splashing in the water. Turned out to be *Skrreee!* although I didn't know her at the time. She had swooped down to pick up what she thought was a fish and snagged it, but it turned out to be the plastic rings for a six-pack of beer that someone had thrown into the river. It was stuck on a rock, and she had gotten her leg twisted in it.

"*Skrreee!* was unable to free her leg and would have either died of exhaustion or some other predator would have gotten her.

"She panicked when she saw me coming and tried to beat my head with her wings. I kept at it until I was able to pull the rings free of the rock they were stuck on, then grabbed her legs so she didn't fly away with the damn thing still stuck to her. And although she raked at me with her talons, I managed to avoid the worst of it, pulled the ring off of her leg, then held her up and threw her into the air.

"She flew up and away, way high up, then circled, flew over my head, and settled in a nearby tree. She started screeching at me, and I started to understand her after a while.

"She told me there was a man trapped in the water, as she had been, not far from there, and did I want to kill it for supper? She was repaying me, see.

"I had her lead me to the man – and damn me if we didn't get much the same reaction as I'd had from *Skrreee!* The man started waving and shouting at me as if to scare me off. I walked over to the bank opposite where he was and sat down, just looking at him. His leg was trapped between a log and a rock – literally between a rock and a hard place – and his canoe was overturned and had floated ways down the river.

"I sat down and watched him flail away for a while until he gave up and settled down and sat awkwardly, panting from pain and exertion, his body at an awkward angle because of his trapped leg.

"Then I spoke to him, which I knew would freak him out.

"'Looks like you could use some help there.'

"His jaw dropped, and he looked for a moment as if he were going to faint.

"'I know it seems unlikely, but I really am a talking polar bear. And no, you're not losing your mind.'

"He stared at me for a long time, then said, 'Have ya come fer me?'

"I laughed, which seemed to unnerve him even more, then said, 'Well, I did come because my friend the hawk,' and I nodded towards *Skrreee!*...said you were stuck. I came to see if I could help. Would you like my help?'

"He just stared at me some more, then gulped, and finally nodded, 'I don' see as how I got anythin' to lose, so...yes, please, hep me.'

"I swear he spoke like that. So, I waded out to where he was, and he flinched away from me. I looked over the problem, then reached down and lifted the log wedged against his leg by the water pushing against it. That freed his leg, and he pushed himself back and fell into the water.

"His leg must have been hurt worse than he expected because he floundered in the water. I threw the log towards the shore, then waded in and grabbed him around the waist, and hauled him up to the river bank.

"When I placed him on the bank, he just sat there, panting, for a while, then said, 'So, you ain't gonna eat me, ere ya?'

"I chuckled again and said, 'No, I'm allergic to humans. They give me a tummy ache.' And I rubbed my belly.

"He threw back his head and laughed. 'Don' blame ya a bit. I've a hard time stomachin' most folks mysel'.' Then he stuck his hand out, 'I'm Riley. I do odd jobs 'n deliveries 'round here. Pleased ta know ya!'

"I put my paw out and gently shook his hand.

"Well, I helped him get back to his truck, and fortunately, it was his left ankle that had been bruised, so he was able to drive home. But he came back two days later with five pounds of bacon and sat there, calling for me, until I showed up.

"'Wanna ta thank ya fer what ya did fer me. Doc says I was a dam' fool fer being out here alone, but nothin's broke, so ain't no harm done. If'n I can do somethin' fer you, ya ask it, okay?'

"I took the bacon, thankfully, then said, 'Can I order stuff, human stuff, through you, so can you bring it up here?'

"Well, he looked at me strangely all over again, then nodded and said, 'Yep, I kin do that.'

"'And don't tell anyone, okay?' I added.

"He laughed, 'Trust me fer that! Tried ta tell Doc, and all he thot was I had me a con-*cussion*. Didn't believe a blind word I tried te tell 'im. No, yer secret's safe wit' me – I don't wan nobody to lock me up in no looney bin!'

Bear chuckled again. "And *that's* how I get human supplies."

Bear sat back and looked at Girl, waiting for a reaction.

She giggled, then looked thoughtful. "But where do you get the money to order stuff?"

Chapter 13: Fires In The Field

"That," Bear said, "is another story for another day. But if you think about it, the answer should be fairly obvious. And no," he held his paw up. "I'm not going to discuss it, so don't go asking the questions I know are hammering behind those lovely lips of yours."

Girl stopped, then giggled, "Well then, may I ask if you really think my lips are lovely?"

Bear stopped in his turn, then grinned. "Good enough to eat." And he gave her a glowering look that she just knew was supposed to be ferocious but failed by several leagues. She giggled even harder, then squealed when he pushed her over with his shoulder and straddled her, making a loud, snarling sound.

"OOOH!" she pretend-cried, "Somebody *save* me from the 'rocious, ravening BEAR!' Oh, oh, oh." And she waved her hands around, patting them on his chest as if trying to fend him off, then collapsed into even more giggles, eventually turning on her side and curling up in helpless laughter.

"Aw, shucks. You ain't no fun! How can I terrorize you if all you do is laugh at me?" He continued to loom over her.

Her laughter slowed, then she looked up at him with a taunting smile. "Bear?"

"What?" he said crossly.

"THIS!" and she started tickling him under his forelegs.

"No! No, don't...Oh, stop it, STOP IT!"

Bear rolled over, away from her, but she got up on her hands and knees and pursued him, tickling him mercilessly.

For his part, he had to be cautious. He could bash her head in with a careless blow or crush her with his bulk, neither of which he wanted.

So, he allowed himself to be pursued while he rolled over and over, seeking to escape but really just playing a part.

She finally relented, and the two friends lay, panting, on the grass, laughing together.

"Bear?"

"What *now?*"

"Thank you."

"For what? Never mind...you're welcome. Just don't try that again, or I shall be *forced* to resort to *extreme measures!*"

She snorted. "Right. A cutting remark. A sarcastic jibe. A *rude witticism!*"

Bear, lying on his back, let go a moderately loud *ROAR!*

Girl jumped, startled. "Oh shit! You *almost* scared me, Bear!" Then she started giggling again, which rapidly turned into guffaws.

Which, of course, set him off again. Eventually, they were both gasping for breath and holding their sides.

When they finally stopped for a second time, both of them had aching sides and exhausted diaphragms. Their reactions were born of relief and were cleansing.

Finally, Bear rolled over and lumbered up on all fours. "Well, we should be getting home. Can you walk, or do you want to ride?"

Girl sat up, gave Bear a strange look, swallowed, and said, "I think I'd better walk if you don't mind."

Bear shrugged, "Not at all."

Girl scrambled up, walked over to Bear, put her hand on his back, patted his fur, and said, "Let's go!" And off they went.

They were lounging in the great room after supper, just kibitzing with each other and laughing together. There was a new easiness between them, born of the belly laughs they'd shared, and they both seemed to seek chances to touch one another in gentle affection.

Bear looked at the window, then sat up, almost dumping Girl on the floor. "They're here! I was afraid we'd lost them. Come on!"

He jumped up and went for the door, then turned to look at Girl, who, having been unceremoniously dropped to the rug, was lying there, one hand on her chin, her body laid out behind her, looking at him sardonically.

"Well, come on!"

Giving an exaggerated sigh, she made a great show of lumbering up, aping his behavior, then rocking forward, walking on hands and knees, mimicking him.

"Cute. Now, get up, smart ass!"

Grinning, Girl got up and walked to the door, then the two of them jumped down the three steps from the porch and into the meadow.

Where Girl finally understood what Bear had been going on about.

"Fireflies!" she shouted. "I haven't seen any fireflies since I was a kid! I used to *love* them!"

She started running around the meadow, chasing them, capturing them in her hands, then releasing them again. She suddenly looked more like six than sixty-three, and Bear was charmed by the look of delight on her face.

She finally found a rock and settled on it out in the meadow, just watching the blinking light show around her. Bear lumbered over and sat next to her, and she leaned on him.

She pushed herself upright and looked at him. "Bear? Did you do this for me?"

Bear chuckled, "Gosh, you have a lot of faith in how much influence I have with Mother Nature, don't you? No, I'm as delighted as you are. But I've seen them before up here – just not as often as I would have hoped." He snorted. "Humans are destroying their habitats."

He shifted his weight. "When I was a kid, we'd have fireflies every summer, sometimes for many nights. But as I got older, I saw them less and less frequently. As an adult, I didn't even think about it – until one night, my wife, family, and I were staying at a campsite in...um...rural Pennsylvania, I think it was. And there they were.

"I hadn't thought about fireflies in years at that point. But all of a sudden, I felt truly sad that they had disappeared from my life." He went silent for a long time, looking off into the distance.

And Girl knew, without asking, that it wasn't just the fireflies that he missed.

Chapter 14: The Purpose of Life

The two friends lay on the warm meadow grass on their backs, watching the fireflies, with the other night show – the stars – beyond them. They had been chatting, but eventually, the conversation ran down, then eventually stopped.

Finally, Girl said, "Bear?"

"Yes, Girl."

She paused, which Bear hated. She would open a subject and then stop, or appear to be asking a question, and then pause midway through it. He decided to wait her out.

"A while back, you said you knew the purpose of life. What did you mean?"

Bear thought for a moment, then said, "Actually, I didn't say I knew the purpose of life. Instead, I said I *understand* the purpose of life. Not the same thing."

"Okay, so...what did you mean?"

Bear paused for a while, then said, "There's a slim book of only about 150 pages called *Man's Search for Meaning* by Viktor Frankl. Frankl was a Viennese psychiatrist before World War II, but more importantly, he was a *Jewish* Viennese psychiatrist, which meant that when the Nazis occupied Austria, Frankl wound up in Auschwitz, one of the German death camps.

"The book is short but harrowing. The first third talks about how the Nazis sleep-walked people to their deaths by holding out hope every step of the way. The second third of the book describes what it was like to live in hell. The third part of the book is about what it's like to be set free from hell – and it's nowhere near as easy as you might think. The book is well worth reading, but let me focus on one specific part of it.

"Frankl said that people who lost purpose died. Someone would just give up, and neither the entreaties of their friends nor the beatings of the guards could make them get up. They had decided they were going to die, and they did.

"When asked by their friends, they would say something like, 'Why should I live? What can I expect of life?' And if you tried to answer that question, you lost them, because there is no answer, then or now.

"Frankl said that the only way to answer that question was with a better question. He said you had to ask *them*, 'It doesn't matter what you can expect of life, what can life expect of *you?*' If you could engage them in that question, you might save them. And if it sounds familiar, it's because Jack Kennedy's speechwriter, Ted Sorensen, had read Frankl's book.

"But that question turns the telescope around. Most people look at the world and say, 'What can I expect life to give me?' And there is no answer to that question. Yet, if you ask, 'What can life expect you to give?' you turn the telescope inwards and force them to look at themselves.

"So, Girl, what can life expect of you? What is it that you have that needs to be done, that someone else needs from you, that the world can expect you, and you alone, to do?"

Bear paused.

"What can life expect of *you?*"

Then he stopped talking.

There was silence for a long time after that. Bear was determined to say nothing more, to force Girl to think about it and answer.

Finally, she said, "I...I don't know the answer to that, Bear. I'm not sure there is anything life can expect of me. I'm...well, nothing."

Bear heaved his body up so he could face her. "You haven't heard a thing I've said the whole time you've been here, have you?"

He got up from the meadow and walked slowly back to the cabin.

Girl, surprised, eventually scrambled up and followed him in, closing and bolting the door after her. "Bear?"

He ignored her, slumping down on the rag rug in front of the fireplace and closed his eyes.

"Bear, did I offend you somehow? I'm really sorry if I did. Forgive me?"

Bear neither moved nor spoke.

She sank down, cross-legged, in front of him and put her hand on his head. "I'm sorry, Bear. Really. What did I do? *Please,* Bear."

Without opening his eyes, Bear said, "You insulted my friend. I'm not sure I can forgive that."

She drew back. "Oh, Bear!" But she didn't know what else to say.

When Bear said nothing more, she got up slowly, wiped a tear from her eye, went into her bedroom, changed into her nightie, and got into bed.

But sleep wouldn't come, so, after tossing and turning for what seemed like hours, she dragged her blanket and pillow off her bed, into the great room, and lay down with her head propped up against Bear's tummy.

Bear made no move nor sign, but continued his deep breathing, as if asleep – although she was pretty sure he knew she was there. She stared into the fire for a long time, until finally, it danced her to sleep.

The next morning, she woke to find her head propped up on her pillow but flat on the floor. The door was open, and Bear wasn't there. Feeling stiff from sleeping on the floor, she got up and went to the door. Bear wasn't at his accustomed place on the porch, so she pulled her blanket out onto the porch, put her knees up, feet tucked next to her bum, and wrapped the blanket around up to her nose against the cool morning air. The sun hadn't yet peeked over the ridge tops to her right, but the high clouds were pink and beautiful, heralding the approaching dawn.

And she waited.

The sun had long risen, and Girl had been able to shed her blanket with the warming of the day when Bear finally rounded into view from behind the cabin.

"Good morning, Girl."

"Good morning, Bear."

"Have you had breakfast yet?"

She shook her head no.

"Well, go on in and get some, okay?"

She thought about starting a conversation but decided that if he wanted to broach the subject, he would. Meanwhile, she would respect his obvious wish and not raise it.

She came out somewhat later carrying a large bowl of oatmeal, with some walnuts, plus some berries Bear had brought back for her that he called Saskatoon berries. They were delicious – and she wondered why she had never even heard of them before, let alone found them in the stores.

She returned to her rocking chair and ate slowly, watching the day unfold.

Finally finished, she laid her bowl aside and said, "Bear, I'm sorry."

"For what?"

"I don't know, but your opinion is important to me, and I did something you didn't like." She sighed. "That's not true. I know what I did. I said I was nothing. I know that's not true, but sometimes I feel that way. And I know what you've told me, about myself, and about how my presence has, well, you said I had saved you."

She turned towards him, "Bear, you've become very important to me, and not just because you've saved my life at least twice. I worry about you, more than you know.

"What you were saying about purpose – I get it. Honest. And one of the things life can expect of me is to help you. I'm not sure how, but I know that.

"*That* is part of my purpose."

Chapter 15: Less

Bear snorted. "What's part of your purpose?"

"You are."

"What about me?"

Girl looked at him, a puzzled expression on her face. "I'm...not sure yet. But I am certain you are part of my purpose. Just as, I suspect, I am part of yours."

She smiled. "By any chance, are you a prince bewitched into a bear? I mean, if I kiss you, will you turn into a prince?"

Bear snorted again, "No, but knowing my luck, I might turn into a frog."

"Oohhh...shall we risk it?" She got up and started to walk towards Bear, puckering her lips.

Bear turned his head away from her and said, "Get away from me! Do you think I want to be turned into a dang frog?" But he started laughing.

She kept walking towards him, arms out in front of her, making "MUAH, MUAH, MUAH" sounds and pursing her lips.

Bear jumped off the porch, laughing, and Girl followed behind him, arms out, making kissing sounds, until finally, Bear collapsed on the ground, rolling and laughing, finally yelling, "Stop! Stop it! *STOP!*"

Girl kept coming forward, moving like a zombie-wannabe, "MUAH! MUAH! MUAH!" then finally collapsed on top of him while he faux-struggled to get away from her.

She worked herself forward over his body, giggling the while until finally, she got close enough that she could kiss him. She grabbed his muzzle, pulled it around, and kissed him on where his lips would have been – if he'd had lips.

She paused, making goo-goo eyes at him, fluttered her eyelashes, then wrinkled her nose and said, "YUCK!"

She jumped off him, wiped her mouth, and said, "You have *really* bad breath!" And she kept wiping her mouth with the back of her sleeve.

Bear leaned up on his elbow, "Yeah, but I'm still better than a frog! Have you ever *tasted* one of those things? *Yech!*" And Bear made spitting noises towards the grass. That caused them both to collapse on the ground, laughing helplessly.

When they finally stopped, he lay back, put his forepaws by his head, looked up at the sky, and started to sing.

"Oh, tell me why the stars do shine...

"And tell me why the ivy twines...

"And tell me why the sky's so blue...

"Then I will tell you, why I love you!"

Girl started to speak, but Bear held up his paw, continuing to sing:

"Nuclear fusion makes stars to shine...

"Heliotropism makes ivy twine...

"Rutherford diffraction makes skies so blue...

"Glandular hormones are why I love you!"

Now Girl started to laugh. "I'd never heard *that* version! Where on Earth...?"

Bear leaned on his elbow, "Call it the 'Scientist's Love Song,' I guess. I have no idea where I heard it. Just some of the useless junk that clutters up my head."

He heaved himself up from the grass. "Come on. It's time you did some meditating."

"Why do I need to meditate?"

Bear just looked at her, then kept walking.

Finally, she shrugged and scrambled up to follow him. The two friends walked along the trail, finally arriving at the outlook where they had spent a foggy morning dreaming the world into existence.

"Sit comfortably," Bear said, "Tailor fashion is fine. But make sure you are comfortable because you won't be moving for some time. P.B.S.," he said.

"P.B.S.?"

"Posture, Breathing, and Stillness, keys to this form of meditation."

Girl settled herself in a tailor's seat, wriggled until she was comfortable, cleared her throat three or four times, then looked at Bear and nodded.

"Now, close your eyes – mostly. Leave them open a bit, looking at something close to your legs, in front of you. The idea is to meditate, not to fall asleep."

She did as he asked, focusing on a broken twig about a foot in front of her.

"Okay, now breathe in slowly to a count of four."

Girl inhaled as Bear watched her chest inflate.

"Now hold your breath for a count of four."

Bear counted to four in his head.

"Now exhale slowly to a count of four."

Bear waited and watched.

"And hold the exhale for a count of four." Again he waited.

"Now repeat...four in, four hold, four out, four hold...and again. Just keep going around until it's time."

Girl wondered, *time for what?* but said nothing, continuing to breathe and count. She found her thoughts wandering, and at first, she fought them. But, over time, she found it easier to just let them come into her head, and then let them go again. Eventually, she stopped noticing them.

Meanwhile, her breathing gradually slowed, and her muscles slowly relaxed; shoulders, ankles, jaw, knees, butt, and finally her back and neck.

She lost track...

"Girl," a voice said.

The thought entered her head, and she let it leave.

"Girl."

There it was again. Interesting.

"Girl, come back to me, please."

That was even more inte...oh...

She listened this time, to see if it would happen again. It did.

"Girl, it's Bear."

Ah! That name...and it was a name, not just a noun. Bear was...oh, yes. *Him.*

"Hi, Bear," she said, a smile spreading across her face, eyes still mostly closed.

"How do you feel?"

Her mouth turned up in a very small grin, "With my hands."

She heard a deep rumble of laughter. "I see enlightenment hasn't stopped you from being a smart ass."

The grin widened. "Silly Bear. Enlightenment means *being* a smart ass."

She didn't hear him nod his head but imagined it. "Very Zen. A koan, even. 'To be enlightened is to be a smart ass.'" She heard the chuckle again.

"Hello, Bear. Are you enlightened, too?"

"I'm not sure bears can be enlightened. What do *you* think?"

The grin widened some more. "Well, I know at least one Bear who is a smart ass, so...why not enlightened as well."

Again the chuckle. "Thank you. I think."

"Did you want something, Bear?"

"Oh, many things, Girl. Which is why my attachments keep me from enlightenment. How about you?"

"Hmm...I think I'd like a strawberry ice cream cone, Bear."

"With sprinkles?"

She shrugged, which seemed like an odd thing to do. "Why not? I mean, if you're going to give up Nirvana for strawberry ice cream, it as well have sprinkles too, don't you think?"

She heard the deep rumble of Bear's chuckle once again. "Do you think strawberry ice cream is worth giving up Nirvana for?"

"Oh, definitely. I mean, if you're going to lose your chance at eternal peace, it might as well be for something worthwhile, right?"

She opened her eyes all the way and swiveled her head to look at Bear. "You're beautiful, Bear," she said softly, and was surprised to find tears forming in the corners of her eyes.

Bear smiled, nodded his head, and said, "So are you, Girl. That's what I've been trying to tell you."

She looked at him steadily for some time, then finally said, "Thank you. For many things. For everything. Without you, I would have nothing, I would *be* nothing – so, thank you for everything."

"And thank you, Girl. For purpose – and life. For everything." Bear stirred, then said, "Would you like to get back?"

Girl inhaled slowly and deeply, then exhaled and said, "I'd like to stay on the mountaintop, but my friend, Bear, tells me that enlightenment is found in the marketplace, so I guess we'd better go...find some strawberry ice cream."

Bear got up, misquoting the *Tao Te Ching*, "Even to seek strawberry ice cream is to go astray. The Way that can be known is not the Great Way...to strawberry ice cream."

"Oh," Girl sounded disappointed. "Then I don't want the Great Way. Let's go back to the cabin."

Bear chuckled again, "Unfortunately, the Way to the cabin is not the way to strawberry ice cream, either. Come on." He got up and walked over to her. "Or I'll let you smell my breath again."

She grimaced back from him, arms up as if to fend him off, "No! Not that!" feigning horror. But she scrambled up, chuckling in her turn, wiped her hands on her butt, then nodded. "Let's go."

The two friends strolled together in silence. Girl felt different, somehow. Lighter, less concerned, less...yes...just *less*. She was content to amble along, keeping pace with Bear and occasionally rubbing her hand along the fur on his back.

When they got to the cabin, they naturally assumed their normal positions, Girl rocking in her chair and Bear seated in his accustomed place at the end of the porch.

They sat and contemplated the mountains for a time, and Girl felt she could easily just keep watching forever – except that soon it would be sunset, and the temperature would start dropping.

Finally, she sighed and said, "I guess I'd better rustle up some grub, else I'll wind up going to bed hungry."

Bear pondered briefly, then said, "Hmm...grubs are nice. I know a place where we could get some if you like."

"Oh, yuck, *Bear!*"

Bear looked at her for a moment. "Have you tried some? If not, then how can you say you don't like them?"

She just shook her head, "I'll leave that particular delicacy to you, thank you *so* much."

She got up and went into the cabin, and Bear went off to go forage for his supper. Come to think of it, he thought, grubs sounded pretty good, so he wandered off in that direction.

The two friends sat on the porch and watched the almost-full moon rise. Bear noticed it first when it looked as if the lady in the moon was peeking between the tops of the mountains surrounding the lake. He pointed it out to Girl, and the two of them watched her lift herself into the sky, even as the sky around them darkened into dusk and transformed itself from blue to velvet.

Eventually, Bear looked over and noticed that Girl had fallen asleep in her chair – again. She seemed very much at home in the rocker, for which he was grateful. He waited for her to be well away, then padded over, lifted her up, and carried her into her bedroom. She stirred, smiled, crossed her arms, and leaned her head against his chest as he carried her into the cabin.

He gently laid her on the bed, pulled the covers up over her, and said, very softly, "Good night, Girl. Nothing but good dreams, okay?"

Her smile deepened, "Night, Bear. You, too."

He padded out to his place on the rag rug, slumped down on the floor in front of the fire, heaved a deep sigh, looked into the flames for a while, then closed his eyes – and slept.

It had been a very good day.

Chapter 16: Fireweed, And Rain On The Roof

When Girl awoke, it was twilight, and the sun hadn't quite risen yet. She yawned, stretched, then realized how good she felt. She rolled the covers off her, then sat up, tailor fashion, and started the controlled breathing Bear had taught her...

Bear returned from his morning rounds, expecting to be greeted by Girl, sitting on the porch in her rocking chair. He was disappointed that she wasn't there but expected to find her inside, getting her breakfast. He padded up into the cabin and looked around the great room but still didn't see her.

He walked quietly towards her closed bedroom door, listening. Hearing nothing, he went closer, straining to hear in order to avoid awakening her unnecessarily. Finally, he was standing just outside her door and listening. After a moment, he heard a slow, controlled exhale – and realized she must be meditating.

He turned and padded away, returning to his accustomed place on the porch, waiting.

He watched the day unfold for quite some time, then bestirred himself and padded back into the cabin, listening outside Girl's room. After a while, he heard the same quiet exhale and decided he had better check to see if she was all right. He cautiously pushed her door open and padded inside.

She was seated in her nightie, tailor fashion, with peace on her face and her whole being radiating calm. He hated to disturb her but wondered if she had had anything to eat.

"Girl," he said.

She neither moved nor indicated that she had heard.

"Girl, it's Bear. Please come back to me."

"Yes, Bear, I'll come back for you." And she opened her eyes, which remained focused on something that only she could see, far in the distance, then smiled. "You're beautiful."

"Have you had any breakfast?"

"I will, once I'm finished meditating."

Bear considered, "What time do you think it is?"

"Why it's not even..." and she looked out her window. "Bear, how did it get so light?"

"When did you wake up, before you started meditating?"

"It was...I'm not sure, but it was before sunrise. What time is it now?"

Bear chuckled, "It's mid-morning, Girl."

She slowly shook her head. "No, it can't be. I only just started..."

She turned her head and looked out the window. "Mid-morning?"

"Yup."

"Really?"

"I certainly hope so, or else the Sun has gotten himself all messed up."

She took a deep breath and said in a very small voice, "Oh."

She put her hand on her tummy. "That would explain why my tummy seems so...hollow."

Bear chuckled again and said, "Come on, Girl. Let's get some food in you."

"I hadn't realized how hungry I was, Bear. I can't believe I just ate all of that!" She looked at the remains of an enormous breakfast with feelings of mild dismay.

Bear chuckled. "You needed it. Now, what would you like to do today."

She looked at him, "Do?"

Bear chuckled again. "I seem to recall *someone* complaining to me that 'just sitting' wasn't doing anything."

She colored, then said, "Well..." then stopped, uncertain what to say.

"Why don't we go look at some flowers, Girl?"

"Flowers?"

"Yes, you know...pretty things that have no purpose other than to make people happy. Like you. You make *me* happy."

She colored again, but riposted, "And who says you're a 'people'?"

He chuckled yet again, "You did."

She shoved her chair back and stood up, "Okay – flowers! Let's go!" Changing the subject seemed to Girl the best way out of this.

Bear laughed, then stood up and padded out of the cabin. "Follow me."

Sometime later, they sat on a ridge, overlooking a river valley. The valley was enormous, stretching for miles in both directions that they could see and more miles across from one side of the valley to the other. The river wound back and forth through it, leaving banks of rocks and silt. Clearly, at other times, such as the Spring, it ran much faster and vastly overflowed its current banks.

But the most stunning part of the already remarkable view was the waves of some kind of purple flower, immense quantities of it. As the wind blew through the valley, the flowers rippled, as if they were being combed by giant, invisible fingers.

"WOW!" Girl said. "Wh...what is all *that?*"

"That is generally called fireweed, although it has various names in various places. It grows here later in the summer. Beautiful, ain't it?"

"Isn't it," Girl corrected quietly without realizing quite that she had it. Bear snorted, then chuckled.

She sank into a tailor seat and stared at the waves of flowers waving in the continuous wind. Bear sank onto his hind haunches next to her and kept her company.

Sometime later, Girl shook herself and looked up at Bear. "This is quite mesmerizing, isn't it?"

"Ain't it," Bear corrected, snickering.

She looked sharply at him, then giggled, "Ain't it," she agreed.

"Yes, it's one of the benefits of the job, scenes like this."

"Oh, Bear, there are so many beautiful things here! I can see why you like..." Girl trailed off abruptly.

Bear sighed, "It's okay, Girl. There are compensations.

"Oh, look!" Bear called, pointing with a paw, "There's *Skrreee!*"

Girl looked up at where Bear was pointing, and at first, didn't see the red-tailed hawk gliding overhead, then did.

"How do you know it's your friend and not some other hawk?"

Bear pulled back and looked at her as if she had asked a foolish question – as she somehow felt she had. "Because it's her. How do you know a girlfriend of yours in a crowd or from a distance?"

"Well, by the shape and color of the hair on her head or the clothes she's wearing...wait, do you mean you can see the differences between one hawk and another – from here?"

Bear held her gaze, "Do you mean you can't?" He sighed. "I forget how different human senses are."

Girl was thoughtful for a while, then said, "Bear, I know this is going to sound stupid, but..."

"You're thinking I could be of great use to zoologists."

"Well...yes, actually."

"How?"

"By...oh. I was going to say 'talking to them,' but that's not going to happen, is it?"

Bear just shook his head.

Girl bit her lip, started to say something, then stopped again. Finally, she shook her head. "I'm sorry, Bear."

"For what? You've done nothing but good things for me."

"I'm...I'm sorry I can't be of more help, is all."

Bear grinned, "Except possibly for Riley...and I'm not even sure about that...you've done more for me than any other living human. You have nothing to be sorry about."

Girl looked out over the vast expanse of the river valley, bedecked with fireweed for a long moment, then noticed that the shadows were starting to creep over the valley. Night falls quickly in the mountains, so...

"I guess we'd better go now, Bear." She inhaled deeply, then sighed.

"Yup, guess so. Do you want to ride?"

Girl started to say no, then changed her mind and said, "Please."

When she climbed onto his back, instead of riding as if he were a horse, she leaned forward and hugged his back, clinging to him.

What he didn't see were the tears rolling down her cheeks.

When she awoke the next morning, it was to the sound of rain drumming on the roof of the cabin. She looked out at the grey day through the window and decided she must have slept in. The rain clouds above made it dark, but there was still light in the sky, which meant that she had slept later than usual.

She stretched, then turned, placed her feet on the floor, got up, and went to recycle some of last night's water. While there, she washed her face and hands, then walked back to the bedroom.

She stopped and looked into the great room, and, as expected, the door was open, and Bear was nowhere to be seen. He often went out early to forage for food, usually coming back shortly after she was awake. She didn't know how he managed on so little sleep. He usually put her in bed at night and was gone when she awoke – but maybe polar bears had a different kind of metabolism than girls did.

She returned to her bedroom, picked up the digital watch she didn't use much anymore and set the timer for twenty minutes. Then she settled herself and began breathing and counting, as Bear had shown her. She'd learned that if she meditated without some way of marking time, she could go deep in and have a hard time transitioning back to Real Life – whatever that was.

This time, the sound of the rain helped her scatter her thoughts, and she went deep anyway.

When the timer went off, she reached over, grabbed it, and shut it off while keeping her eyes closed. She took a long, cleansing breath, then listened to the sounds of the cabin. The rain was continuing, but she heard nothing else. That meant that either Bear was not back yet, or that he was seated out on the porch.

Regardless, she decided it was time to be up and doing. She remained in tailor position, called easy seat in yoga practice, and opened her eyes. She moved nothing else; she just let her eyes remain out of focus at first, and then gradually, they began to fasten on specific items. The window. The chest of drawers. The doorknob. The chair.

She started to gently move her neck, rotating it, then slowly cricking it: left ear to left shoulder, right ear to right shoulder. She inhaled her hands above her head, palms flat, in an upward salute, then exhaled them back to prayer position, then inhaled her hands up again, exhaled down, repeating several times.

Next, she inhaled her hands up, then brought her elbows down to shoulder level, forearms pointing up, and upper arms parallel to the ground so her arms looked like goalposts, hands open, and pulled back in half-angel. She repeated this several times. Next, she inhaled her hands up, then, sitting up straight, twisted left, her right hand to her left knee, left hand on the bed right behind her, arm straight, and looked as far back at the wall as she could. Next, she lifted her hands above her again, and repeated the twist to the right. After holding for a few seconds, she put her hands up, facing front, them brought them into prayer hands at heart center.

Deciding to do some more yoga, she got up and changed into a t-shirt and hiking shorts that were the closest thing she had to a yoga outfit, then paced, bare-footed, deliberately and with awareness, into the great room, standing and centering herself on the rag rug, facing the door and cold hearth.

Inhaling up again, this time from a standing position, she went through a full sun salutation three times, then continued on to other asanas.

By the time Bear ambled into the cabin, Girl was lying in Shavasana, also called corpse pose – the meditation period at the end of yoga practice. He stopped, surprised to see her lying in the center of the rug and seemingly dead, but then saw her chest slowly rising and falling. He guessed she had been doing yoga, walked slowly over towards her, and sniffed up and down her torso, ending by exhaling through his nose over her face.

"Bear, you have no class. Can't you see I'm meditating? And your breath still stinks."

Bear sat on his hindquarters and chuckled deep within his chest. "Oh, you're alive! I was thinking I wouldn't have to hunt for a while but could feast on raw Girl!"

Her mouth twitched, but she kept her face still, and her eyes closed, then said, " *You*...are a *louse*."

She propped herself up on one elbow and opened her eyes to look at him. "Do you seriously mean to tell me that you would *eat* me?"

He tilted his head to look at her askew, "Well...only if you were dead."

She leaned forward to smack him on the nose, but he turned away to avoid it, chuckling.

She launched herself at him, tackling him and yelling, "KIAI!"

But no sooner had she started grappling with him when she jumped back and said, "Bear! You're all wet! YUCK!"

He laughed deep in his chest, then shook himself, like a dog just out of the water, sending raindrops flying everywhere.

"OH! BEAR! STOP IT! Damn! Now *I'm* all wet!" She wiped her face clear of the rain expelled from his fur.

He looked at her and laughed again, looking at her, and said, "I disdain to answer. You're *always* 'all wet'."

She paused for a moment, then launched herself at him again, hitting him in the side with a flying tackle.

He hardly moved. She weighed about 130 pounds, and he weighed almost 1500 – more than ten times her weight. She knew this, but she made up in ferocity what she lacked in mass – or brains. He kept laughing as she tried to push him over, which just made her madder. Which just made him laugh harder.

Finally, he allowed himself to be pushed over on his side, at which point she yelled, "Aha! Now I've got you!" and jumped on him, trying to apply a wrestling pin on an animal massively bigger than she was.

He let her grunt and strain for a while, huffing, puffing, and trying to do impossible things. Finally, he leaned up, propped himself up on one foreleg, and said, "When you're *quite* done..."

She collapsed, with her back on his chest, panting and puffing. "There! I guess I taught *you* a lesson. And don't you forget it!"

He dropped his head back on the rug, laughed harder, and said, "Forget what?"

"Oh! *BEAR!*" She smacked him on the stomach with her palm, then jumped up and stomped off to the bathroom, slamming the door. A while later, she emerged, wrapped in a towel, her hair wet, and marched down the hall to her room, then slammed the door to her bedroom.

Meanwhile, Bear went outside and shook himself again, sneezed once, chuckled to himself, then padded back into the great room and set about making a fire in the hearth.

The two friends were seated in the great room by the dining table sometime later. Girl was working on another jigsaw puzzle she'd found in the back of the storeroom, and Bear was pointing out pieces she'd overlooked. His paws were too big to manipulate the pieces, so both were getting impatient.

Finally, she shouted at him to knock it off, she was *quite* capable of doing a stupid jigsaw puzzle without his help, *thank you very much*, and would he please go catch a fish or something?

He stalked off in a huff, grabbed the rag rug from where it was suspended between two chairs in front of the fire, and pulled it back on the floor, preparatory to lying down on it again.

He lay there for a while, feeling hard-done-by, until finally, she sighed, then walked over and sat down in front of the fire, her back to his stomach, and started stroking his muzzle.

"I'm sorry I shouted at you, Bear."

"I'm sorry you shouted at me, too, Girl."

She chuckled, crossing her arms on her chest and leaning back on him.

The two friends sat there, staring at the fire and listening to the rain pounding overhead.

They were at peace, both with Nature and each other.

It was a lovely feeling, for both of them.

Chapter 17: Bartholomew

The next day was a quiet one. They didn't want to venture too far out because everything was wet. Brushing against a bush left Girl's clothes soaking wet in patches and Bear's fur wet in clumps. After a short walk they decided to spend the day indoors, which they did – Girl continuing work on her jigsaw puzzle, and Bear...well, Bear did what Bear did. Mostly out on the porch, just sitting.

After several hours, as things started to dry out, Bear got up and wandered off into the bush. Girl knew better than to ask where he was going – he was foraging for food – never a simple task. His bulk was so great that he needed a lot of food every day, and most of the time, he contented himself with fish.

But he confided in her that fish wasn't enough. Polar bears usually get a great deal of fat as part of their nutrition – although not as much in the summer months, when the temperatures are high – and fish were mostly pretty lean. And in summer months, it was often a matter of staying cool enough, of keeping his body temperature down. On such days, Bear would often disappear and come back wringing wet, having swum in the lake or lay in one of the rushing rivers nearby.

From time to time, he went on a serious hunt for big food, not just top-up fish. Often, this was elk, which were plentiful in the Rockies, but it could be almost anything that Bear could catch. He was an excellent hunter, possessing both the natural patience and cunning of a polar bear, but also the knowledge and intelligence of a human.

Today was a big hunt day. Bear hadn't said as much, but she could tell by his grouchiness that he was feeling especially hungry. So, when he padded off into the woods at a higher-than-usual pace, Girl guessed he was going for a big meal.

She never asked because she knew that she would be squeamish about what he caught – and yet, she knew his metabolism didn't give him any choice in the matter. Both friends instinctively knew it was a subject best not discussed.

So, when Bear came wandering slowly back into the meadow, and Girl, who was sitting on the rocker on the porch, saw him, she could tell by his gait and by the extra weight of his stomach that he had caught and eaten something big.

He hardly spoke to her but wandered into the cabin's great room and collapsed onto the rag rug in the center. Shortly thereafter, he was asleep, snoring like a...well, like a bear.

She smiled to herself, happy that he was getting what he needed, then continued to sit out on the porch, by herself for a change.

She found that being on her own was a very different experience from "just sitting" with Bear. At first, it seemed the same, but as time went on, she felt like she was hearing things she didn't when he was with her.

She could hear crickets – at least, she thought they were crickets – but there was a background sound, too, a kind of roaring, that surprised and confused her. She didn't know what to make of it, where it was coming from, or why it was happening. It was unchanged if she turned her head to try to locate it. It was almost as if it was everywhere.

Finally, after puzzling about it, she gave up and just accepted it.

Many hours later, Bear padded slowly onto the porch and slumped down in his accustomed place at the end, yawning, and undoubtedly still digesting whatever he had eaten. The two friends sat in quiet companionship for an unmeasured time until Girl felt that perhaps she could risk talking to a possibly grouchy Bear.

"Bear?"

He yawned, "Yes, Girl."

"What is that sound I'm hearing?"

His head swiveled towards her. "What sound?"

"I...I'm not quite sure how to describe it. It's like a high-pitched roaring sound, kind of like the sound of ocean breakers rolling in, but constant, not rhythmic."

Bear thought for a moment. "Which direction is it coming from?" he asked.

"That's part of the problem – it doesn't seem to be coming from anywhere. No matter where I turn my head, it's always the same."

Bear chuckled, and Girl suddenly felt as if she was going to be shown up as being a fool.

"Well, I could talk about the background radiation of the cosmos, as discovered by Wilson and Penzias in...was it 1964? But that really wouldn't help very much. The truth is, Girl, it's all in your head."

She looked at him crossly. "You're trying to say I'm imagining it," she stated flatly.

Bear chuckled again, then said, "Nope. I mean, it is literally in your head. Let me tell you a story."

"Is it a true story?" she asked.

"How would I know? I'm only a Bear! And besides, 'What is truth' anyway?" He chuckled even harder. He was clearly enjoying this.

"Once upon a time, there was an elderly couple that lived in Chicago in a flat next to the El – the elevated trains that..."

"I know what the El is, Bear," she said peevishly.

He chuckled again, which annoyed her even more.

"Well, every night at 3:47 a.m., a train would come rumbling through, making an ungodly racket – and they always slept right through it they were so used to it.

"Then they retired and bought a lovely cottage on a lake in the middle of nowhere, congratulating each other on what a quiet setting it was.

"Then, the first night, at precisely 3:47, when everything was completely silent, the man sat bolt upright in bed and shouted, 'What the heck was THAT?'"

Bear sat and waited, chuckling.

Finally, Girl said, "Oh...kay...so what you're telling me is that it's what I'm *not* hearing that I'm hearing – or something like that. Is that right?"

Bear nodded. "Have you ever had a ringing in your ears after being in a noisy environment?"

Girl nodded, "Of course."

"Well, that's what you're hearing – the accumulated ringing in your ears of all the years of living in a noisy environment – and now living in a quiet one. Your ears are trying to rid themselves – ringing if you will – from all the crappy sounds you unwittingly pollute them with living in the city."

Girl rocked back and forth on the chair. "But why is it so *loud?*"

Bear chuckled yet again, "It's not. That's the ringing sound of your ears trying to get back to a zero state. If you will, it's the sound of silence!"

Girl thought for a while, looking at Bear and rocking, then said, "Hunh. Well, all I can say is that quietness is awfully damn noisy!"

Bear chuckled again – annoying her – then trotted down the steps and wandered off into the woods.

She was waiting for him when he returned. She was feeling happier. Peace – now that she knew what it was – was bringing her to a state of contentment that she found quite appealing. She even wriggled in her seat at the sensation.

So, when he appeared again and seemed to be humming, which was always a good sign, she was feeling happy that he was back. Not wanting to spoil his mood, she smiled at him and waved.

He looked at her and smiled, "Well, hello there! You're looking cheerful!"

"I'm always pleased to see my favorite Bear," she dimpled.

Bear looked around behind him, "Why? Has Winnie the Pooh showed up or something?"

"Oh, stop it," she laughed.

Bear heaved himself up onto the porch, walked slowly over to Girl, and laid his muzzle on her lap. "Or did you mean...someone else?" he asked quietly. She rubbed the fur on his nuzzle, then leaned down and kissed it.

"Silly old Bear. You know I mean you."

"Silly – young – girl, yeah, I do."

The two friends stayed like that for a while, then Bear lifted his snout and said, "Would you like to meet my friend, Bartholomew?"

Girl said, "Sure! I mean, I'm amazed that you *have* friends, but..."

Bear barked, a short, sharp sound that caught Girl by surprise. She jumped and shrieked. "Oh! BEAR!"

He chuckled, "Don't get smart with me, young lady! Come on," he turned and walked down off the porch.

"Wait!" she called, "I need my boots. I can't go barefoot!"

"Why not," he asked, "I am."

She stuck her tongue out at him and tried – unsuccessfully – to blow a raspberry at him.

"My, my! Talented, aren't you?" he chuckled.

She ducked back inside and came out a few minutes later, tucking her shirt into her waist, then brushing her hair out of her face.

"Oh, you don't need to get all gussied up for Bartholomew. He really won't care what you look like, trust me."

"Bear, *I* care what I look like, okay? Now, let's go find this friend of yours – if he really exists, that is."

Bear chuckled deep within his chest, then turned and lumbered toward the woods. Girl jogged until she caught up, then walked beside him, her hand smoothing the fur on his back.

They ambled through the forest on what Bear called a "real track" as opposed to a "human track," as if humans didn't really know what they were doing in the mountains – which she suspected was true.

They chatted about what they saw – how some leaves were turning brown around the edges on the deciduous trees, how the days were getting a little shorter, what a lovely breeze there was today, what it was like in the mountains in winter – "Beautiful, but really cold – at least for humans," was Bear's comment – and much besides.

Finally, they came to a rather scrubby part of the forest. They were walking by a marsh, complete with cattails, scummy, algae-covered water, and the call of frogs. Girl commented that the ground was getting squishy underfoot and wondered if it didn't bother Bear.

"Nope, feels kinda nice. Not many pedicure artists around here to take care of my feet, you know."

Girl thought for a moment, then said, "Bear, I don't know anything about bear claws, but if you'd like me to give you a pedicure and can tell me what feels good, I'll try."

Bear stopped, swung his head up to look at her, smiled, and said, "Well now, that's right neighborly of you. I accept – later. But we're almost at Bartholomew's place now." He kept walking.

Not long after, they came to a rock face with what looked like a cave. "Now we wait," Bear said and sat down, "It won't be long."

Girl found a small rock and perched on it. She hoped it wouldn't be too long, as the rock was a bit pointy, and she wasn't very comfortable on it.

Shortly after that, Bear said, "Okay, here they come!"

Girl stood up, rubbing her bum, but said, "They?"

Suddenly, a cloud of bats emerged from the cave mouth and started swooping up from into the sky like a plume of smoke. Girl shrieked again, then put her hand to her mouth. "Your friend is a *bat?*" she asked.

He looked at her, "Sure. I'll bet they're better friends than a lot of the people you know!" Then he turned back towards the cloud of flying mammals and gave a loud moaning sound.

Immediately, as if flipping a switch, one of the bats turned sharply away from the cloud and moved with surprising speed right at Bear's head. Bear sat with a quiet grin as the bat swung around, looping past his head repeatedly, getting close in, far out, and back again.

Then it started to do the same with Girl. She gave a sharp yip and pulled her hands in close around her head and hair.

"He won't bite, will he?" she asked Bear.

"Hmmm...well, let's see..." Bear got up and walked around Girl, sniffing. "Well, you sure don't *look* like an insect, and you don't *smell* like an insect...and I'm pretty sure that, screaming like that, you don't *sound* like an insect, so...I'd say the odds were pretty good that he won't bite you.

"But you never know..." he added with a deep chuckle.

Girl stood up straight, dropping her balled fists to her side, "OH! You're so *infuriating!*"

Bear hung his head, laughing deep within his chest, and said, "It's a gift," then continued chuckling.

Finally, having looped around the pair several times, Bartholomew came to light on Bear's head, opened his mouth, and appeared to say something. Girl thought she might have heard a high-pitched sound, but it could easily have been her imagination.

Bear's eyes rolled up towards the top of his head, looking very comical as he did so, and said, "Hi, Bartholomew. Yes, this strange-looking creature is a friend of mine, and yes, I know I have strange tastes in friends, but she's mostly harmless. Her name is Girl, but you can call her...Girl." And he chuckled again.

Girl walked closer to Bear and looked carefully at the palm-sized dark creature perched on Bear's head while staying about a meter away. "It's a pleasure to meet you, Bartholomew." She wondered if she should hold out her hand or something, but decided it might look threatening, so didn't.

The bat launched into the air, flew around her several times again, and landed on her shoulder. Girl gave a quick yip, then clamped her mouth closed again, trying to hold herself steady. Bartholomew opened his mouth again, and this time, Girl was sure she heard something, but it was so high-pitched that she could only just hear it. The bat launched itself off her shoulder, circled several times, and landed on Bear's head again.

"Hey, he likes you! And he didn't even take a bite!"

Girl scowled at Bear, but said, "So, how did you two meet? I mean, how much does a Bear have in common with a bat?"

Bear looked at her, "Well, for one thing, we're both Mother Nature's creatures."

Girl waited, then said, "Yes, that's true."

Bear twisted his head to look at her askew and said, "You're not believing in Mother Nature, are you? The Person, I mean, not the idea."

Girl hesitated, "Bear, I'm not sure I believe in talking *bears* – and I'm talking to one!" She sighed, "If you say she's a friend of yours, I will believe in her."

Bear nodded, "So, she *can* be taught! Good!"

He turned his eyes up to look at Bartholomew again, "I found Bartholomew trapped in some bushes a while back. He had been flying near them, flew through a spider's web, ripping it apart, but it deflected him into the branches of a sticker bush, and he was caught there. I happened to be nearby, heard the thrashing, and went to investigate.

"When I saw him, he was a wee little thing, not the robust adult you see before you now, but a tiny little beastie. I was able to use my claws to free him – although I did get a couple of prickles, ouch! – and he finally was able to fly free.

"He flew up high and far, circled for a while, then flew back, buzzing around me, and finally landing on my head."

Bear chuckled again, then said, "He said he could show me where there were some particularly delicious mosquitoes if I wanted some. I declined with thanks and said they were a little out of my weight class. But we got to chatting.

"He's a whiz at all kinds of bugs, although bats have their own names for them. They even have a name for humans – although I won't repeat it in polite company – but he said I was a different kind of bear, and he was pleased to meet me, and what kind of insect did I like to eat?"

"Well, I finally convinced him I didn't eat insects, which he thought was weird, but finally accepted, and we got to talking about other stuff."

The bat started working its mouth and moving its wings slowly back and forth. Bear cocked his head as if listening to something Girl couldn't hear. Then, in a flash, Bartholomew was gone.

Bear got up, stretched by dropping his forequarters down, arching his back, then smacked his jaws together and said, "Well, we'd better be getting back.

"Bartholomew said he thinks this winter is going to be harsh. He explained that the insects were getting panicky but that it was awfully early for them to be doing that – but that the last time they did, we had a particularly nasty winter."

Bear heaved a deep sigh, "Just what we need. A hard winter. Oh, well. Not much we can do about that just now. But I'd better start laying in some supplies, I guess. I'm glad we came to see him." And he turned and started to walk back the way they had come.

After a moment's hesitation, Girl turned and caught up with him. "Bear?"

"Girl?"

"Do you really believe a bat knows how hard the winter is going to be?"

He turned to look at her, "But he didn't. He said the insects were getting panicky. And, yes, before you ask, I do believe he is probably right. You would be surprised at how carefully attuned animals are to the seasons. Humans used to be, but...well, science is all very well and good, but it means humans aren't listening to themselves or to Mother Nature anymore."

The two friends walked along silently for a time, then Bear said, "Go ahead. Ask the question you're dying to ask. I know you will eventually."

Girl hesitated, then said, "Did you really mean what you said about...Mother Nature being a person?"

Bear stopped, sat, and turned to look at her. "Okay, now listen to me, Girl, and listen carefully. Mother Nature is not a 'person,' she is a 'Person.' And you must speak of, and to, Her, with *respect*, understand me?"

Girl wasn't quite sure what to do but realized that, for once, Bear was completely serious. Finally, she nodded and said, "I promise Bear."

"Good. Now, it's starting to get dark, so let's get back to the cottage."

But Girl spent most of the trip wondering about this...Person...Bear called Mother Nature.

The next day, after arising from her bed and cleaning up, Girl headed out to the porch to see if Bear had returned from his morning forage – and found that he had.

"Good morning, Girl," he said when he heard her walk through the door. "And how are you this morning?"

"Oh, I'm light-to-variable with a chance of showers. How about you?"

Bear's head swiveled to look at her. "Not quite as much of a smart-ass as you seem to be today, but otherwise good, thanks. I think we'd better stick close to the cabin today."

Girl considered, then said, "Sure, no problem, but how come?"

"*Skrreee!* flew by to say that there were hunters in the area. Since it isn't hunting season yet, I'm guessing they're looking for your ex, the troll – and whatever happened to him."

Girl paused, and her heart skipped a beat. "He had four brothers. They will certainly come looking for him. Did, uh, she say how many of them there were?"

Bear blinked, "More than one. *Skrreee!* doesn't really have much of a grasp of numbers. But I wish you'd told me about his brothers. I had thought there'd be a search party but that they would chalk it up to an accident and let it go. Brothers, though, might decide they wanted more of an explanation than that and might search longer and harder."

He turned and looked off into the distance, obviously thinking. "I'd better lay in some food for me. Do you have enough to get by for the next week or so?"

Girl thought, then said, "I'd better go check," and turned and walked back into the cabin.

Bear heard cupboards opening and closing, then the fridge, and shortly after that, Girl returned. "I can get by for a week – although I'll run out of milk, even the shelf-life stuff – and could stretch it to perhaps ten days if I have to. After that, I'll be back to oatmeal, peanut butter, and canned goods, which we can stretch for much longer. How long do you think we might need to hunker down?"

Bear stared at her for a while, then said, "It's more complicated than that. Come and sit down, kid. We need to talk."

Girl settled slowly into her rocking chair. "Any discussion that starts with 'We need to talk,' ain't gonna be good. So, go ahead; hit me."

"I told you before that we need to get you back to civilization. Winter is no place for a human in the Rockies. And there's a deadline, too – they close the roads at the end of September, and even Riley doesn't usually come up here after that. So, no food, no transport – and lots of bitterly cold weather."

Bear slapped his side and said, "I'm built for it, but you...no, you're just a dainty, hot-house flower, kid."

Girl's eyes started to fill. "Bear, this is the first place in decades where I've felt safe, where I've felt *at home!* Please don't make me go, please!"

Bear took a big breath and exhaled noisily. "Girl, you have no idea how much I want you to stay. I've been so terribly lonely. Yes, I have animal friends, only a few of whom you've met, but it's not the same. And you are a joy and a delight, someone I am glad to know for your own sake.

"But it's not a matter of choice, don't you see? You *have* to leave. You would not survive here in the winter. It's just too dangerous – and not just because of the winter. If the troll's brothers are looking around here, they may be looking for you, too. For both of us, really.

"I know you've been comfortable here – at least, I've tried to make you comfortable..."

"Yes, I've been very comfortable here, Bear. It's been home, a home I've never really had before. Thank you," Girl said, tears now rolling down her cheeks.

"...but it's only been a temporary respite, a safe haven in a time of storm. But you *must* leave. You see that, don't you?"

Girl nodded glumly, "Yes, I know. I don't like it, but I know."

She looked up, "But, Bear, where will I go?"

Bear looked at her. "You must have had some plan before you tried to escape from the troll."

She nodded, "Yes, I have a sister. But I can't *live* with her. And I had made plans for if I escaped – for *when* I escaped...but...," and her voice died away.

Bear shook his head, "Then you can start there. And I suspect that once you tell your sister what your life was like, you'll be able to stay with her while you figure out what you want to do from there. I doubt she'll throw you out after three or four days, Girl. Even if you are a brat."

Girl was looking sad, then her head jerked up. "OHH!! You're so...*annoying!*"

Then she smiled at him through her tears. "You got me again, didn't you?"

He chuckled, "Yup. Just keeps gettin' easier all the time!"

Then his smile collapsed, and he looked off at the mountains again.

She looked at him for a long time while he studiously ignored her.

"Bear?"

"Girl?"

"If I agree...to go, will you tell me...about what happened?"

Bear's head swiveled towards her, and he looked at her for a long time. Then his eyes closed, and he sighed. "Yes, okay. I'll tell you. But not yet."

Girl nodded. "Me, too. Not yet."

Bear heaved himself up and loped off into the woods. She knew he was going to forage for food – but she also knew that wasn't his main reason for leaving.

She shook her head sadly. Did this really have to end?

Chapter 18: Bear's Nightmare

Girl was asleep in her room that night, figuring that she was disturbing Bear's rest by lying snuggled against him.

She woke up, not knowing why, and sat up in bed, listening. Hearing nothing, she lay down again, closed her eyes, and tried to go back to sleep.

Then she heard it again. Slowly, she drew back the covers and stood up by her bed, and heard a low rumbling noise.

Quietly, she walked out to the great room to see Bear asleep on the rag rug by the fire.

She stood there for a while, listening, and was about to turn and go back to bed, when his form jerked, and she heard it again.

It didn't seem possible, but Bear was...whimpering...

His body jerked again, and he started twitching, as if trying to move and failing.

Girl crept quietly over to Bear's head, knelt down, and started stroking the fur behind his head.

At the first touch, he jerked, then calmed down as she continued, his eyes still firmly shut. As she continued to stroke his fur, his twitches continued to lessen gradually. Girl sat, cross-legged near his head and lifted it onto her lap.

Bear's mouth opened slightly, revealing long, white teeth.

Girl crooned softly and said, "Shhhh, now, shush. It's OK, I'm here. It's all right, Bear."

After a moment, Bear's eyes moved and opened a slit, "Maddie?" he said.

"Yes, dear one. I'm here."

Bear's eyes closed again. "I thought I'd lost you."

"Never, my friend. Never. I'll always be with you."

Bear seemed to settle down and soon was breathing calmly and evenly, apparently asleep again.

Girl kept stroking his head and muzzle, all the while getting stiff and cold.

When she finally thought he was safely asleep again, she gently laid his head back on the rug, cautiously scootched back from his sleeping form, and got up. She stretched to get the stiffness out, rubbed her arms to warm them, and then walked back to her bedroom.

She got into bed, pulled the covers up over her, and hugged herself to get warm.

When she was warm and almost asleep, a tear rolled down her cheek, and she whispered to herself, "Poor Bear."

Chapter 19: Shelter

Aside from that one side trip, Bear and Girl stayed close to the cabin. Bear consulted with *Skrreee!* every morning about the hunters, and every morning she repeated that they were still in the area.

Girl was out in the meadow one afternoon, gathering some wildflowers for a centerpiece when she heard something. Quickly, she crouched down and turned slowly towards the sound, only to see four men off in the distance – the troll's brothers – come into the clearing.

Although her heart started pounding wildly, she knew better than to make any sudden moves. Instead, she lowered herself slowly and quietly onto the ground and lay flat, head turned away from where they had been. She knew that movement and eyes both attracted human attention and wanted to offer neither to these particular individuals.

She listened as best she could, and, unfortunately, heard the sound of their tramping feet getting louder. She gulped but could think of nothing better to do than stay still and keep quiet.

It seemed as if they were coming straight for her – by coincidence, most likely, because if they had seen her, they would be calling to her or to each other. Instead, there was only the steady, tramping sounds of their boots getting louder.

She wondered what would happen if they found her and worried that she knew exactly what would happen.

Suddenly, she heard the scree-ing cry of a stooping hawk, echoed by cries of the four men. Then, she almost heard a high-pitched squeaking and more cries from the men. The men were calling and shouting to each other, cries of surprise and anguish, and equipment dropped to the ground. Very shortly after that, she heard them swearing and cursing, then the sound of quick steps, now moving away from her, and into the forest.

She lay quietly, breathing hard but keeping it as noiseless as possible. She had no idea how long she had lain there, or how long she should lay there, but decided that longer was better than too early, so continued to lay still. The only problem was that she really needed to pee, whether from fright or natural causes, she wasn't sure.

Then she heard something else – a quiet slithering as if something was parting the grass. As it got closer, she felt her heart in her throat and wondered what it could be.

"Girl!" It was Bear, whispering urgently. She turned her head and saw him, flattened on the ground, looking at her. She turned her head down, and her eyes filled with tears of relief. She moved her body around and started to eel her way toward him. He waited until they were head-to-head, then whispered in her ear, "Follow me back to the cabin, but stay low and keep as quiet as you can, okay?"

She nodded, relieved to let him take the lead and decide what to do. He slowly moved his body around so he was facing back towards the cabin, then started to crawl, slowly but surprisingly quietly, back that way.

She followed him, crawling as he was, paying attention only to what she could hear and thinking of nothing but the next movement forward.

Finally, Bear stopped, slowly lifted his head, and turned it, scanning the area. He turned to face her, then quietly said, "Follow me." He slowly crouched up, moved over to and up the stairs onto the porch, into the doorway, then waited in the open door while Girl followed him.

Once they were both inside, he quietly closed the door and bolted it, then waved her towards the storage room. She shook her head no, moved quickly off to the bathroom, did what was needed, and then walked, crouched over, to the storeroom. She opened the door, and scooted to the far end, sitting tailor fashion, with her back against one of the shelves. Bear quickly followed, lying on his side, with his head towards her. "Shhhh," he whispered. She nodded.

The two friends waited, seemingly frozen. As much to reassure herself as him, Girl started stroking his head, feeling the coarse texture of his fur beneath her hands and feeling the rise and fall of his great chest. After doing that for some time, she impulsively leaned forward and kissed him on the top of his head.

He twisted his face towards her, smiled, nodded, but said nothing.

She wondered what he was waiting for, then, after what seemed an age, heard the scree-ing sound of a hawk again. Bear got up, turned to face her, and patted the air down with one paw, indicating that she should stay where she was. She nodded and remained sitting.

Bear opened the storeroom door, padded out, then closed it quietly behind him. Girl waited in the room, wishing she were with Bear. Just his presence seemed to make her feel safer and happier. But she waited.

Finally, Bear appeared at the door again and motioned for her to come out. "*Skrreee!* says they've gone. We'll keep quiet just in case, but I think we're safe."

Girl shivered, walked over, and hugged Bear. "How did they find us, Bear?"

Bear chuckled, deep in his chest. "It's more like, why *didn't* they find us, Girl? They've been systematically searching this region, according to *Skrreee!*, and were bound to come back to this area as this was near where his body was found. You did just the right things, dropping slowly to the ground and staying there. You're a smart girl, Girl, and you have a good head on your shoulders.

"They were headed right for you – did you realize?"

Girl nodded, then swallowed hard, "Yes, I heard them."

"I was watching from the cabin, but couldn't do anything. I was almost going to break cover and run away from the cabin to draw them off when *Skrreee!* swooped down and buzzed them, then looped up again and down over them. Just as they were starting to pull their shotguns up to aim at her, Bartholomew flew at them from shoulder level, flying into each of their faces and disrupting their aim, then flew away.

"They looked like Keystone Kops for a while, dropping their shotguns, floundering around, and then running off in the direction *Skrreee!* went." Bear chuckled again, and Girl began to feel better. "She circled way high up, so they couldn't shoot her, and kept an eye on them. When they headed back towards their pickup and drove off, she circled back here to let me know. She's going to keep watch for a while, but believes they've gone."

Girl sighed, then sat down next to Bear. "Are we ever going to be safe, Bear?"

Bear looked at her. "I don't think you understand what just happened, Girl. You were *protected.* Do you think that it just happened that *Skrreee!* was watching them, and Bartholomew was flying this way? No, Girl. Someone likes you – other than me – and I'm pretty sure I know Who that is." And he waited, looking at her.

"Mother Nature?" Girl finally asked.

"That would be my guess, Girl. Although *why*...that's perhaps a harder question. But if *She* likes you, that will help a whole heap in keeping you safe."

Bear slumped to the floor, on top of the rag rug, "Besides, *I* like you, and I'll do my darnedest to keep you safe."

Girl's eyes filled with tears, "I know you will, Bear. I don't know *why* you will, but I know it." She looked up at him and kissed the tip of his nose. "Thank you." And she cuddled into his body, up against his stomach, feeling safe once again.

Chapter 20: The Owl and The Porcupine

It was a lovely day in the Rockies. Bear and Girl had broken their fast, and were sitting in their favorite places on the porch, watching the mountains grow. There was a light breeze, and a leaf blew onto Girl's lap, where she sat on the rocking chair with her feet on the seat, her knees up high, and her chin resting on them.

She smiled, picked up the leaf, and looked at it.

"Bear," she said.

His head swiveled towards her, "Girl?"

"Look at this leaf. It's beautiful!"

It was red and had wondrously articulated veins running through it.

She turned it to the front and saw a shiny, bright red texture.

"It's a maple leaf, Girl. You know – like the one on the Canadian flag?"

She giggled, and it made her seem like a little girl – which, in many ways, she was.

"They didn't do a very good job drawing it. This is far more beautiful, Bear!"

Bear stood up and lumbered over to where she sat to look at it. She held it up to his gaze and turned it slowly so he could see both sides.

"Hunh," he said. "I guess it's time," he said cryptically. "We need to go see someone, Girl. Would you rather walk or ride?"

She dropped her forehead and slowly looked up at him with a smile on her face. "May I ride, please, Bear?"

Bear smiled. "Of course, Girl. Climb aboard."

She scrambled off the rocking chair and onto Bear's broad back, her legs straddling him, barely making it over the sides.

Bear lumbered down the steps and headed off in a direction they'd not gone before.

They started singing as they went, songs from campfires and arias from operas, then finally fell silent.

Girl's face broke into a grin; she squeezed Bear's middle with her legs, stretching up and shouting, "AH...E-AH-E...AHHH!" and thumping her chest with her fists.

Bear rumbled his laugh. "What are you, Tarzan?"

Girl swung down so her face was next to Bear's while she clung to his fur.

"No, *me JANE!*"

Bear laughed and picked up speed – "So what does that make me? Hathi the elephant?"

"No, Bear...that's *The Jungle Book*! Different author, different story. Silly!"

Bear's laugh rumbled again, "Oh, ex*cuse* me!"

The banter kept flying back and forth until finally, Bear stopped by a great oak tree. He lifted his muzzle and howled. "AAHHHRRROOO!" then pawed the bark of the tree.

There was a long pause where nothing seemed to happen, then a quavery voice said something that Girl – remarkably – understood, even though it was in no language she had ever heard before. "What is it now, Bear?"

Bear looked up, Girl looked up – and a Great Horned Owl looked back at them, its face seemingly suspended inside the trunk of the tree.

"Owl, this is Girl. Girl, this is Owl."

Owl blinked, then said, "Bear...this is...most irregular. Are you sure you know what you're doing?"

Bear's laugh rumbled again, "Not really. No more than usual."

"Oh, well...in that case. Wait there."

There was a scrabbling noise, then a whiffling sound, and the enormous Owl glided gently down to the ground, landing some ways away from Bear.

Owl was half Girl's height – large for a bird – but this was no ordinary bird. This was Owl, the wisest resident of the Forest. He stalked awkwardly around Girl, his head turning and twisting as he circumambulated her.

"Hmmm...," he said. "This is a strange one. How did you get it, Bear?"

Bear chuckled deep in his chest. "I found her by the side of the human road."

Owl's eye fastened on Bear. "Really? So, they threw her out, did they?"

Bear shook his great head. "No, Owl. She escaped from them."

Owl's head swiveled back toward Girl. "Well, perhaps she is cleverer than she seems, then."

Owl stalked around her again, then stopped by Bear, peering up at him.

"Bear...is she...quite *safe*, do you think?"

Bear chuckled even more loudly. "Yes, Owl. She is quite safe. And quite lovely. You'll see."

Owl's head swiveled towards Girl, then back towards Bear. "Well," was all he said.

He closed his eyes, and Girl began to wonder if he had fallen asleep.

133

Finally, he opened his eyes. "Yes, Bear, you are right. She has escaped from them. And they were particularly brutal towards her – rather as they are towards us." He regarded Girl and blinked his great eyes. "She has been hurt by them. And she needs healing."

Owl closed his eyes again, but this time Girl felt as if she were being examined...deeply.

Finally, Owl opened his eyes and turned toward Bear. "I think she should see Porcupine."

And he hopped off, opened his great wings, clattered back up to the hole in the tree trunk, then vanished inside.

Bear ducked his head, walked over to Girl, and said, "As I had hoped. Porcupine is our healer. But she is very shy and would never have seen you if Owl hadn't said you should."

Girl was puzzled but trusted Bear, so she kept her peace.

"Come now, Girl. Get on my back. We have a ways to go, and it is getting late."

Girl climbed on Bear's back, grasped two handfuls of fur, and Bear began first to walk, then to trot, and finally to run through the forest.

This caused a commotion. Animals poked their heads out and chittered, calling to Bear, who ignored them.

They went on and on...until Bear, with his chest heaving, finally began to slow to a trot, then to a walk...

...and eventually stopped by an old, dead tree.

Beside it was a rotting log. Bear rapped on the log three times, then cautiously backed away, making sure that Girl stayed on his back.

At first, nothing seemed to be happening. Then there was a rustling sound, and shortly after that, Porcupine emerged from the log with spines bristling, blinking into the light.

"Who is it, and what do you want this time? Can't an old woman get any sleep? If this is the chipmunks again, here to complain about their paws, I will BITE them!"

Bear chuckles again, "No, Porcupine, it's me, Bear."

Porcupine stopped, blinked in a way that showed Girl that the old girl couldn't see very well, then sniffed.

"You're not alone, Bear. How dare you bring a *human* with you!" she began withdrawing into her rotting log again.

"Wait, Madam Porcupine. Owl said you needed to heal her. She escaped from the humans."

Porcupine stopped and blinked at them as if trying to focus. "Escaped, you say?"

"Yes, Madam P. But they damaged her."

Porcupine started forward. "Those....*savages!* They have hurt so many of my children. How *dare* they? Even to their own kind?"

She stopped short of Bear. "Let me smell her closely, Bear, so that I may know her."

Bear turned to Girl and said, "It's okay, Girl. Slide down and stand still. She won't hurt you."

Porcupine sniffed again, "Hurt her? I should say not! Are *we* savages? Hunh!" And she sneezed dismissively.

Porcupine waddled around Girl, her quills rattling inches from Girl's flesh. Any one of them brushing her would have wounded her – but none so much as grazed her flesh.

Finally, after Porcupine had made a complete circuit, she stopped, nose pointing up towards Girl's face.

"My dear...wait, I can't call you a...human," Porcupine's tone implied that to do so would be a dire insult. "What shall I call you, child?"

Bear cleared his throat, "Call her Girl, Madam P."

"Girl," Porcupine mused, "Yes, that will do. My dear Girl, they have been quite dreadful to you, haven't they? Awful creatures, stinking things with no manners!"

She sneezed again as if to discharge their smell from her nose. Then she stood for a long while as if thinking. Girl held her breath and held quite still.

Finally, Porcupine sighed deeply and said, "Girl, I will give you one of my quills. Will you take it?"

Girl glanced back at Bear, who was carefully still, giving no sign.

"Madam Porcupine, I would gratefully accept anything you gave me, with thanks."

Porcupine looked up, squinting, at Bear, "Well, at least she has breeding, I'll give her that."

Turning back to Girl, she said, "Now, Girl, very cautiously, put your hand forward and find the quill that is closest to my left ear. It will not sting you."

Girl leaned forward very slowly, looking carefully, and found what she thought was the appropriate quill.

She pointed at it. "This one, Madam?"

Porcupine sneezed again, "I can't see my own ear, dear. You will have to choose. Choose wisely, Girl."

Girl thought and looked again very carefully. "Yes, I believe it is this one," and she carefully tapped it with her finger, causing it to move slightly.

Porcupine shivered, and all the quills on her back shook. "Yes, my dear. Carefully grasp it and pull it gently from my head."

Girl carefully wrapped her hand around the quill she had selected and gently pulled on it.

It didn't move at first, then slowly, like from a bottle of molasses, came free.

136

Girl held it up. "I have it, Madam. Now what?"

"Why scratch your tummy with it dear. It will sting a bit, but it will heal you. Over time."

Girl turned and looked at Bear, but he gave no sign.

Girl pulled up her shirt, baring her firm stomach, and ran the quill over it.

A red welt appeared, and it stung...for a moment.

But very quickly, the welt started to fade – and Girl felt a sense of euphoria permeate her.

'Ohhh..." she said and began to fall backward.

Bear quickly caught her and placed her gently on the ground.

Girl smiled up at him. "Bear," was all she said, raising her hand and rubbing his muzzle.

Bear smiled down at her. "Yes, Bear."

Bear looked up at Porcupine. "My lady, thank you. You have been gracious and kind. We will not trouble you again."

"Oh, fiddlesticks, Bear. You always bring the most interesting ones to me. And they always need my help – and your care."

She waddled over to him and raised her front paw. "This one especially needs you. Take good care of her, Bear. She is...," Porcupine hunted for the word in her aged brain, "...unique."

Then she turned and waddled back to the log. There was a scraping sound, and she slowly disappeared into it.

Bear gently lifted the now-sleeping Girl onto his back and carefully trotted back to the cabin.

Climbing the steps, he took Girl into her room. He removed her boots and socks, then gently placed her in bed, pulling the blanket up over her.

He stepped back a pace and looked at her. She was breathing quietly, her face was smooth and seemingly at peace.

"Madam was right, Girl," Bear said quietly, "You are unique."

He regarded her for a moment longer, then turned and went out to the rag rug, walked around it, collapsed with a sigh, and went to sleep.

Chapter 21: Porcupine's Gift

The next morning, Bear woke up and blinked. It wasn't quite light outside, and the cabin was quiet. He stood up and padded into Girl's room as silently as he could. She was sleeping peacefully, and her face was calm, even serene.

Bear smiled, went into the kitchen, and prepared some fruit and honey – all sourced from near the cabin. He had not raided the beehive but asked the bees if he and Girl might have some, and as he had asked politely, they were happy to oblige.

He laid it out on the table, awaiting only their patroness, when Bear heard something. He stopped, unsure of what he was hearing, then turned and padding quickly towards Girl's room.

Gently, he pushed the door open and was shocked to find Girl, curled up in a ball, weeping. No; sobbing uncontrollably.

Bear, puzzled, padded across to the bed. "Girl! What's *wrong* Girl?"

She was unable to speak, she was weeping so hard, her face a mask of pain and anguish.

Bear put his front paws on the bed and nudged her with his muzzle. She moved violently, and turned away from him, "Leave me alone! I'm terrible, I'm awful, I'm...*human!*" She screamed the last word in a horrible, rasping, screeching voice.

Bear dropped back down onto the floor, unsure what to do, afraid to leave Girl alone, but well out of his depth. Finally, he sat back on his haunches and waited, reasoning that she couldn't cry forever and would run down eventually.

And she did – although it was a long time in coming.

Finally, she rolled over, her head upside-down, hanging off the bed, eyes red, staring at Bear. "Oh, *God*, Bear! Why have we been so horrible? *WHY ARE HUMANS SO...* "She had balled her fists, her face turned bright red – then she collapsed, exhausted, and went limp.

Bear moved over to her, settled himself, and picked her up. She was a rag doll in his arms, as if she had no bones at all. He stood on his hind legs and carried her out to the porch, pushing the door open with his rump, then cautiously placed her in her rocking chair, arranging her so the chair would support her, and not cause her to slip to the ground.

He turned his back to her, pushed up against the chair to prevent her from spilling forward out of it, listened, and waited.

Finally, he heard a despairing sigh. A hand came out and started to stroke his fur. "You're well rid of being human, Bear; well rid. We are...*despicable!* I see that now – and I'm part of it."

Bear moved so that he was facing sideways, half towards her, half towards the mountains, unsure what to say. "I...I take it that it was Madam Porcupine's quill that did this?"

Girl, shook her head, her eyes red and full of sorrow. "No. All it did was to open my eyes to the world around me, the world I have so long been blind to." She bowed her head, "It...it showed me that *I* am human."

Bear looked at her, waiting to see if she would go on, then eventually nodded, "Yes, you are. Let he – or she – who is without sin cast the first stone. You are not without sin. No one is.

"Porcupine eats grubs – which are other animals. I eat fish, elk, small mammals – and if I could get them, seals. Owl eats field mice and small birds. There is sin enough for all."

But Girl was shaking her head. "Not so. You – and Porcupine, and Owl, and *Skrreee!* and the others take what they need. We humans take what we *want* whether we need it or not. We...are so...*greedy*, Bear." And she sighed.

She was sitting up now, her chin on her knees, hugging them to her, her face red and swollen.

Bear regarded her, thinking. Finally, he said, "In the Book of Judges is the story of Gideon. The Midianites were looting the land and taking the crops, leaving the people of Israel in despair for their future. Gideon was seeking to escape, I believe, when an angel of the Lord appeared to him, and said, 'Hail, thou mighty man of valor, the Lord is with you!'"

Bear grinned sheepishly, "I may be getting this wrong. I'm going by memory, okay?"

He drew himself up and continued, "But Gideon said, 'If the Lord is with us, why? Why do the Midianites kill our people and burn our land?'

"The angel looked at him with burning eyes and said, "Go! Go in this thy power, and save thy people.' And vanished."

Bear stopped, and Girl waited.

Finally, she said, her mouth sketching the ghost of a grin, "I don't get it."

Bear shrugged, "Neither do it, but I learned it in Sunday School, and now seemed as good a time to use it as any."

Girl threw back her head and laughed, caught by surprise.

She was still exhausted from her earlier ordeal, so she quickly stopped and looked at Bear with fondness. "Bear? You have another meaning, don't you."

Bear nodded his great head. "Yes. The world is as it is, Girl. But you have the power to do something about it." And he stopped.

Girl looked at him, waiting. Yet, when he said nothing more, she lifted her head off her hands and said, "Me? I'm nothing. I'm nobody. I...I can't even go *home.*"

Bear raised his head to her level, so his eyes were boring into hers, and said, "'*Go,* in this thy power, and save thy people.'

"Girl, you cannot change the past. It is done. But the future – *that* you can change. How much you change it – that's up to you. But I know this, from everything you have told me: you have put more into the world than you have taken out of it. You have touched the people around you with grace. You have lifted people up and blessed them with your thoughts, your actions, and your presence. You have spread goodness wherever you have gone. And you have asked for nothing but acceptance and a measure of respect.

"Yet, the world has given you the back of its hand in return, sometimes literally. It is no wonder you are frightened and feel alone and neglected.

"You are...there's no other word for it...wonderful. Full of wonders. Girl, in the time you have been with me, you have healed wounds I didn't know I had. You have befriended animals who fear and loathe humans – something I did not think possible. They accept you as an animal – and that is an *astonishing* accomplishment.

"And you did the same among the people with whom you lived, even though you yourself were being beaten down, sometimes physically, sometimes mentally, by cruel and ugly people.

"I know you are familiar with the term – the *human* term – *namasté*. It means 'I salute the light within you.'

"Of the people I have known, your light is among the brightest I have ever seen. You don't see it because it is always there with you, so it vanishes into the background. But you are grace-ful: full of grace. And you bestow that grace on those around you.

"Girl, I have told you before that you are beautiful, and each and every time, you have disputed that fact. But your beauty shows not only upon your face, it shines through your words, your actions – your very being. *That* is why the animals accept you."

Bear looked deep into the troubled eyes before him and saw continued disbelief. He shook his ponderous head. "You still don't believe me. So – ask the animals. Any of them. Ask them if they trust you and if they accept you. Animals do not lie – it's not in their natures. Ask them."

So, in the days that followed, wherever the two friends went, Girl would ask, "Do you trust me? Do you *like* me?" And the animals, few of whom could speak as Bear or Owl or Porcupine could, would cock their heads, look at her strangely, then run towards her and climb up her arm to nuzzle her hair, or rub themselves along her legs, or fly around her and land on her head, tickling her scalp with their claws, or lick her with their rough tongues – which made her giggle.

Eventually, she accepted what Bear had said.

But not quite.

"Bear?" she said one evening, as they lay on the rag rug before the fire.

Bear lifted his head. "Girl."

"I will accept that I'm not...bad. For a human."

Bear looked at her, then huffed, "Hunh," and laid his head back down on the rug. "Girls," he said, dismissively, closing his eyes.

Chapter 22: Henry and The Rascally Rabbits

Bear came rumbling into the great room of the cabin, muttering to himself. He threw himself down on the rag rug in the center of the room, gave a huge sigh, and closed his eyes.

Girl, who was making herself some lunch, said, "Is everything okay, Bear?"

Bear ignored her.

She walked gingerly over to him and stood nearby. "Bear?"

"WHAT?" he shouted.

Girl jumped back. This was most un-Bear-like behavior. "I'm sorry, I didn't mean to disturb you – but you seem unhappy about something. May I help in some way?"

Bear collapsed back onto the rug, continuing to grumble, but said nothing else. Girl walked to the door and peered out, but saw nothing unusual. She looked back at Bear – who now had one eye open, looking at her.

He lifted his head and said, "If you must know, it's those *damned* rabbits again!"

Girl looked out at the meadow in front of the cabin but saw nothing and no signs of any rabbits. "Sorry?" she said.

Bear heaved another big sigh, then said in a very huffy voice, "I was just trying to lie in the sun on the meadow, but each time I was almost asleep, a rabbit would come over and pull my tail, then scamper away. I could hear the wretched animals giggling among themselves." He huffed again and shut his eyes.

Girl stared at him. "Rabbits?"

"Rabbits!" he confirmed.

"Bear, I'm sorry, but...aren't you a lot bigger than any rabbit? Why aren't they scared of you?"

"Because they're agile, and I'm not. Sure, I could eventually run one down, but they're just barely a mouthful and not worth expending the energy on. And they know it. Ever since one of them tried tweaking my tail and got away with it, it's become a game for them. 'Bullyrag the Bear' they call it. Or some such.

"Rabbits!" he said dismissively, then shut his eyes.

"Could someone help you with them? Maybe...Skreee or whatever your hawk friend's name is? She could swoop down and grab them."

"She doesn't like rabbits. They make her jumpy." Bear huffed again. Then, suddenly, he lifted his head. "Wait... I know someone who *does* like rabbits. He'd be perfect! Oh boy! That's *it!* Thank you, Girl!"

Girl looked uncertainly at Bear, then said, "You're...welcome? I'm not sure what I did, but I hope it helps."

Bear started chuckling. "Oh, it will." Then he opened one eye. "I hope you like mischievous people because that's Henry!"

145

He closed his eye again and was soon sound asleep on the rug.

The next morning, the two friends were sitting out on the porch, watching the shadows move along the mountains as the sun rose higher. Bear had already been out to forage for breakfast and came back chuckling, but refused to say why. Girl had had breakfast and was waiting to see if Bear would suggest some kind of outing...which he hadn't done so far. Instead, he sat there with a silly grin on his face.

Girl was wondering what he was up to and had finally worked up the nerve to ask him. She turned towards him and said, "Bear...," then stopped.

Bear swiveled his head to face her and said, "Yes?" but nothing more.

Girl was speechless. There, sitting on top of Bear's head, was a fox. The fox's grin matched Bear's own – yet, Bear did not seem to be aware of the fox.

Girl giggled.

"What?"

Girl just pointed over Bear's head.

Bear looked back behind him, then up, and said, "What? What are you talking about, Girl?"

Meanwhile, the fox was mimicking Bear's words. Girl giggled even harder, bending forward in the chair.

"WHAT? What's going on, Girl?"

After gasping, and finally getting some air, "You...you have something on your head," she finally said.

Bear's eyes traveled up. Just then, the fox leaned down, gazed into Bear's eyes, then kissed Bear on the nose.

Bear reached up to grab the fox off his head, but the fox leaped nimbly down to the ground, swaggered over, and climbed up into Girl's lap.

He kissed her on the nose, too, then turned around, tromping around on her lap, and made himself comfortable.

Bear, meanwhile, flapped his paws as if flummoxed that he hadn't been able to grab the fox, then straightened up, collected his dignity, and said, "Girl, this is Henry, the Arctic fox. Henry, Girl."

The fox swiveled to look up at Girl, scanning her up and down, nodded, settled down and apparently went to sleep.

Bear shook himself, harrumphed, then said, "Henry...as you might have guessed...is a bit of a trickster. He's *just* the person I need to fix those rascally rabbits!"

Girl started stroking Henry, who opened one eye, sighed, and then closed it again.

"He's really quite lovely, Bear." Henry's face split into a grin, but he kept his eyes shut.

Bear grinned, "You might not think so when he starts playing tricks on you!"

Girl just looked at him but continued to pet Henry.

That afternoon, Bear lumbered out into the meadow, humming ostentatiously, then settled down in the sun-soaked grass, making as much noise as possible.

Girl didn't see Henry anywhere but suspected he was around. She sat on the porch, rocking and waiting to see what happened.

A while later, when it looked like Bear had gone to sleep, Girl noticed a movement in the grass, which seemed to be heading toward Bear's hindquarters.

Bear started up, and Girl surmised that something – probably one of the rabbits – had pulled his tail.

Then there was a tussle in the grass, and Henry popped up, holding a rabbit in one paw, a big grin on his face and his tongue lolling out.

He trotted around and held the struggling bunny in front of Bear. Bear reached for the rabbit, but Henry held it away and then thumped his own chest.

"Sure, Henry. If you want the damn thing, go ahead. Too much fur, and not enough meat for me."

Henry nodded, then disappeared again into the grass, holding the rabbit, which continued to struggle.

Bear settled down and seemed to go back to sleep.

He was settled there for a while when Girl saw another disturbance in the grass and decided that the lesson hadn't taken, that another rabbit was sneaking up on Bear.

Bear started up again, angry this time, and grabbed for his rear end – coming up empty.

But instead of a rabbit hopping away, it was Henry, sitting off to one side, smirking at Bear.

Bear relaxed. "Did you warn them off?" he asked.

Henry just nodded, then patted his tummy.

Bear settled back down on the meadow grass, then started a bit when Henry climbed up and made himself at home on top of him.

Girl giggled as quietly as she could, but Henry lifted his head, looked at her and winked.

Chapter 23: Henry Goes Without Saying

Bear lumbered contently towards the cabin after a long, sunny nap – even though Henry had been lying on top of him. Henry trotted along beside Bear, tongue lolling out, looking sleek and smug.

Henry trotted up the steps to the cabin, stepped triumphantly inside, circled the rug twice, and then settled down comfortably in the center.

Bear looked at him, somewhat bemused but with a satisfied smile on his face after outwitting the rabbits. He settled into his favorite place on the porch and looked over at Girl in her rocker, a smug look on his face.

Girl smiled at him and said, "Very clever, Bear. You sure showed those rabbits who's boss!" Her sentiment was slightly spoiled by her suppressed giggle, but Bear didn't deign to notice.

Bear nodded as his smile broadened, then looked off at the mountains opposite.

After Girl had had her supper, the two friends wandered out into the meadow to watch the stars come out. Bear settled down into the grass, and Girl leaned back on him, gazing into the infinite. They were silent for a long time, watching their favorite show.

Finally, Girl began to get both sleepy and cold, so they called it a night and wandered back to the cabin, with Girl putting her hand on Bear's back to help her navigate the hummocky ground in the dark.

They walked companionably up into the cabin, only to find that Henry was nowhere to be seen. Bear turned back to look at Girl, who shrugged.

"Maybe he went home?" Girl said.

"Maybe...," said Bear. "He comes and goes without saying. He's unpredictable and more than a bit of a scamp. Oh, well. Good night Girl." he said, rubbing his head on her side.

"Good night Bear. Sleep well." And she walked off to her bedroom.

She started to get undressed, taking her nightie off the hook on the back of the door, struggled into it, then turned towards the bed, drew back the covers...only to find Henry curled up there.

"Henry!" Girl said sharply. "What are you doing in my bed?"

Henry lifted his head, looked at Girl for a moment, then reached up with his mouth, pulled the blanket from Girl's hand, flipped it up over himself again, and nestled back into the covers, closing his eyes.

Girl snorted, then whipped the covers off the bed, dropping them down to the foot. She placed her hands on her hips and said, "MY covers, MY bed! Now get off!"

Henry raised his head, looked at the covers at the foot of the bed, then – Girl would swear – shrugged, lay back down, and closed his eyes.

Girl opened her mouth to say something, then decided that actions would speak louder. She reached in and lifted Henry up...

Or at least tried to. Henry wriggled out of her grasp, jumped back down onto the bed, and curled up again, closing his eyes – then stuck his tongue out at Girl before settling himself back into his comfy position.

Girl reached in again and took a firmer hold on Henry, lifted him, turned, and dumped him on the floor with the intention of shooing him into the great room – but Henry was faster and scrambled around her, then leaped back into bed before Girl could close the door on him.

He lay curled on the bed but now kept his eyes open, regarding Girl, and with a smile on his face.

Girl was tempted to get Bear to help her, then decided to try one more thing.

"You know, Henry, when I was a little girl, and I didn't want to get up in the morning, my older sister, who was *very* mean, would tickle me...like this!" And she leaned over and started digging her fingers gently into Henry's sides, tickling him.

He started kicking his feet, then scrabbling to move back towards the wall, trying to get away to no avail. Finally, he leaped up, jumped off the end of the bed, grabbed the blanket in his mouth, and quickly pulled it out into the great room.

He walked over to Bear, who seemed to be mostly asleep, curled up next to him, and flipped his mouth up in a quick snap, causing the blanket to settle over his body.

He stuck his snout and head up over the blanket, looked at Girl, stuck his tongue out again, then closed his eyes, a satisfied smile on his face.

Girl decided that she didn't want to wake Bear by fighting with Henry over the blanket, so she walked out into the great room.

Henry raised his head to track her movement, but when he saw she was heading for the couch rather than him, he dropped his head back down.

Girl took the worn blanket from the couch, walked back to her bedroom, and remade her bed with it, then pulled it open, and lay down. She was a little cooler than if she had had her own blanket, but it was a pleasant night, so she didn't worry about it and quickly fell asleep.

She woke in the night, needing to get up and pee but feeling as if the blanket had gotten particularly heavy on her legs. She started to get up, only to find Henry curled up next to her legs in the bed, with her original blanket drawn most of the way over him.

She carefully extricated herself from the bed, tiptoed to the bathroom, then returned – and found Henry occupying the top of the bed again.

She chuckled to herself, then shoved him down on the bed, wriggled herself into position, pulled her own blanket up over her and Henry's apparently sleeping body, leaving one hand over the covers.

Henry lifted his head, licked her hand, sighed contently – and they both went to sleep.

Chapter 24: Bear's Story

When Girl woke the next morning, she realized from the position of the sunlight streaming into the cabin that she must have slept in. She stretched, yawned, and started to swing her legs out of bed – then realized that Henry wasn't curled up on the bed.

She got up, figuring she'd see him in the great room, so went to the bathroom, then returned to her room to get dressed, and walked out into the great room.

She found no one there, but the door to the porch was open, so walked out, grabbed the door jamb with one hand, and swung around, expecting to see Henry with Bear.

And saw neither. Feeling deflated, she plunked herself down on the rocking chair and sat for a while, watching the day grow and brighten. Sighing, she felt the wonder of it all over again.

Finally, when neither of her friends appeared, she got up and went in to make herself some breakfast. She was quite liking oatmeal again, after years of forgetting about it, especially with nuts, raisins, and those Saskatoon berries when Bear could find some. She prepared the bowl, then took it out to the porch to eat it, pulling her sock-clad feet up onto the seat of the chair and balancing the bowl on her knees.

She was just finishing when she heard Bear's whiffling sound, the sound his large lungs made when he walked. She put her bowl down, stood up, and smiled at the white form moving through the meadow toward her.

He saw her, nodded his head, but kept coming, then stopped by the edge of the porch, right in front of her, looking up. "So, how are you today, sleepyhead?"

Her smile broadened, "I'm feeling really good, thanks, Bear. But Henry was missing when I woke up. Isn't he with you?"

Bear gave a hearty huff that she interpreted as a laugh. "Nope. Henry goes without saying, as the saying goes: when and as he pleases. He's mercurial, as you found out, and funny, and a good friend. But a bit of a trickster."

Bear stepped his front paws onto the porch so that his eyes were level with Girl's. "He must really like you. He doesn't normally tease someone as hard as he did you. And he slept alongside you. I don't think I've seen him do that with anyone else. Especially not a human."

Bear climbed the rest of the way up to the porch and took his accustomed spot on the end. "But then, you're not like most humans."

He swung his head to look at her again. "Since becoming a Bear, I've come to realize just how selfish and destructive humans are, as if they were the only ones living on this planet, and they could just take anything they wanted."

He stopped for a moment, then looked out at the mountains and was silent for a time. "At times, it makes me ashamed that I was a human," then fell silent.

Girl held her breath, then decided she had nothing to lose. "Bear, how did you come to be a bear?"

He was silent, but Girl could hear his breath wheezing in and out of his chest – a sound she never normally heard.

Finally, he swiveled his head towards her. "It...hurts me to tell it, but I'll try. I may have to stop, Girl, if that's okay with you?"

She looked at him solemnly and nodded.

He looked back at the mountains, then took a big inhale and let it all out in a rush.

"Maddie and I – Maddie was my wife – were hiking hereabouts. We loved the mountains and were good hikers. We also loved each other very much. She was the love of my life."

He stopped, then snorted. "That's such an easy thing to say, and people say it all the time." He heaved another sigh. "But it was true."

Bear looked off to his right into the far distance, then straight ahead again. "When we set off, the Ranger told us that there had been an unusual sighting – a huge, white bear. No one had gotten a good look at it, so they weren't sure if it was an albino brown, black or grizzly bear, or a polar bear that had somehow wandered this far south.

"They had searched for it diligently all Spring and Summer, but had never been able to find it. They occasionally found tracks, but the tracks seemed to vanish after a while, as if the bear had evaporated, leaving neither tracks nor trace.

"They'd tried to enlist the help of both the Western Plains Cree and the Dane-zaa, the Indigenous peoples who live in this area, to track the animal. These were the descendants of the original humans who settled here thousands of years ago. But when these First Nations people heard the story, they all refused to help, every one of them, and wouldn't say why.

"We thought it was some kind of local legend and dismissed it – although we took all of the usual precautions in bear country. This wasn't our first rodeo.

"By the fourth day of our hike, we had forgotten all about the stories.

"Then we heard a man shouting in an angry voice. We carefully picked our way through the bush to the clearing where the sounds were coming from and saw a white hunter with a shotgun pointed at an enormous white bear who was staring down the hunter, teeth bared, showing no fear. The white bear stood over a bleeding brown bear, who was sheltering her cubs. And it wasn't hunting season...

––––––

Maddie glanced at me, then pushed forward and ran into the clearing.

"What the hell do you think you're doing?" she yelled at the hunter.

I scrambled after her. There were two dangerous carnivores and a criminal with a shotgun, and I didn't see any way she would be safe running into a mix like that.

I ran after her and tried to grab her, but she shook me off.

Both the white bear's head and the shotgun swung toward her. She ignored both and walked straight between the two, then turned and faced the hunter. The shotgun was now pointed directly at her chest. And this enormous white bear was breathing down her neck.

Maddie had always been incredibly brave, much braver than me, and also absolutely intolerant of wrongdoing. Now she was putting herself in harm's way – literally – without knowing what was going on.

But she had an innate sense of what was *right*, and she had decided that the man was wrong, the bear was right, so she acted on that.

"Look, lady, I don't know who the hell you are, but you need to get out of the way. That's a *bear* behind you, a big one, and you are going to get yourself torn to shreds."

"And you were going to kill at least one of them, if not all of them, and I won't let you."

The hunter – a tall, gaunt man with a grizzled beard – snorted, then said, "I don't rightly see how you gonna stop me. Now *move!*"

She stood there, resolute, and just shook her head, then reached up to grab the muzzle of the shotgun.

I saw the anger on his face, how his jaw clenched, and how the muscles in his wrist were tensing, so I jumped forward and pushed her out of the way – just as the shotgun went off.

Things got a bit hazy after that. I think the hunter turned and ran. I know Maddie dropped by my side, screaming.

But besides all that, it was as if I was outside myself looking at everything – and the white bear was with me.

Then I sensed another...well, Presence, a Woman, I thought. A very *powerful* Woman, and She was looking at both of us, shaking Her head. I *knew* Her, but I didn't know *how* I knew Her.

"Oh, My children," she said, shaking Her head, "Why do you do these things?" She looked at both the bear and me, then sighed. "And you are both mortally wounded. I cannot save either you – but perhaps I can save you both together."

She looked at me. "Would you rather die, James, or live as a polar bear?"

Strangely, I felt no pain – and no fear. I pondered for a time – I don't know how long – then nodded and said, "Life is a treasure. I would like to live – as a polar bear if I must."

She turned to the white bear. "And Bear, would you rather live with this human, or die alone?"

Bear was still for some time, then seemed to say, "Live," he turned to me, "even with him."

She nodded, then turned back to me. "This is most unusual, but I am prepared to do this because you both were willing to sacrifice yourself for another. And your mate, Maddie, was willing to sacrifice herself for a person who is not even your animal. This is rare, very rare. And commendable."

"Very well. But you must leave at once. James, I'm sorry, but you must not speak with Maddie. She will think you are dead, and unfortunately, that is how it must be."

Now I felt sad – but for Maddie, not me. Yet, I had no choice. I just nodded.

She clapped her hands very loudly, and I collapsed, feeling as if I had disappeared.

Only to feel myself getting up, pushing myself up on four legs with unaccustomed strength against surprising weight. I swiveled my head to look at Maddie, who looked odd, shocked, and unutterably sad.

I turned and lumbered away, gradually picking up speed and finally disappearing into the brush. I rushed headlong, neither knowing nor caring where I went, until finally, exhausted, I stopped.

I slumped down and would have cried – except I found I couldn't remember how.

Finally, I got up and started walking. I wasn't sure why I was walking in the direction I was, but something led me. Eventually, I broke into a clearing, a meadow, and there, in the center of the meadow, was the cabin.

It was the cabin I had inherited from my Dad, who had inherited it from *his* Dad. But *that* cabin had been in the Appalachians, not the Canadian Rockies. Maddie and I had spent many summers there and many weekends and vacations in other seasons, too.

Puzzled and not a little scared, I walked cautiously towards it, padding up the steps, and pushed the door open.

As it swung open, I could see that it was Dad's cabin – or mine, now that he was dead.

I was home. I didn't know *how*, but I was home.

———

Bear was silent for a long time, then turned towards Girl. Her hands were covering her mouth, and tears were streaming down her face. And, strangely, Bear found that he could finally cry again.

He collapsed onto the floor of the porch. Girl leaped off her chair and hurried over to him, kneeling down, laid her head on his side, stroking his fur, and crooning. They stayed that way until it got dark, and they were both stiff and all cried out.

Chapter 25: Mother's Nature

The next morning, the two friends were quiet with each other. After saying good morning and after both had foraged for breakfast, each in their own way, they retired to the porch, Girl to her rocker, Bear to his favorite spot at the end of the porch, looking at the mountains.

After a while, Bear got up and said, "I'm going to go for a walk. Like to come?"

Girl thought for a moment, then nodded, unwound herself from the rocking chair, and skipped down the stairs, then turned, waiting for Bear to join her. After he lumbered down the stairs, one by one, she put her hand on his back, ruffling his fur, and the two friends set off.

Bear seemed just to be rambling, with no set destination in mind, which was fine with Girl.

Eventually, after the silence had stretched on for a while, Girl spoke up. "Bear...when you told me about what happened to you and, and the...bear, you mentioned a, a...Person, a Presence."

Bear walked on slowly without acknowledging Girl's implicit question.

"And a while back, you said something about Mother Nature...*liking* me, protecting me."

Bear looked over his shoulder at her, nodded, but continued walking.

"Bear, would you...uh, please tell me more about Her?"

Bear kept walking, and Girl kept walking alongside him, but now his walking seemed directed as he turned a couple of times onto well-worn animal tracks. Finally, he came to a quiet overlook, with the stream far below and the mountains far above, and sat.

Girl found a nearby rock, pulled herself on top of it, settled in with her feet drawn up, arms wrapped around her legs, her chin on her knees, and waited.

After a time, Bear said, "I told you about how a Presence appeared when both the polar bear and I were shot by that hunter."

Girl nodded, silent.

Bear was quiet for some time, then said, "That...Presence was, I believe, Mother Nature – at least, that's what I call her in my head. And no, I don't know what I mean. I just...know...that She was unusual and, uh, well *powerful* is the word that comes to mind."

Bear took a deep breath and huffed it out. "She certainly saved my life...and that of the polar bear she saved with me. And I have no idea how that could be done."

His head swiveled to face her. "But it seems clear to me that She likes you. Small things, many of which you haven't noticed. Like chipmunks aren't afraid of you, or butterflies are happy to land on you, or that *Skrreee!* seems to like you – and she's a cold-hearted carnivore. And Henry...well, I don't think I've ever seen Henry take to *anyone*, animal or human, as he took to you.

"They *know* you. They know you through *Her*. And I believe She thinks you have a pure heart, and that you try to help others. And sometimes you help others even when it hurts you."

Bear looked into her eyes. "And I like you. You truly are a special person." His mouth split into a grin, "Plus you're kind to old bears. That's gotta count for something, right?"

Girl looked at him steadily, then rose, vaulted off the rock, crossed to Bear in a bounding leap, and hugged him tightly.

"I don't know why Mother Nature likes me, Bear. I don't know what I could possibly have done to deserve Her affection. But I do know that I like you.

"You. You saved me. And I will never forget you for it."

Bear rubbed his muzzle against her. "And you saved me, Girl. You saved me, too."

The two friends hugged for a while, then Bear pushed himself up, "How about we go splash in the hot pools for a while? It'll give me a chance to see you naked again!"

And, not waiting for an answer, he turned and started trotting into the bush, hurrying towards the hot springs. Girl grinned at his retreating back, then turned on her foot and jogged after him. After all, she usually got to pull his tail when they were splashing in the water – and she felt that made it an even trade!

Chapter 26: "Once Upon A Time..."

"Bear..." Girl called.

Bear lifted his head from the rag rug in the great room but said nothing, then put his head down again.

"Bear!"

Sighing, he got up. It was a cold, wet, windy day: dull, drab, and bone-chilling, and all Bear wanted to do was to lie by the fire. But no, Girl had to go exploring the cabin.

He padded around, looking for her, and finally found her at the back of the storeroom.

"What?" he said, sounding annoyed.

"Bear, there's a box back here. What's in it?"

Bear snorted. "How would I know?" and started to turn back to the great room.

"Bear! Please help me get it down – or else I'll climb up on a chair, slip, and break my fool neck!"

"Well at least that way, I'd get some peace and quiet," Bear grumbled to himself.

"What?" Girl said.

Bear sighed. "Nothing. I'm coming."

He reluctantly padded into the store room and pushed Girl out of the way – none too gently, although she giggled, which irritated him even more. He reared up, slid the box down into his other paw...then had to juggle to keep hold of it as it was much heavier than he expected.

Finally, he set it down on the floor with a thump, turned, and wandered slowly back into the great room, letting his irritation show, then slumped onto the rug with a long-suffering sigh and closed his eyes.

"Bear..."

Looking weary, he opened his eyes, then squinched them tightly shut, hoping he could pretend he hadn't heard.

"Bear!"

"WHAT!"

"Well, you don't have to shout! This box is heavy."

Bear ignored her.

"I said..."

"I *know* what you said. *So what?*" Bear replied crossly.

"I can't carry it into the other room."

"Well, neither can I – from here. And I'm going to stay here – *sleeping.* So, please *be quiet!*"

There was a silence that Bear could only interpret as sullen that lasted for almost twenty seconds.

"Bear..."

He lifted his head and shouted, "WHAT?"

"There are *books* in here, Bear!" the voice said excitedly. "*Wonderful* books!"

"Big frickin' deal. Books. Hunh." And he laid his head down again.

There was a long period of silence, during which Bear could hear a steady procession of *thump*, pause, *thump*, pause, *thump*...he presumed as she was taking books out of the box and depositing them on the storeroom floor.

Finally, the noise stopped, and shortly thereafter, Bear heard footsteps coming slowly into the great room. He tried to pretend he was sleeping.

Girl sat down next to Bear and tried to snuggle into his belly, but he crossly wriggled around, so all she got was his paws and hind quarters.

She didn't seem to mind but leaned back anyway. He heard a dry creaking sound as if something old was opening, then silence, followed by what sounded like heavy pages turning slowly.

Bear squinched his eyes shut, scowled, and pretended he didn't hear, but now sleep was just *not* going to happen. He heaved a great sigh – which Girl ignored.

Finally, when the silence seemed about to explode, Girl flipped several pages, cleared her throat, and read, "*The Wind in the Willows*, by Kenneth Grahame, illustrations by Ernest H. Shepard..."

Bear lifted his head and glared at Girl.

She ignored him and carried on reading, "*The Mole had been working very hard all the morning, spring-cleaning his little home. First with brooms, then with dusters; then on ladders and steps and chairs, with a brush and a pail of whitewash; till he had dust in his throat and eyes, and splashes of whitewash all over his black fur, and an aching back and weary arms...*"

She kept reading, page after page, and gradually, Bear relaxed. First, he gave up trying to sleep. Then he started listening. And finally, he turned so Girl could snuggle into his crescent-shaped tummy and lean back on him.

And so, the two friends passed the cold, wet, rainy, miserable afternoon in companionable enjoyment.

And when Girl finally put down the book to start supper, Bear lifted his head, held out his paw to stop her, looked at her, and said, "Thank you, Girl."

And he licked her nose.

She blushed and hurried off to the kitchen area.

But she was happy.

And so was he.

Later that evening, Girl was sitting on the floor, thumbing through all the books that had been in the storeroom box.

Bear kept wandering in and out, knocking over the book pile each time he passed.

Finally, Girl picked up one of the heavier books and smacked him on the butt as he walked by.

Bear pretended to be hurt and crawled across the carpet, whimpering, one eye on Girl to gauge her reaction, while crying crocodile tears. "Boo hoo hoo..."

Girl said, "OOOHHHH!!! You are *so* infuriating!" then got up, went over, pummeled his stomach to make a crescent pillow on his tummy, sat down, scrunched around, then started to read *Peter Pan* to him.

When she wasn't looking, he smiled to himself, then leaned over and licked her ear again.

Which is one way he showed affection – but which she *hated* as it both tickled and got *Bear slobber* all over the side of her head!

She turned and smacked him again, this time with the flat of her hand, wiped her ear with the palm of her hand, then went back to reading.

He chuckled loudly, then settled down to listen.

Soon, they were both transported to Neverland...until Girl noticed that Bear had fallen asleep and was snoring gently – for a bear.

She got up quietly, leaned over, kissed him on the ear, then tiptoed into her own room...and was soon fast asleep herself, dreaming of flying and fairies.

The two friends slept contentedly while the stars above twinkled at them – especially the second star to the right...

Chapter 27: Reading and Writhing

Girl had found the boxes of books from the storeroom to be a treasure trove. Bear had long forgotten they were there, although he, too, had plundered their wealth when he was a boy, then discarded them when he reached his mid-teens.

Girl was distinctly older than that but found that reading them let her pretend she was a child again, and rediscover a time when life seemed simpler, fresher, and more promising. As such, she plunged into them with a greater delight than the stories themselves might have warranted.

For her, they were a way she could try to reclaim part of her life, to relive it, and draw parts of it back from the awful reality it had become.

Bear was glad she was delighted – although he had to admit that Girl with a book wasn't much company. Still, when he nudged her, she would lie on her stomach on the floor with her chin in her hands or lay on her back, holding the book in the air above her, and read aloud to him.

He missed reading. One of the many things he missed being a Bear. And it was lovely to have her read. She conveyed all of her own delights as she read.

But she couldn't read aloud all the time – plus it diluted her joy as it slowed her progress through favored stories – old friends she was revisiting, especially the Oz books.

So, Bear would go out on the porch and sit, communing with the mountains. Or he would slump inside on the rag rug, watching Girl read, a gentle smile playing over his face.

Then, one morning, as she was reading *Treasure Island*, by Robert Lewis Stevenson, she suddenly stopped, sat upright, and said, "Bear, why didn't *you* read these books? You enjoy it when I read them to you!"

Bear raised his head off the floor and said, "Well, there are actually two reasons. The first is that I had forgotten that those books were even there. And the other reason is that I can't read."

Girl's head turned sharply towards him. "I'm sorry?"

Bear dropped his head and turned away.

"I can't read, Girl. I can see the pages of the book, and I can see black marks – but I can't figure out what they mean. Even when I already know what the words say, I can't recognize them. It's as if they are in an alphabet I've never seen before."

Girl sat stock still, staring at Bear. How could it be that her...hero, this person who meant so much to her, who *was* so much to her, could not read? She knew he must have done at one point. But why not now?

"Why?" she barked, far more abruptly than she realized she should have done.

Bear turned his head away and returned it to the floor.

Girl got up, walked over to Bear, sat on the floor next to him, and leaned against him.

"I'm sorry, Bear. That must have sounded...nasty. I didn't mean it to."

She leaned against him, and rubbed her face against his fur, then sat up, but continued to smooth his fur with her hand, stroking him gently.

"Bear, you could read when you were a human, right?"

Bear grunted, which she took as agreement.

Girl was silent, stumped. Finally, Bear lifted his head and said, "I've been trying for...forever to read that peanut butter jar over there." He lifted his muzzle and nodded at a corner of the room.

Girl looked and saw a glass jar lying in a corner that she had never noticed before. She got up, went over, and picked it up. It did, indeed, say "Peanut Butter" with a brand name.

She slowly walked back to where Bear was once again lying and sat down beside him. She held it out to him and said, "What do you see?"

Bear stared briefly at the jar, then turned away. "Gobble-de-gook," he said. "Nothing." He swallowed and looked down, not meeting her eyes. "As near as I can figure it, I have some kind of a hybrid brain – part man, part bear. And a bear's brain can't recognize letters. It doesn't have the programming."

Girl put the jar down beside her, away from Bear. Then she picked it up again and looked for the "Best by" date. It was many years in the past.

She put it down and almost said something about the date – then stopped, realizing that it might be something else he didn't want to talk about and that one bad thing at a time was enough.

"I'll read to you Bear, as much as you like. Promise."

He lifted his head and put his muzzle on her leg. "You're a lovely lady, Girl. And I am so lucky to have met you."

He lifted his head again and laid it back on the floor. "But I'm used to it. Please – read for your own enjoyment. I enjoy *that*."

Girl sat, stroking Bear's fur, tears forming in her eyes, but she realized that her being sad would not help Bear. Plus, she found herself feeling strangely...vulnerable. Bear could do *anything*. He had saved her at least three times. He kept her alive against all odds. He had risked his own life for her, yet, she could do nothing for him.

Then, a thought occurred to her.

"Bear," she said softly.

He lifted his head, "Girl."

She grabbed his muzzle, pulled it towards her, and kissed him on the mouth – what would have been his lips – then waited.

He started chuckling. "You thought you could turn me back into a prince again, didn't you?"

She sat looking at him, crestfallen...then started to giggle. "Yeah, I guess I did." And she began to laugh.

Bear started laughing, too. "But you see...the problem is, I never *was* a prince, so you couldn't turn me back!"

Girl started giggling even harder, as did Bear. Soon, the two friends were rolling on the floor, helplessly holding their sides, laughing.

Finally, a long time later, they stopped and lay, huddled together on the floor, happily exhausted.

"I do love you, Bear."

"Me too," said Bear.

Chapter 28: Shimmering Curtains

Bear awoke with a start, then strained to listen.

Something was wrong, but Bear wasn't quite sure what, or what woke him up. He swiveled his head left and right, listening.

Then he heard it. It was Girl, and she was weeping.

Bear got up, and padded towards her room, then stopped. The sound wasn't coming from her room. It was coming from the bathroom. He turned and padded that way, then stopped outside the door.

He heard sobbing. Girl was sobbing.

"Girl?" he said softly.

The sobbing stopped. There was silence for a time. "Bear? What are you doing up?"

"I...thought I heard something, Girl. Are you okay?"

He heard her sniff. "I'm fine. I'm FINE! Now, go away."

Bear thought for a moment. "I'm going back to sleep, Girl. Wake me if you need me, okay?"

"Sure," she said. "I'll do that. Now go away!"

Bear slumped down on the floor, just outside the bathroom door and shut his eyes. He didn't actually go to sleep, but dozed, half-listening to Girl and what she was doing.

He heard her start to get ready to leave, so he squinched his eyes tightly shut and pretended to snore.

The door opened, and Girl came hurrying out of the bathroom – and tripped over Bear, precisely as he had planned.

"BEAR!" she shouted. "What are you doing here?"

Bear lifted his head and looked at her, apparently in surprise. "Sleeping?"

She glared at him...then collapsed on top of him and started weeping.

Bear didn't know what to do, so he wrapped his forepaws around her and just held her while she wept.

Finally, she stopped.

Bear continued to hug her, then had a thought.

"Get up on my back, Girl."

She looked at him quizzically. "What?"

"Please, just do as I ask, okay? For once?"

Reluctantly, she climbed on his back and hung on, face down, legs dangling down his sides. He lumbered up onto all fours, walked to the front door, unbolted it, then pushed it open and padded down the steps into the meadow.

Walking well away from the cabin, he finally slumped down onto his stomach, Girl on his back.

"Look up," he said.

Girl twisted around on his back, one hand holding a fistful of fur, and looked up at the stars – only to find they were not as easy to see as she had expected. Instead, there were shimmering curtains of green, with tinges of red and even yellow, often shading into blue, suspended in the air.

"What?..." she began, then stopped, stunned by the beauty of it.

"My friends, the Northern Lights. They come to visit me regularly, and I thought you might like to meet them."

Girl collapsed back on Bear's back, looking up, and fastened her gaze on the spectacle above, fascinated.

Time passed, but she had no idea how much. She was enraptured by the shimmering lights, dancing above them. They seemed so close, and so real, yet so...magical, out of her experience.

Finally, they faded away, seeming to wave as they left.

Girl sighed, breathed to herself for some time, then said, "Thank you, Bear. You always know what to do."

Bear lumbered up and started back to the cabin as Girl re-arranged herself into a sitting position on his back.

"No, Girl, I don't. But what I do, I do from love. You are my friend, and whatever you need that I can provide, I will."

Girl leaned forward so her front was clasped to his back, eyes leaking, and put her arms around him.

"Thank you, Bear. You're amazing."

"You're welcome, Girl. I know."

Chapter 29: Life After Death and Ice Cream

The two friends were lazing out in the meadow, allowing the Sun to warm them while they idly discussed life, the universe, and other stuff. The conversation had lagged for a while when Girl spoke up.

"Bear," said Girl. "Do you have dreams when you sleep?"

Bear looked at her and smirked. "Yeah, I dream of fat, fresh seals, waiting to be caught and eaten!"

Girl smacked him on his shoulder. "No, I mean *real* dreams."

Bear's smile faded, "Sometimes."

"What are they about?"

Bear's head dropped. "Mostly about things that were...and which never can be again."

Girl was silent for a time, then said, "Bear?"

Bear looked up at her again, "Yes, Girl what is it now?"

Girl looked down, "Nothing. Just...I promise I will find a way to help you."

Bear looked away, swallowed hard, looked back at her, and started to speak, then stopped. He stared at her for a long time, then finally said, "Thank you, Girl. I'd appreciate that."

Girl finished braiding the flowers she had picked, then placed the crown of flowers on Bear's head.

His eyes moved up as if he were looking at the flowers. "Get this thing off me!"

Girl put her hand to her mouth and giggled. "But you look so GOOD in it!"

Bear tossed his head, throwing the crown of flowers off to one side. Then he stood up on all four paws and pushed his nose so that it just barely touched hers. And growled.

She giggled again, kissed it, then jumped up and ran back into the cabin, slamming the door...giggling the whole way.

Bear looked after her, then muttered, "Girls!" and slowly followed her.

Later that afternoon, Girl was lying on the sofa, reading a Zane Grey novel, when she dropped the book on her lap and looked over at Bear.

"Bear?" Girl asked.

Bear lifted his head from the rag rug, not so much because of the question but because of her tone of voice.

"Yes, Girl."

"Where do you think we go when we die?"

Bear thought for a moment, then said, "Hoboken," and dropped his head back to the rag rug.

Girl dropped her head and giggled, "BEAR!"

He looked at her out of the corner of one eye, then sighed. "Girl, do I look smart enough to answer that? Really?"

Girl nodded. "Yes."

Bear lifted his head and stared at her. "Hunh."

He turned his head away and was silent for a while. "Well..." he started, then paused again. "Girl, I could tell you what Robert Heinlein said, through one of his characters, Lazarus Long..."

"Yes?"

"You'll know soon enough, so why worry about it."

She snickered, "But that's cheating!"

Bear nodded, "Yes, it is."

She looked down at her lap, then up at him again, "Bear...I know you don't know..."

"Too right, honey child!"

"...but what do you *think?*"

Bear heaved a heavy sigh. "I think...that what my father and my brother thought is too unlikely."

He paused, until Girl said, "Go on."

"They thought that once you died, that was it – there was nothing more. You just...vanished. POOF!"

Girl waited, then said, "But...?"

Bear looked back at her, "But I think that avoids the central question, the one I asked Ram Dass: 'Is spiritual existence real?'"

Girl said, "But he didn't say it was! He just said there was no objective evidence of it!"

Bear nodded, "Yes, but think about that for a second. If there is no spiritual existence, then...what are we?"

Girl looked puzzled. "I...I don't get what you mean, Bear."

Bear nodded again, "Because it's too obvious. It's right in front of you, all the time. Are we just lumps of meat, animated by random neurons firing away in a semblance of rationality? That's what atheists would have us believe. And make no mistake – atheism is a faith. Atheists make a positive declaration of faith that is unprovable: 'I believe there is no God!' But they have no proof."

Girl cocked her head to one side, "That...that's not quite all to the argument – and you're getting off topic."

Bear snorted. "I was hoping you wouldn't notice. It's easier to demonstrate that atheism is a faith than that spiritual existence is real.

But think of this: Who is at home here? Who are you, and who are you talking to? Are you a female human, speaking to a bear?

"Or even if I were still a man, are you a separate entity, a human woman, speaking to a human man? Or are you this...person, communing with another person?"

Bear shifted position restlessly, "It's not just two lumps of meat sending sound waves back and forth at each other that is happening here, Girl. It is two *souls* communing with each other."

Bear went silent. Girl, looked off into the distance, chewing her lower lip.

Finally, she shook her head, "That's not proof, Bear."

Bear looked at her, "I never said it was. What I'm asking is for you to understand yourself – your *essence*. Are you a lump of talking meat – or are you something more?"

Girl looked pensive again, "I'm more," she finally said firmly.

"Yes, you are," said Bear. "And so am I."

The room was silent for a long time.

Then Bear heaved a deep sigh and spoke again, "Do we have any ice cream left? I think that's more important."

Girl threw her book at him, then launched herself from the sofa across the rug and hugged Bear around the neck.

"OH! *You* are just *spoiled!*"

She got up and walked towards the kitchen. "I'll go check."

Chapter 30: Girl, Not Frog

It was mid-morning, and Bear was seated on the porch, watching the mountains grow – or not, as the case might be. Girl was seated in her rocking chair, reading, with her knees curled up under her chin. After a while, she put her book down and said, "Bear?"

Bear's head swiveled towards her, and said, "Frog?"

She shook her head and said, "What? I'm not a frog; I'm a girl!"

Bear chuckled, "I know. I just wanted to see if you were awake. Besides, I was getting bored saying 'Girl' when you said 'Bear.'"

She tilted her head sideways and looked at him, mouth crooked in a smile, "You're weird, you know that?"

Bear chuckled, "Well, sure. How many other talking bears do you know, eh?"

She stared at him but her smile broadened.

"Bear?" she repeated with a laugh in her voice.

He sighed, and said, "Girl? Or is it Frog? I get confused."

"*Ribitt*," she said, then burst out laughing, smothering it with her hand across her mouth.

Bear pretended to be cross. "Look, if you're going to interrupt my 'Very Important Watching,' at least make it worth my while, okay?"

She kept her mouth covered with her hand and laughed, then cleared her throat, "Ahem! Uh..." She looked blankly at him, "I've forgotten what I was going to say, Bear! You disrupted my train of thought!"

Bear chuckled, "Didn't take much, did it?"

"BEAR!"

He looked away and laughed.

"I was *going* to say that...well, I appreciate what you've done for me, but now, I think I'm gonna take it all back!"

Bear looked at her and smiled, "So, you're going to take back something you've never said? Oh dear. I'm *wounded!*" And chuckled again.

She smiled, got up, walked over to him, kissed him on the forehead, and said, "Silly old Bear. Do you have any idea how much I...well, I love you?"

His head swiveled to look at her, and he gazed fondly into her eyes, then said, "Yes."

She looked at him for a moment, then slapped him on the shoulder and cried, "*Bear!* I'm trying to be *cereal* here!"

Bear looked fondly at her, then leaned forward and kissed her on the nose. "I know, Girl. And believe me – you have no idea how important it is to me. You are...I don't even know how to say it. But whatever it is, you're it."

Girl threw back her head and laughed. "That's one of the many things I love about you Bear – you have an absolute *way* with words. I think."

She leaned her head forward and placed her forehead against his, hugging his neck. "Silly old Bear." Then she walked back to her rocking chair, sat back down, and pretended to read so he couldn't see the tears in her eyes

Bear sighed and turned back to look at the mountains so Girl couldn't see the tears in *his* eyes.

Later that day, after supper, the two friends started the trek home. They had visited the waterfall, and while Girl had not gone into it this time – too cold in the gathering shadows – she had once again marveled at its ethereal beauty. The spray created rainbows in the air, and the shiny rocks and moss made everything seem otherworldly.

They made their way back towards the cabin, stopping from time to time to greet or speak with one or another of the creatures in the woods, all of whom now seemed quite comfortable with Girl, and many of whom wished to climb up on her, or cuddle up next to her.

It got to the point that Bear had to push some of them off.

He said, somewhat huffily, that they seemed to like her more than him.

Girl laughed at him and said, "Well, what do you expect? I'm better looking!"

Bear stopped and turned his head slightly, giving her a side-eye.

"Hunh," was all he said then kept on walking.

She giggled but caught up and ran her fingers through his fur.

"Silly old Bear. They all love you. You know that."

Bear lifted his head haughtily and looked straight ahead. "Humph."

"Bear! They love you! You *know* that!"

Girl stopped, then said, more quietly, "Besides, I'm not sure if they really know me. If they did they..."

She stopped speaking and looked down at the ground.

Bear waited a moment, turned and walked back, then sat on his haunches, looking directly into her eyes.

"Girl, you are a lovely creature. They know that. I know that." He sighed. "I just wish that *you* knew that."

He turned side-on to her and said, "Get on kiddo. I'll give you a horsey-back ride home."

She looked at him through her eyelashes, a slow smile spread across her face, then she leaped on and shouted, "Ride 'em, cowgirl! *YEE-HAA!*"

And smacked Bear on the rump.

Bear looked at her, sat down, dumping Girl on the ground, where she fell – thump! – on her bum.

Bear wheeled around, put his face into hers, and growled, "Are you *sure* you want to do that?"

Girl giggled, "Absolutely!"

Bear tried to look fierce, but eventually, she got to him, and he started giggling, too. Soon the two friends were rolling on the ground, laughing so hard they could *Bear*-ly breathe! Finally, they collapsed in the grass, leaning on each other and huffing quietly in the aftermath.

Bear got up, and, at his urging, Girl got back on him.

He carried her to the cabin, up the stairs, and to her room.

By this time, everything that had happened over the last couple of days came falling in on her. She was exhausted.

He gently placed her into bed, pulled up the blanket, kissed her forehead, and said, "Sleep now, Girl."

She closed her eyes, put her hand up to his muzzle, and said, "Bear?"

"Yes, Girl."

"I'm still better looking than you..." and her face spread into a slow grin, even as her eyes were closed.

Bear huffed. "Maybe so, Girl. Maybe so."

He padded softly out of the bedroom and heard her start to snore. Quietly.

Late that night, Bear's eyes opened, but he didn't know why. He lifted his head and listened, then sniffed the air.

Everything seemed right – there were no indications of danger or difficulty. But something...*something* had disturbed him.

Slowly, he lumbered up and quietly padded off to see if Girl was all right.

Her door was closed, so he stopped, and listened.

He could hear her breathing, and smell her. She seemed fine.

He padded back to the rag rug and was about to slump down again...but felt...odd. He walked slowly to the door of the cabin, then paused. He was strangely afraid to go outside, but finally pushed the door open, and walked out onto the porch.

He sniffed the air and smelt...nothing. The air was clean and bright. He looked up at the stars; they were beautiful...but they were not why he was awake.

Slowly, reluctantly, he stalked out onto the meadow grasses. Finally, he sat and looked at the sky...and waited.

Nothing happened. Nothing stirred. The night was...still.

Then, he cocked his head and listened. There was no sound...but...

"Mother, please..." he said.

Bear, She replied, *You cannot keep her. She is only yours for a time.*

Bear's head dropped and hung there for a long time, then he raised it and tried to speak. "I know, Mother, I know. But..." He fell silent.

Yes, Bear...go on, She said, kindly.

"Mother...please look after her for me?"

The wind caressed Bear's head, and said, *Of course, Bear. When have I ever not looked after My children?*

Bear's eyes filled with tears. "Thank you, Mother. She means...so much to me."

Mother Nature stroked his head and looked at him fondly.

I never intended to cross one of my creatures with a human...but, Bear, you have continually surprised me.

Bear was silent, not knowing what to say or, indeed, what was expected of him. Mother Nature lifted his head to look into Her eyes. She leaned forward and touched Her head to his, then lifted and kissed him on the forehead.

I will look after her, Bear, and slowly, Her presence vanished, leaving only a sense of peace and fulfillment.

Bear stayed where he was for a long time.

He grew cold and stiff, but still did not move.

Finally, he heaved a great sigh, got up, and very slowly walked back to the cabin. He mounted the steps, one-by-one, and walked wearily through the door.

He very quietly padded to Girl's door and stood, silent, outside, listening and smelling her presence.

Finally, he walked back to the great room, and slumped down on the rug, letting the fire finally warm him.

He gazed into the leaping flames, wishing it were otherwise than it was, until he heard Mother's voice in his head.

Oh, Bear. You, of all My creatures, are the kindest. Do not fear, and be at peace, My lovely child. I promised I would look after her.

He gazed into the flames and huffed.

Mother chuckled, *Silly old Bear. Sleep now. You deserve it.*

He closed his eyes at Her bidding, but his heart was heavy, and tears leaked onto the floor.

Finally, he slept.

Chapter 31: Help in Trouble

The day had been lovely. The two friends had hiked down to the lake as Girl thought the day was hot enough to try swimming – or at least wading. Yet, when they got there, walking carefully from the trail, down the scree to the lakeside, Girl was...surprised. She had removed her boots and dipped one foot in the water, then squealed at how cold it was.

Bear just chuckled, so she turned on him. "You *knew!*" she said in an accusing tone.

"I did tell you it was fed by glaciers, as I recall. But *NOOO*...you insisted that it was hot enough that you just had to dip your tootsies in the water." He chuckled again.

Impulsively, she leaned down and splashed him with the flat of one hand, a determined look on her face.

His smile just widened, then he leaped into the water, right in front of her, with a big splash, drenching her front.

Her mouth opened in a big O – and she screamed. "You *bastard!* That's COLD!"

Bear, chuckled again, then turned and waded further into the water, eventually swimming away. Then he turned and faced her, floating on his back. "Come on in! It's lovely...if you're a polar bear!"

She was sitting, dejectedly, on a rock, then stood up, leaned forward, and blew him a raspberry.

"Oh, very adult, I'm sure," he chuckled.

She turned and started to march back up towards the trail.

Bear quickly swam back to shore, and padded out of the water, following her up towards the trail, "Girl!" he called urgently.

She ignored him, and continued to walk as quickly as she could up the scree, back towards the path.

"GIRL!" he called again, then put his head down and moved as quickly as the terrain and the slippery scree would allow him.

She continued to ignore him, and had almost reached the path when she came face-to-face with a brown bear cub. She stopped dead, with conflicting emotions going through her head. Part of her said, "Aww...he's so cute!" but another, saner part said, "Where's the Mama?"

She found the answer to that last part when she heard a roar from behind her. She quickly turned and saw a much bigger bear starting to run towards her.

Mama Bear looked angry, and was picking up speed.

Girl tried to think what to do. She decided that running uphill was a bad idea, and running to one side or another would allow Mama Bear to catch her, leaving back downhill as the only possible avenue of escape.

She turned to run back downhill...and saw a third bear bounding towards her, up the slope.

Her hindbrain didn't take in the details, only that she was between three bears, two of which were much bigger than she was, and were running hard towards her.

She screamed and crouched down, covering her head with her hands, dividing her attention between the Mama bear and the other bear running up the slope at her.

That last bear...which now registered in her mind as being white...suddenly leaped towards her, and she was sure she was going to be lunch – after being torn to shreds.

But Bear bounded in front of her, landing between Mama Bear and Girl, growling. He reared up to his full ten feet and roared with his mouth wide open, sounding so loud and so close that it terrified Girl, even though she now had now recognized her friend.

Mama Bear stopped short, then reared up to confront Bear, roaring in her turn.

Bear looked down at Girl, and spoke to her in an urgent tone. "Quickly, slide down the scree, back towards the lake. And don't even *look* at the baby, okay?"

Girl quickly did as Bear asked, sliding down the scree, scraping her hands but moving as quickly as she could.

Bear, dropped down on his paws, and backed carefully down the slope, away from Mama and baby bear. The Mama quickly lumbered over to its cub, and the two of them raced away up the mountainside.

When Bear finally caught up with Girl, back at the lakeside, she was sobbing, head down and in her hands. He cleared his throat to say something, but she jerked her head up and opened her mouth to scream...then saw Bear, and threw herself at him, wrapping her arms around him, "Oh, *BEAR!*"

She sobbed. "I'm...I'm so sorry. Thank you. I..."

He cut her off, panting slightly at his exertion – and adrenaline. "It's okay, Girl. You didn't know, and I should have warned you. This is Mama Bear's territory, but I thought we wouldn't be here long and she would steer clear of us. My fault. I led you into a dangerous situation without preparing you adequately. I'm sorry, Girl."

She pushed herself back and said, "No. I knew this is wild country. I should have known better, but my pride was hurt, and I..."

Bear chuckled. "So, how long are we going to stand here and argue over whose fault it was? Come on. Let's get you home."

And the two friends walked carefully – for they were both winded from the exertion and adrenaline – directly back to the cabin.

That night, after supper, Girl declined to go out and look at the stars. Bear knew something was up, but she would not open up about it, insisting she was fine and just needed an early night.

Bear walked her to her room. She leaned over and hugged him. "You saved my life – again. Thank you."

"You're a lovely Girl, and there was no way I would let anything happen to you. Now, good night – and only good dreams, okay?"

She smiled at him but said nothing, then went in and closed the door behind her.

Bear stood for a moment, looking at the door uncertainly, then padded back to the great room, found a comfy position with his head turned towards her door, then lay down, being warmed by the fire, and finally slept.

Sometime later, he woke, hearing muffled cries. He got up, padded over to Girl's door, and listened.

"No...No!...please...please don't! I...I didn't. I wouldn't!...No! PLEASE! NO!"

Bear pushed the door open quietly and padded softly into the room.

Girl was asleep, but tossing on the bed, clearly caught in a bad dream, wrapped in the blanket, arms up and holding them as if to protect herself from...something? Someone?

Bear looked at her and wondered what to do, then said, in a low voice, "It's all right, Girl. Bear is here. I'll take care of it. Shhh...shh, shh, shhh..."

He kept it up, and gradually, her struggles slowed, then stopped.

He stayed where he was for a while. Then, her eyes opened a slit, looking cautiously out at him as if afraid of what she was going to see.

"B...Bear?"

"I'm here, Girl. You're safe. I'm here, and I'm not going anywhere. You're safe."

She reached out and touched his muzzle. There were tears in her eyes. "Thank you, Bear. You're my knight in shining white...fur."

Bear chuckled deep in his throat. "It's okay, girl. I'll sleep here next to you. You'll be safe. I promise."

She looked at him with sleep-laden eyes, then said, "Bear?"

"Girl?"

"May...may I sleep with you? Please?"

He thought for a moment, then said, "Of course. Come out into the great room. Bring your pillow and blanket."

She slowly got up, grabbed her pillow with one hand, and her blanket with the other, trailing it on the floor behind her, following him into the great room.

Bear draped himself on the rag rug, but in a crescent shape, with an opening in the middle. She looked at him briefly, then plopped her pillow down on the floor inside the crescent and climbed into the curve of his body.

She pushed the pillow part-way up him, so she was leaning with her head and pillow on his stomach, her legs stretched out on the floor in front of her, towards the fire. She pulled the blanket up to her chin, then turned and looked into the large, liquid eyes staring back at her.

"Bear?"

"Yes, Girl."

She paused for a long time, then said, "Thank you."

He paused in his turn, "You're welcome, Girl."

She closed her eyes and very shortly was breathing slowly and deeply.

Bear's eyes stayed open for much longer, staring into the fire. His emotions, which he had suppressed for so long, were stirring again, and he felt a bittersweetness that both hurt and soothed him.

Finally, he slept.

Both of the friends had nothing but good dreams for the rest of the night, each comforted by the presence of the other.

Chapter 32: Thunder and Frightening

The next night, Bear was awoken from a sound sleep by a human torpedo as Girl thumped into his side, quivering. At first he was puzzled, but then, when he heard the crash of thunder overhead, he realized that she must have been frightened by the noise.

He stroked her head, "It's okay, Girl. It's only thunder." That didn't seem to help, and every fresh flash of light and crash of thunder seemed to produce an electric shock in her body, causing her to dig further into Bear's tummy.

She was shaking and whimpering.

"It's *okay*, Girl. I'm here. I'll keep you safe."

He continued to stroke her hair, and eventually she stopped shaking as badly, although she did keep trembling and jumped each time there was another crash. He huddled around her, hugging her close, murmuring soothing sounds.

Eventually, the storm passed, and Girl slowly started to relax.

Finally, she heaved a deep sigh, then sat up, wiped her eyes, and, looking at the floor, said, "I... I'm so sorry, Bear. I didn't mean to disturb your sleep."

She sniffed, then continued, "It's silly really. I ought to have grown out..."

Bear put up his paw, "Stop it, Girl. We all have things we can't stand. Thunder and lightning just happen to be one of yours. It's okay. I understand."

Girl, tried to smile, without notable success, then slowly started to get up. "I...I don't think you do understand, Bear," she said, looking at the floor.

Bear waited, but she said nothing further. "If you want to tell me, I'll listen," he said. "Or not if you'd rather not talk about it."

She stood for a long time, staring at the floor, not moving. Finally, she exhaled. "It was something *he* did," she began.

Bear thought for a moment, then decided she meant her former husband, the troll. He kept still, waiting to see if she'd go on.

"He...he knew I was afraid of thunderstorms and used to laugh at me when I would shiver each time there was a crash.

"Then, one day, when he was drunk...and mean...he grabbed me during a thunderstorm, dragged me outside, and threw me in an old dog cage we had on the property – outdoors. He locked the cage, left me there, and walked away, laughing."

She was shivering now. "Bear, it was awful, truly just..."

She gulped, and tears started coursing down her cheeks. "I was completely soaked, and cold, and crying, and screaming, and scared out of my mind...I ..."

She couldn't go on but broke down, collapsed on the floor, and started sobbing uncontrollably.

Not knowing if it would make any difference, Bear gathered her in and hugged her to himself, rocking her and crooning wordlessly. She turned her face into him and continued sobbing until she was exhausted. She went limp, barely breathing.

After a long while, she looked up at him, her face a mess, her eyes miserable. "Thank you, Bear, for listening."

All Bear could do was shrug, then thought for a minute.

"Girl, would you do me a favor?"

She looked at him, "Yes, Bear. Anything. What?"

"Would you get your blanket and come sleep here? I was getting chilly, now that the fire has died down."

Girl looked at him, and was going to say something, then stopped, bit her lips, then said, "Sure, Bear. I'll be right back."

She walked quickly back to her room, and as quickly returned, almost running...and would have knocked the wind out of him had he not been anticipating her arrival.

She snuggled down into his tummy and pulled the blanket over her, with one foot sticking out – as usual.

Bear smiled, pulled the blanket over her foot, smoothed her hair, and said, "Good night, Girl. Sweet dreams."

"Mmm..." was all she said, exhausted and already mostly asleep, her face finally smoothing out into something like peace.

Bear smiled to himself, kissed the top of her head, then lay back down...and stared at the ceiling, impossibly, helplessly angry at her former husband but glad the troll was dead and out of her life.

Finally, he took a deep breath, tried to shove the thoughts from his mind, and eventually fell back to sleep, holding her all through the night.

Chapter 33: The Spirit Bear and the Star Girl

Some days later, Bear woke up later than usual and stretched along the rag rug. He rolled on his back and looked up at the ceiling, the beams crisscrossing along the open space between the floor and roof. He lay there, luxuriating, feeling lazy, and no longer alone.

After a while, he wondered why he wasn't hearing Girl, so rolled over and got to his feet. Padding over to her room, he started to give her some smart-ass greeting but stopped once he was through the door. She had the sheet and blanket pulled up to her chin, her eyes closed, and her face pale – too pale.

"Girl?" he said softly.

Nothing happened. He moved slowly closer, "Girl?" he said with more urgency. Her eyes fluttered open, and she smiled weakly, "Oh, hi Bear. How are you?"

Bear moved forward and placed his nose against her forehead. It felt hot.

"You've got a fever. How are you feeling?"

She coughed slightly, then said, "No, I'm fine, really, Bear..." and broke into a coughing fit.

Bear sat, "No, you're not. But who can I call? And how?"

After a moment, he got up and padded from the room.

Girl closed her eyes, and time passed. She wasn't sure how much time, but when she opened them again, Bear was sitting there, looking concerned.

He didn't speak but just watched her, his eyes wide.

Girl heard footsteps on the front stairs and said, "Bear...Bear! There's someone at the door!"

Bear nodded, got up, and padded out of the room. He returned, followed by a man with long, dark hair and strong features. The man walked very tentatively into the room, eyes fastened on Bear. He was dressed in cargo pants and a sweatshirt with the sleeves pushed up. He swallowed hard, then looked at Girl and said, "Why am I here?"

Bear looked at him and said, "She's sick. Owl said that you can help her."

The man stared at Bear. "*Owl* said...?"

Bear nodded.

"Who *are* you?" he asked Bear, wiping his face. "And are you...*talking?*"

Bear nodded. "Yes I am. Or else you're having one hell of a nightmare. Now, she..." he nodded at Girl, "...is sick and needs your help."

The man's head turned to face Girl. He licked his lips and seemed about to say something, then came over to her, knelt down, and gently took her wrist.

He felt her pulse, but unlike doctors, he didn't compare the pulse against a watch or listen with a stethoscope. Instead, his eyes closed, his head bowed slightly, and he held her wrist as if meditating.

He stayed that way for many minutes, then leaned down to her face and sniffed, inhaling deeply, then sat back, thinking.

After a long time, he lifted his head, leaned forward, and stared closely into each of her eyes, then sat back in his heels in thought. Finally, he nodded, said, "Bark," got up and left without saying anything else.

Bear sat, unmoving the whole time, waiting.

Girl stared after him, then finally said, "Bear, who is that man?"

Bear shook his head but didn't answer.

After a long time, the man returned, "I need to boil water."

Bear immediately got up, and the two left the room.

After a time, Girl could smell something astringent, herbal, and clean.

The man returned, cradling a mug in his hand like some precious object. "Drink" was all he said while presenting the cup to Girl.

Girl looked at Bear, who nodded, so she took a sip.

At first, it tasted bitter, but then it seemed to soothe and open up passages in her lungs.

She slowly drank it, a sip at a time. When she reached the bottom, she found herself wishing there were more.

The man took the mug, nodded to her, then looked at Bear and said, "May...may I ask a boon?"

Bear nodded.

"Would you...would you come to our fire next full Moon. I'd like our Wise Woman to speak with you."

Bear stared at him, then slowly nodded. "Yes – but only if no one outside your group ever hears of this."

The man looked at Bear, then nodded.

The two looked at each other, and then the man held out his hand to Girl. Tentatively, she took it, but instead of shaking it, he bowed over it.

"You are a Blessèd One. Thank you."

He turned on his heel and left. Shortly, Girl heard the door close.

Bear sat there, a serious look on his face.

Girl stared at him, then finally said, "Blessèd?"

Bear nodded. "The Spirit Bear is said to have a companion from the stars. She brings blessings to the Earth and Her children."

Girl stared at him, tears forming in her eyes. "That's a lot to live up to..."

Bear moved over to her and then touched his forehead to hers. "You are not only blessèd, you are a blessing."

Chapter 34: "You're So Damned Reasonable"

Girl was sitting on the rocking chair on the porch, reading yet another Zane Grey novel, while Bear sat, staring out at the ageless mountains. At least, Bear surmised, she was pretending to read.

She was sprawled across the rocking chair, one leg over one arm of the chair, the other barely touching the porch, her back to the other arm of the chair, but Bear realized she wasn't concentrating.

Finally, she slapped the book closed, slammed it down on the porch, jumped up and leaped off the porch. She walked purposefully off towards the forest.

Bear got up and followed – as he knew she knew he would. He had warned her about going into the forest alone, and he knew she remembered. She wanted to talk to him. Or shout at him, more likely. So he followed, loping easily behind her as she steamed into the woods.

As the trees thickened, he closed the gap between them, not wanting her to be too far ahead. Finally, she got to their favorite lookout, overlooking the lake, with the waterfall off to their right and the sun's shadow just starting to creep up the far edge of the mountains.

She plopped herself down on her sitting rock, pulled her feet up under her knees, and rested her chin on her knees, huffing.

Bear plodded slowly into the clearing, sat slightly back from her to avoid impinging on her view...and waited.

Finally, she said, "Why do you do it?"

He waited.

She turned and glared at him. "I said, 'Why do you do it!'"

Bear smiled, "Why do I do what, Girl?"

"See! You're doing it again! Why are you always so darned *reasonable* about everything?"

She whipped around again to face the lake, burying her chin in her knees and peeking over their ridge at the mountains.

Bear got up, moseyed over to her, placed his muzzle in her lap, and whispered, just loudly enough so she could hear...

"Because I know it makes you mad..."

Then he backed away and snickered.

"OH!"

She sat bolt upright and glared at him. "I suppose you think you're funny, right?"

Bear shrugged. "That depends on who's listening, I suppose. Do you think I'm funny?" And he made a funny face at her.

She glared at him again, then burst out laughing.

"Darn you!" she said, "You always make me laugh when I want to be mad at you."

Bear nodded. "I know. It's most unfair of me."

"OH!!"

She launched herself at him, landing on his right shoulder and slapping at his back.

Bear sat still, letting her go on... until finally she wound down, and clung to him.

He nuzzled into her side. "Done?"

"Um-hmm"

"Shall we go home?"

"No. I want to watch the sunset."

Bear thought for a moment, about the dangers of being out away from the cottage at night in the forest, then nodded, "Okay."

Girl unwound herself from him and reseated herself on the rock.

Finally, after a long spell of silence, she said, "You are always so patient. It's not fair!"

Bear looked at her, then got up, knelt in front of her, waited a moment, then touched his forehead to hers.

She closed her eyes and clenched her fists, breathing hard.

Then gradually relaxed. First her fists, then her face, and finally, she opened her eyes. "Bear, what am I going to do?"

"About what?" he asked.

"About leaving you," she said, almost whispering, turning away.

Bear smiled gently, "But you're not."

"What?"

"You're not leaving me. You're going to find your life. I'll still be here."

She was quiet, her mouth muffled into her sleeve, then finally said, "I'm not sure I have a life."

Bear shook his head, "No – but you will. Trust me."

Her eyes filled with tears, which she made no move to wipe away.

"Bear?"

"Yes, Girl."

"I'll... I'll miss you."

He nodded. "I know. And you know I'll miss you. But we will see each other again."

She waited, then said, "Promise?"

He nodded. "Promise."

"Okay. I can leave then when I have to."

Bear thought for a moment, then nodded. "Yes – but we need to talk about what life you're going back to. Okay?"

She got up and placed her hand on his back, "Yes Bear. But not yet."

He got up, and the two friends walked back to the cottage through the twilight. She stopped halfway up the steps, turned, and looked at the mountains, fading into the dusk, soon to vanish completely until morning.

She sighed, then followed Bear in – and closed the door.

Chapter 35: Girl and the North Wind

Girl woke up and looked around. It was dark, and all she could see outside were stars. She got up and padded down the hall to the bathroom, finished up, and started to walk back to her room, but paused as she passed the great room, and listened to Bear snuffling as he slept.

She smiled to herself. He was so warm and wonderful. And yet, so silly at times.

For no reason that she could think of, she padded quietly through the room, grabbed the worn blanket on the sofa in passing, and slowly opened the door to the cabin, slipping outside, then pushed the door closed softly after her.

She crept cautiously to the edge of the porch, settled carefully on the top step, and looked up at the mass of stars overhead, pulling the blanket around her and cradling her arms to stay warm. She leaned against one of the posts and sighed. *They are so beautiful,* she thought.

And so are you, she heard.

She straightened up and looked around but saw nothing. She felt a cool breeze on her cheek and pulled her blanket closer.

No, you weren't imagining it, Girl. I'm here.

"Who are you? *Where* are you?" Girl said.

I'm the North Wind, Girl. And you're Bear's friend that everyone is talking about.

Girl was confused. "Who... who's talking about me?" she asked.

There was a sound that might have been a chuckle.

All of Bear's friends. They all like you.

Girl smiled, even as she shivered, then wondered.

"Why do they like me?" she couldn't help asking.

Because, the North Wind answered, *you are good for him. He's been so lonely all of these seasons.*

Girl felt tears prick the corners of her eyes. "How many seasons?" she asked. The North Wind was silent.

Girl waited, then decided to ask something different.

"Is there anything more I can do for him? He has been so kind to me."

North Wind was quiet for a time, then, *You're doing it. You keep him company and make him laugh. You warm his heart.*

There was a sound like a sigh.

Bear hadn't laughed for many years...until you came. He used to be quite grumpy, even when he was helping others of his friends. You make him laugh, and make him happy.

Girl smiled to herself. "Then we're even. He makes me laugh and happy, too."

Take care of him, Girl. And take care of yourself. And if you need something, or a message taken to someone, call on me.

Tears started to roll down Girl's cheeks, "Thank you, North Wind. I will."

Good night, sweet Girl. Sleep well.

And Girl felt that she was suddenly alone again with the stars

She gathered the blanket around her shoulders, softly crept back into the cabin, went to her bedroom, pulled the bed blanket and pillow off, and dragged everything into the great room. She gently laid them down on the rag rug next to where Bear was snoring, made herself a warm nest, and quickly went to sleep.

Snoring...quietly...

Chapter 36: How Old Is Bear?

Girl finished the Zane Grey she was reading and let it flop on the floor with a thump. She looked up and noticed it was quite late, yet, surprisingly, Bear had not set the fire. Instead, he was slumped on the floor, staring off into space.

"Bear?"

He didn't reply.

Girl got up, walked over and knelt down next to his head. "Bear?"

Bear flicked his eyes up towards her and then back down again.

"Bear, are you okay?"

He ignored her.

Girl stayed where she was, stroking his fur and wondering what to do.

Finally, she got up, patted Bear on his head, and went off and laid the fire. Finding matches on the mantle, she struck one and lit the fire on the first try. She stood back, hands on hips, watching the flames leap up. When she was satisfied that it was well and truly started, she turned back to Bear.

She walked over behind his back and knelt by him, then started stroking his fur. She began by his rump and gradually worked up towards his head, stroking the fur and massaging the muscles underneath.

She was surprised at how hard his body was – but then reflected that it wasn't really that surprising. When she got to his neck, she stroked for a while, then kneaded the muscles around his neck, working deep into the thick roll of muscles around his shoulders.

For the first time, Bear made a noise.

It was a deep, almost whinnying sound, sort of like a sigh with a groan mixed in. Girl smiled and kept going, stroking the fur on his great head.

She moved around so she was next to his muzzle and gently stroked along the fur along the muzzle, then ended by leaning forward and kissing him on the tip of his nose.

His eyes flicked towards her, and, seemingly against his will, he smiled...then let out a deep sigh. "I'm sorry, Girl. But I miss them sometimes, and it...it just gets to me."

Girl mused, and realized Bear had to be talking about his family. "How long has it been, Bear? Could I perhaps go see them for you?"

Bear snorted.

"And tell them what? That I've been turned into a Bear by Mother Nature?"

He snorted and turned his head away. "Besides," he said quietly, "they will probably be dead."

Bear turned back to Girl. "How old do you think I am, Girl?"

Girl rocked back. She had never thought about it.

"I...I don't know."

Bear turned away again. "Girl, I became a Bear before you were born..."

The words hung in the air.

Girl was astonished. He must be...very old. Much older than she ever imagined.

She looked around the cabin and noticed that everything was vintage for the first time. Nothing was new. Nothing had been new when she was a little girl. Tears formed in her eyes. There really was no way he could go back, even if, by some miracle, he could change back into a man.

She leaned forward, placing her cheek against his shoulder and hugging him. "I'm sorry, Bear. I didn't know."

"I know, Girl..."

The two friends were silent, staring into the fire as the flames leaped up, painting their faces red and orange. The clock ticked, and the flames began to burn down...

Finally, Girl got up stiffly and stretched. She went to her bedroom, changed into her pajamas, grabbed her blanket and pillow, and dragged them along the floor, sleepy-eyed. "Move over, you big furball."

Bear's eyes glanced up at her, and he smiled.

Grudgingly, he moved to make room for her. She flopped down on the floor, nestled into his tummy, pulled the blanket over herself, snuggled into her pillow and heaved a deep sigh. Bear mimicked her, giving a deep sigh...

...then there was a deep rumble as he chuckled deep in his abdomen.

The two friends watched the fire burn down, eyes wide, thoughts to themselves.

And the stars overhead kept watch.

Until finally, slowly, gradually, their eyes closed.

And they slept.

Chapter 37: First Snowfall

Girl woke up that morning, and was surprised that it was as bright as it was in her bedroom. She sat up in bed and looked out the window. Somehow, it seemed brighter outside. She got out of bed, wrapped the blanket around her, and wandered out into the great room.

For once, the front door was closed, and Bear was not on the rag rug – or anywhere inside.

She walked to the front door and opened it to find that it was *snowing!*

And Bear was frolicking and running around, trying to catch snowflakes!

She laughed out loud to watch him!

He saw her and stopped and said, "Come on out! It's SNOWING!"

She laughed and called, "I have to get dressed!"

He stopped and looked at her and said, "Oh...right. Yeah." He thought for a moment, then said, "Well, hurry up!"

She bustled back into her room, threw on all the clothes she could find, slipped on her boots, and ran out and down the stairs. She ran straight for Bear, who was dancing in the snow, leaped and landed on his back. He reared up like a bucking bronco and stood on his hind legs, pawing the sky, laughing.

Then started galloping around the meadow with Girl clinging to his back.

After a while, she realized she was getting cold and tapped Bear's shoulder, "Bear..."

But Bear kept going, laughing and giggling.

"BEAR! I'm getting cold!"

Bear stopped, panting, and turned to look over his shoulder.

"What?"

"I'm getting COLD!"

He thought a minute, then said, "Oh...yeah, right. I forget you don't have fur..."

Then he chuckled, "Well, not MUCH fur, at any rate."

He turned and padded back to the cabin, then turned and gently deposited her at the bottom of the steps.

"If you go back into the storeroom, at the very back, you'll find a big, old trunk. Drag it out into the great room."

Girl skipped up the steps, ran to the store room and found the trunk, then, with difficulty, yanked and pulled it out to the great room, panting.

Bear sat there, grinning.

"You could have helped, you great, walking rug! Now what?"

"Well, open it, of course!"

She noted that although there was a keyhole in the hasp, it wasn't locked, so she flipped the hasp up and opened the curving trunk lid. "This looks like a treasure chest from some pirate movie," she panted.

"Yo ho ho!" replied Bear, smirking.

Inside was a great pile of clothing of all sorts.

"What am I looking for?" Girl asked

The grin started to fade from Bear's face, "Uh...clothes, women's winter clothing. Probably about your size."

He licked his lips, then looked down, "It's in there."

And he turned and started to lay the fire.

Girl stared at his back for a moment, then started to pull out clothing. Some of it was for a man – a largish man with broad shoulders and narrow hips. And a lot of it was for a woman – about her size. She sorted through the woman's clothing and found several heavier shirts, some cable-knit sweaters, and one great parka in a woman's size, along with several pairs of thick, woolen socks.

She turned to look at Bear, but he was intentionally busy with the fire, so she pulled the woman's clothing out, piled the man's clothing back in the trunk and slammed the lid.

"There! This looks like it might fit!"

Bear wheeled, looked at her, and smiled, "Yeah, it just might. Try it on!"

"Not here!" Girl protested.

"Why not?"

"BEAR! I'm not going to change my clothes in front of you!"

Bear chuckled. "Why?...Oh, never mind. Go get changed!"

Girl gathered up a double handful of clothing and walked off to her bedroom, slamming the door.

She chuckled as she changed – and wondered, at the same time, whose clothes these had been. She had to cinch the waist of the heavier trousers somewhat, and the sleeves were a little long, but overall, they were a pretty good fit.

Slinging the parka over her shoulder, she marched proudly into the great room and shouted, "Behold! Na-Nookie of the North!" And struck a dramatic pose.

Bear looked at her in astonishment, then started laughing. He kept going until he was rolling on the floor.

Girl started chuckling along with him, walked over, and soon found herself lying on the floor alongside him, slapping his side as she laughed helplessly.

The two friends finally wound up curled up together on the floor, still chuckling occasionally.

"Bear?"

"Yes Girl."

"Whose..."

Bear interrupted her. "Not now, Girl. Let's go play!" then leaped up and dashed outside.

Girl got up slowly, a solemn look on her face, watching him go.

Then she changed her expression to a big smile and hollered, "Ready or not, here I come, you big furball!"

Chapter 38: Girl Tells A Story

Girl was sitting on the rag rug, watching the fire flicker and stroking Bear's great head. The two friends were just sitting. They had nothing to say at the moment and had worked into the habit of talking only when they did.

After a while, Girl had a feeling, let it grow, then said, while stroking his head, "Bear?"

"Yes Girl?"

"May I tell you a story?"

There was a low rumble, "I'd like that, please."

Girl gathered her thoughts, then said, "Once upon a time, there was a young princess who lived by the ocean with her mother, father, and older sister. She loved to run along the beach, play in the sand, swim in the water, and get into all kinds of mischief. She grew to be an expert swimmer and a fierce defender of people smaller and in need of help.

"Which was funny because she was quite small herself.

"Yet, no one thought of her as short. Indeed, many scurrilous lads who lived in the area trembled when she roared. She was not to be crossed, and no one even *thought* to harm someone when she was around.

Girl paused. "Go on," Bear said.

"Hmm? Oh, right. She was the youngest of the family, so she would not inherit the castle, wear the crown, or rule the land, so she set out to become the best at something else.

"She was an expert swimmer but not as fast as some others, so that wouldn't work. Then she tried diving and found herself. Her compact, slender, but muscular body was perfect for twisting, turning, and somersaulting in the air. So she became a diver."

Bear stirred. "Where did she dive?"

Girl was silent for a moment, "Oh, she dove off great high cliffs, narrowly avoiding the rocks below and causing the spectators to ooh and ahh at her aerobatics. And they would clap and cheer. And she would pop up and wave at them. She was very happy." Girl stopped again, and was silent for a long time.

"Then what?"

"Then what, *what*, Bear?"

"What happened next?"

Girl sat up, "How would I know? It was far, far away."

Bear sat up, dumping Girl on her bum. "Then how did you know this part?"

"Uh...I, um, heard it from a friend."

Then she looked up, acting as if she was thinking and said, "No, actually, I made it up. That's right. I made it up."

Bear leaned forward until his nose almost touched hers, squinting his eyes.

"Then make up some more," he said in a deep, menacing voice.

"No," said Girl. "I don't wanna."

She lunged forward, kissed his nose, scrambled up and ran off to her room, slamming the door.

Bear watched her go, then chuckled to himself, folding himself back down onto the rag rug.

After the fire had burned down most of the way, Bear heard the bedroom door open and the sound of a blanket and pillow being dragged across the floor.

Bear closed his eyes and pretended to be asleep.

Girl dropped her pillow on his head, then snickered as he flinched but didn't open his eyes.

She arranged the pillow and leaned against his body, covering herself with the blanket.

After a while, she said, "Bear?"

"Yes, Girl."

"Bear, I...I was the princess."

"I know Girl."

"And I didn't want to tell you the unhappy bits."

There was a long silence, and then Bear replied, "I know Girl. But you can skip over them and go on to the part where the princess escapes the evil troll and goes to live in the mountains with her friend, the magic Bear."

There was silence again, and then Bear heard a giggle. "Bear?"

Bear sighed, " *Yes* Girl?"

"Can you make a quarter disappear?"

Bear chuckled, then said, "No, but my kids sure could!"

The two friends giggled together and then quieted down.

The only sounds after that were the crackling of the fire, the hoot of an owl – asked and answered, outside – and the deep breathing of the two friends, asleep.

Chapter 39: Looking for Mother Nature

Bear was asleep on the rag rug, and Girl was curled up in a ball, leaning against his tummy. The fire had burned down low, and the light was dim.

Bear heaved a sigh, feeling a deep sense of peace.

But Girl twitched once, then again.

Bear looked down, and her face was strained, as if she was worried. She started to mumble, then turned. Then she settled, and – to Bear's surprise – tears began running down her cheeks.

Bear watched for a moment to see if she would settle back into peaceful sleep, but if anything, she started crying harder.

Finally, Bear reached a paw over and stroked her hair. "It's okay, Girl. Bear's here. Nothing can hurt you now."

Instead of settling, Girl turned violently away, "No. No. NO!"

"Girl, wake up – you're having a nightmare. Girl?"

Girl turned towards him, her eyes now half-open. "Bear?"

"Yes, Girl. I'm here."

"Oh, Bear!" And she turned into his stomach and started sobbing.

Not knowing what to do, Bear stroked her hair, and made soothing noises. "It's okay, Girl. It's okay. Shh shh shhhh..."

After a while, Girl stopped sobbing and gradually relaxed.

She turned to face Bear, "Oh, Bear. My life has been a waste. It was...awful until I escaped here. You saved me, Bear. You really did. I don't know how I will ever be able to..."

Bear laughed deep in his tummy. "Well, for one thing, you can stop getting my fur all wet!"

Girl looked up at him, tears clouding her eyelashes, and cry-laughed.

"Oh, Bear. You're so silly sometimes! Don't you know your species is known as *Ursus maritimus*? You practically *live* in the water!"

Bear chuckled, "Yeah, but I drown in tears, so cut it out, okay?"

Girl kept her eyes on his, and gradually, her breathing slowed, and she seemed to calm down. Finally, she heaved a deep sigh and buried her face in his side. "Oh, Bear."

Bear gave a very theatrical, heaving sigh, "Oh, Girl."

She chuckled, although it sounded sad. "Bear, I'm sixty-three years old. I have nowhere to go. My home is here – with you. It's the best I've ever known."

She looked up at him, "And you're the best person I've ever known."

Bear gazed at her fondly for a while, then said, "I know."

Girl sat up, "BEAR!"

She slapped him – gently – on the tummy.

"OOfff!" he play-acted, "Not nice, Girl. Not nice!" he said, rubbing the offended part – but his grin belied his words.

She settled back down, curled up against him, eyes focused on the fireplace – and everything beyond it.

"What am I going to do, Bear?"

Bear mused, wondering how to answer.

Finally, he said, "Well, you could go out into the world and see the parts you haven't yet. Would that be a good idea?"

She nodded absently, "Yeah, I guess so. There's so much I want to see. I haven't seen..."

Bear was silent for a long time, then, against his own better judgment, said, "Well, Girl, at least you CAN go see."

Girl thought for a bit, then sat up slowly and looked at Bear. "Bear? What do you mean?"

Bear sighed – for real this time – then said, "Where can I go, Girl? And how would I get there?"

Girl stared at him for a while, then sank back down onto his tummy.

"Oh," was all she said, then fell silent for a moment before speaking again. "Bear?"

"Yes, Girl."

"Could...could I speak to...Mother Nature? Please?"

Bear was silent, then finally, "I don't know, Girl. She comes when She comes, not when I call. Sometimes, I go for years without feeling her presence."

He sighed again. "But we can try. If I promise to think about it tomorrow, will you go to sleep and have good dreams tonight?"

Girl nodded silently, still staring at the fireplace.

Bear stroked her hair, then leaned down and kissed her hair. "Good Girl."

He sighed again, "Good night, lovely Girl. Sweet dreams this time. I'll be in them with you, OK?"

Girl inhaled sharply. "Promise?"

"Promise," Bear said.

"Okay. And Bear?"

"Yes, Girl."

She turned her face up to him. "Thank you."

He smiled, "And thank you, too, Girl. Now sleep, okay?"

Girl burrowed closer into Bear's tummy, "Okay."

And soon, her breathing was smooth and even. She even drooled a little.

Bear stroked her head, looking up at the ceiling, wondering. Who did he know would might be able to request an audience with Mother?

Finally, his eyelids drooped, his breathing slowed...

And he slept.

Overhead, the stars continued to wheel in the sky, and the North Wind blew by, carrying a message...

Chapter 40: Lynx's Death

Bear and Girl were sitting on the porch, allowing the mountains to watch them, when Bear's head suddenly turned up to the sky. "It's *Skrreee!* What's she doing?" Bear asked. The red-tailed hawk was circling around the cabin and squawking.

Bear stood up and lumbered down into the meadow, watching *Skrreee!* circle, and tilting his head to listen.

He straightened up, "WHAT?"

Bear turned to Girl, and said, "Stay here, Girl!" and took off running. But Girl, with her usual stubbornness, took off after him.

Running as hard as she could, she could barely keep sight of him as he crashed through the underbrush, running recklessly down the trails. She thought she'd lost him, then crashed into a clearing – and ran straight into him, THUD.

Bear turned and looked at her, annoyed. "I told you to stay put!"

Girl, breathing hard, looked over Bear's shoulder – and was surprised to see what looked like a large cat growling – at Porcupine! Bear moved to block the cat's view of Girl, then walked slowly toward the pair.

"It's okay, Lynx, you're all right, shhh shh shhh..."

Porcupine was backed against a tree, bristles up, which normally would have caused the other animal to back away. Instead, Lynx was stalking unsteadily towards Porcupine, growling erratically.

Girl looked carefully and thought she saw foam coming from Lynx's mouth. Bear continued walking towards Lynx, "There there, Lynx, you're okay. No one's gonna hurt you..."

"She's not in her right mind, Bear," said Porcupine, "She doesn't smell right."

Bear stopped and sniffed, then slowly started to walk around Lynx to come in behind her, "Porcupine – I think it's rabies."

"What's that Bear?"

"It's a sickness that eats your mind and then kills you. But Porcupine – if she bites you, you'll get the sickness, too."

"Oh. That... wouldn't be good, Bear."

"No. Now, please be quiet and stay still. I'm going to try to lure Lynx away."

Porcupine stopped dead still and said nothing. Bear continued to walk slowly around towards the hindquarters of Lynx. Lynx looked confused and shook her head, a rattle in her throat, then coughed.

When she looked up, it was as if she'd lost sight of Porcupine, then saw Bear moving. She growled and swung her head towards Bear.

Bear, now behind Lynx but still well away from her, stopped and turned head onto her. Lynx shook violently, then yowled once, then again more loudly – and sprung...

Bear dropped low, then caught Lynx's underbelly and heaved her hard and high into the air. Lynx scrambled in the air, howling, then hit a tree and slid down, collapsing on the ground.

Bear lifted a rock in his paws and advanced slowly on Lynx, who was breathing heavily on her back. Finally, when he was close enough, Bear lifted the rock and brought it down on Lynx's head. SMASH!

Lynx kicked twice – then lay still.

Bear slowly backed away, keeping his eyes on Lynx.

"Is...is she okay Bear? What happened?" asked Porcupine.

Bear shook his head, "No, Madam Porcupine. She's dead – I hope."

"You...you killed her, Bear? Was that necessary?"

Bear heaved a deep sigh. "No, Madam P. The sickness was killing her. I just stopped it from killing anyone else."

Porcupine's quills bristled, and she exhaled heavily. "Poor little girl. She was only two summers, you know."

"Yes, I know, Mrs. P. And I'm sorry. Now – it's important that no one goes near her body – not even the kites and vultures, or it will kill them. You can let the ants have her, but no one else. Please, Mrs. P. It's important."

"I know, Bear. I've seen this sickness before." She heaved a great sigh. "She would have killed me, wouldn't she?"

Bear shook his great head. "No, Mrs. P. Lynx would never hurt you. She loved you. But the sickness would have killed you."

Porcupine dropped her head and stood still.

Then she raised it and said, "Thank you Bear. What would we do without you?"

Bear shook his head again. "No, Mrs. P – what would the forest have done without *you?*"

Porcupine took a deep breath. "Wait...you have that...Girl with you. I can smell her. What were you thinking, Bear? Bringing her with you?"

Bear glared at Girl, then turned back to Porcupine, "I didn't bring her, Madam P. She ran after me, even though I told her not to."

Porcupine sniffed, then turned her head towards Girl, even though she was squinting. She sniffed again. "Oh, Bear – be gentle with her. She was scared for you."

Bear swiveled his head and looked at Girl, who was trying to look very small – and failing. He sighed. "I know, Madam P. I know."

Porcupine coughed, "She has great affection for you Bear. If she was another bear...well, we both know what would happen next."

Bear dropped his head, then looked up at her again, "I know, Madam P. I know."

Porcupine turned back to her rotten log, "Well, you children get along home and let an old woman sleep. And Bear?"

"Yes, Madam P.?"

She looked in Bear's direction. "Thank you." Then she waddled back into the rotten log, quills scraping along the trunk.

Bear stood still momentarily, then wheeled towards Girl and stared at her. She straightened up and glared back at him.

"So – do you want to walk, or would you like to ride, Girl?" That was all he said.

Girl swallowed hard, "Uh, ride, if it's not too much trouble, Bear."

Bear shook his great head. "Climb aboard."

Girl clambered up his back and held on tight. Bear took off, walking this time, and headed back to the cabin.

Girl held on tightly, lying close to Bear's body, and thinking about what Porcupine had said, all the way home...

Chapter 41: Bear Gets Hurt

Girl was sitting on the porch, wondering where Bear had gotten to. He was normally back by this time of day, even if he had gone hunting for food. She was starting to get antsy, wondering what she would do if he didn't show up.

He had told her quite categorically that she wasn't safe on her own in the wild, and since she had seen some of the wilder animals, like wolverine, she understood. At the same time, she didn't know what to do if he didn't show up – and it worried her.

She stepped down from the porch and walked into the meadow, looking up. High above, she spotted a hawk circling and wondered if it might be *Skrreee!* She started waving both hands and jumping up and down, trying to get the hawk's attention.

After a minute, the hawk started to circle lower until finally it was circling her, just above her reach. It looked like *Skrreee!*

She cupped her hands to her mouth, "Where's Bear?" she shouted.

The hawk looked at her, twitching its neck, flapping her wings and gaining altitude again. Girl watched as the bird circled higher and higher, then flew off.

Girl stood in the meadow, uncertain what to do. She bit her lip but finally decided she had to stay where she was. Bear wouldn't thank her if she got into trouble and Bear wasn't around to get her out of it. And he would be mad if she wasn't here when he returned.

She didn't like that answer – but she knew it was the right one. She resumed her place on her rocking chair, unconsciously rocking back and forth and worrying. Quite a while later, she heard a sound.

It was a wheezing sound. She stood up and prepared to run into the house and slam the door, afraid that it was a wild animal, or worse, a human.

The sound got louder – then finally, Bear walked slowly into the meadow. Girl jumped down from the porch and ran off to see him – then stopped when she got close.

Bear had blood on his side, and his back had claw and tooth marks.

"BEAR!" she screamed and ran to him.

Bear kept going.

"Bear – what happened?".

Bear kept going.

He was breathing hard, and his head hung down.

Girl was uncertain what to do, and so walked alongside, smoothing his fur.

He stopped, turned his head slightly, and wheezed out a single word, "Water."

Girl raced off to the cabin, and returned with a big bowl, which she had filled mostly with water. A good deal of it slopped out of the bowl, but she had about half left when she got back to Bear. She held it to his muzzle with both hands and let him drink.

He drank noisily and sloppily, until the bowl was dry, then shook himself and sat down.

"Thank you...Girl..."

"Bear...What, what happened? No, never mind. Let's get you to the cabin first, then we can worry about anything else.".

Bear nodded, getting up and resumed his slow walking.

Girl walked alongside him, smoothing his fur, talking to him in a low voice, and telling him how well he was doing, how important he was to her, and how she would take care of him once they were in the cabin.

Finally, they reached the stairs.

Bear put one paw on the stairs and stopped.

"Don't stop, Bear! You're almost there!".

She got behind him, leaned into his right rear and pushed.

And gradually, Bear walked up the steps to the porch.

Girl led him inside and helped him settle himself on the rag rug. She hurried off and got him some more water, placing it by his muzzle.

Then she went back to the kitchen, opened the fridge, got out a plate of several trout that Bear had been planning on having for breakfast the next morning, and placed it in front of him.

"Eat, Bear, please. It will help. Please!".

At first, Bear just lay there, but after a few minutes with the trout smell filling his nose, he stretched forward, grabbed a trout and wolfed it down.

The others quicky followed, then the water, then Bear fell asleep.

Girl quietly boiled some water, got some antiseptic powder and bandages from the First Aid kit, and started first gently washing the wounds, then applying some iodine, and finally, antiseptic powder and bandages.

Bear jerked under her touch at times, but continued to lay still, and sounded as if he were asleep.

Girl looked at the wounds – then noticed that there was also blood on Bear's claws and blood around his mouth. Clearly, he had been in a fight – but why? Girl was itching to know – but knew that what Bear needed now was to sleep and recover his strength.

She quickly ate some food – it didn't matter what – then changed into her nightdress, brushed her teeth, and grabbed her blanket and pillow.

She built up the fire, then lay near Bear without touching him.

She knew he could smell her and that it would comfort him.

Oh Bear... she worried.

She lay on the rag run, with her head on the pillow, and the blanket covering her, watching the fire leap and wondering what had happened.

But she knew she would have to wait until tomorrow....

Girl slept on the rag rug next to Bear that night. Every once in a while, she would open her eyes to see if Bear was still breathing, and every time he was.

But in the morning, when she opened her gummy eyes, she saw Bear looking back at her. He smiled.

"Hey there, my lovely friend," he said.

"Hey Bear – *my* lovely friend!"

He chuckled, then winced.

She sat up suddenly, concerned. "Are you okay, Bear?"

Bear stayed where he was. "Well, yes – and no.

"No, I'm not okay. I hurt in a lot of places.

"But yes, I *will* be okay. I can tell that the wounds will recover. None of them feel hot or feverish, which probably means they're not infected."

He was silent for a moment. "How did I get here?" he asked.

Girl sat up, tailor-fashion. "You walked."

Bear mused for a moment, "Impossible. I couldn't walk."

"You did, Bear. I saw you walking into the meadow down towards the lake and ran to see you. You were a mess, but you were walking."

Bear's eyes stared off into the distance for a moment, then said, "Oh...yeah..."

His eyes closed. "*Skrreee!* flew overhead, and told me you had asked her to find me."

He blinked, "I...I realized that the foolish girl that you are, you would come looking for me. So I got up and started back towards the cabin. I couldn't let them get you."

His eyes closed again, and he was silent.

Finally, Girl said, "Who, Bear? Hunters?"

Bear's eyes stayed closed, "No. Wolves."

Girl remembered a time when a large wolf had approached the edge of the meadow, looked at her, then turned and run away.

"Did the wolves find you, Bear?"

He was silent again for a while, then, "No – they were attacking Mama Brown Bear and her young cubs. Three kept her busy while the rest started attacking her two cubs, trying to pull them away.

"I couldn't let that happen, so I charged the Pack. I think I managed to disable three of them before they even realized I was there.

"Then they turned on me."

Bear was silent again.

Girl leapt up and went and got him some water, which she laid down in front of him. He slowly lifted his head, lapped at the water for a while, then collapsed back on the rug.

"What happened next?"

Bear's eyes stayed closed, "Mama Bear ran off with her cubs."

"OH *BEAR!*"

His eyes opened, "It's okay. It was the right thing to do. Her first allegiance has to be for her cubs."

"But that left you with the wolves!"

Bear was silent.

"How did you get away?"

"I jumped into the lake, just far enough that the wolves had to swim to keep their heads above water. I knocked another two out when they tried to attack me in the water.

"Then they backed off, going back onshore, and waited, knowing I would eventually have to come out, that I couldn't swim or stay in the water forever. They were going to outwait me."

Bear smiled, "But I'm a crafty old Bear. I started swimming for the opposite shore. They started running in that direction once they realized where I was going.

"So, I changed direction and soon had them running back and forth.

"When they started to get tired, they changed tactics and started positioning themselves around the lake, figuring I'd come out near one of them and that one would hold me until the others arrived.

Bear smiled again, "Bad idea. Von Clausewitz would have flunked them for military history. Don't divide your forces, but strike for the heart."

Girl was quiet, waiting.

"Once I had them spread out enough, I swam hard for the furthest one, leapt out of the water, and smashed him down, either knocking him out or killing him – I didn't wait to see – then jumped back in the water and swam out again.

"I did this three times before they caught on, but by this time, they were no longer sure of being able to take me in a fair fight. They left."

Bear was quiet for a long time.

"Then I crawled out of the water, exhausted. And I was bleeding, and the blood loss was starting to make me light-headed. I must have blacked out, because the next thing I knew, *Skrreee!* was screaming at me about you."

Bear turned his head to look at her. "You saved me, Girl. If *Skrreee!* hadn't come looking for me, the wolves might have come back, or some other hunting animal might have found me."

He was quiet for a long time. "How did you get me into the cabin, Girl? I don't *think* you carried me!" And he chuckled, then winced.

"I didn't carry you Bear. I ran and got you some water, then walked back with you, encouraging you, step by step. You were – you *are* magnificent!" And she buried her face in his fur, crying.

"Oh, Bear..."

Bear lifted a paw, and placed it around her shoulder. "Oh, Girl."

It took many days, but Bear did recover. He walked with a limp for some time but eventually recovered entirely. Girl made sure he ate well, and she even started fishing for him down at the lake – although with Bear always nearby.

But she always remembered how close she had come to losing him – and that the only thing that had kept him alive was him worrying about her. It made her cry to realize it – but that was Bear, and she appreciated him all the more for it.

She slept out on the rag rug with him every night, waking several times a night to check on him. And, over time, he would wake up with her, open his eyes, smile, and then go back to sleep.

Mama Bear never thanked Bear – but small offerings of meat started showing up at the edge of the meadow. Girl was never sure whether Mama Bear was doing it – or some of the other animals in the forest, for everyone knew what had happened.

And Bear had a lot of friends.

Chapter 42: Mayflies

Bear was sitting out on the porch, watching the shadows move on the mountains opposite. He felt stillness deep within his bones, and time seemed to halt. Finally, he took a deep breath, exhaled, and looked around at Girl.

She was sitting, as usual, in the rocking chair, with one foot up on the seat with her chin resting on her hands, which were resting on the knee. Her other leg was down, swinging back and forth as the rocker rocked.

But the thing that caught Bear's attention was the tear rolling down her cheek. He pushed himself up, walked slowly over to her, and stopped, his eyes level with hers.

She looked up into his eyes. Bear noticed that her eyes looked sad, and there was one tear rolling down her cheek and another preparing for the journey.

Bear leaned in, and licked the tear, then rubbed his nose against hers.

She smiled, closed her eyes, and rubbed back, but in so doing, dislodged the other tear.

Bear stood, eye-to-eye with her for a while, then finally said, "Come with me." He turned and lumbered down the porch steps, then turned to look at her.

She hadn't moved, but Bear waited, so finally, she rubbed her face, got up, tucked her hands in her jeans pockets, and walked slowly down the stairs.

"Would you like a ride?" Bear asked.

She shook her head, then looked down at the ground. Bear turned and walked slowly across the meadow, then into the forest. Girl followed, slowly at first, but gradually Bear picked up the pace until finally, they were both walking briskly through the forest, down toward the lake.

As they got close, Girl noticed insects swarming around where there had been none before.

"What are they, Bear?" she asked.

"Well, that depends on whom you ask. Canadians call them shadflies or fishflies. But Americans usually call them mayflies."

Girl stopped. "But it's not May."

"Really? I hadn't noticed," smirked Bear. "They don't only come out in May. It depends on when their larvae mature. The larvae live in the lake here for several years before emerging into adult forms."

Girl mused on this for a bit, then said, "But it's closer to Autumn."

"Right. I *had* noticed that, Girl." And he paused, waiting for her to think things through.

She looked out over the lake and up at the mountains, then at the swarms of insects buzzing, seemingly at random.

"So – why did you want me to see this, Bear?"

Bear moved towards her, his head almost on a level with hers, despite being on all fours.

He looked her in the eyes and said, "Because theirs is a short life – but a merry one. You, Girl, looked like you were regretting. And believe me, I know all about doing that."

Bear turned and looked off into the mountains, then huffed dismissively. "But there is nothing to be gained by looking backwards – other than to remind yourself of the good things."

Girl stared at him for a moment and said, "But there were no...well, not many...good things."

"Then why look back at the bad things?"

Girl pushed her hands deeper into her pockets. "What else do I have, Bear?"

Bear took a step forward and trod lightly on her right foot.

"OW!" She pulled her foot back and danced away. "Why did you do that, you silly creature?"

"To remind you that you're alive, Girl. You might not have been, but you've been given a gift, a very precious one."

Bear lifted a paw, and waved it at the mayflies. "And so have they. And they rejoice in it."

He turned back to her. "Girl, believe me, I know regret. But I have come, over the decades, to understand what a gift Mother Nature gave me – and finally to appreciate it."

He sat, then said, "You have life. You have *joie de vivre*. You are breathing, and you should appreciate that, and make the most of it. Plus, you have the rest of your life ahead of you – so be sure to use it, and use it well."

Girl looked down at her feet, then up again at Bear. "I...I know. Really I do. But sometimes I get overwhelmed, is all."

Bear nodded. "That, too, I understand."

He stood for a moment, the turned and said, "Last one home is a rotten egg!" and took off.

"HEY! That's *not fair!*"Girl shouted after him, then turned and shot off after him.

They got back to the cabin, and slumped down on the porch, both breathing hard and laughing.

Girl lifted up and smacked Bear on the rump. "You are a cheater, you cheating cheat of a cheater!"

Bear chuckled deep in his throat. "Yeah" was all he said.

The two friends went into the cabin. Girl made supper for herself, and Bear made up the fire for the night.

That night, they sat out on the porch and watched the timeless stars above them. And that night, Girl fell asleep again, curled into Bear's side.

Smiling.

Chapter 43: A Cold, Rainy Day

The sky was grey through the cabin's windows. The mountains kept appearing and vanishing in the distance, and a kind of hissing sound could be heard on the roof.

Bear had gone out foraging in the morning, as he usually did, and came back grouchy and thoroughly soaked. He stood on the porch and shook himself but still created a puddle on the floor when he came in. He didn't want to lie on the rag rug for fear of getting it wet, so instead, he lit the fire and then lay on the floor nearby.

When he was out foraging, Girl had gone outside to check the weather herself but had quickly retreated into the warmth of the cabin. It wasn't just raining – it was sleeting down: cold, wet, damp, and horrible. She had some oatmeal with tinned peaches and brown sugar, then pulled out a jigsaw puzzle she had done once before and started to sort pieces.

After a time, she gave up, leaving piles of pieces strewn on the table, retreating to the faded red leather sofa with a copy of *Little Women*, and trying to concentrate on reading.

Bear had been staring straight ahead, eyes open, head on the floor. Finally, he exhaled noisily, then lifted his head and spoke.

"Girl, we have to talk."

She dropped the book with a thud. "That never sounds good."

She swung her feet onto the floor, walked slowly over to Bear, and sat tailor-fashion on the rag rug near him, letting the fire warm her side.

Bear couldn't look at her but forced himself to speak, "You know that you're going to need to leave soon."

Girl jumped up, "*Bear!* Not *yet!*"

She ran off to her room and slammed the door.

Bear heaved a deep sigh, then pushed himself up from the floor and slowly walked to the bedroom door.

"Girl, I know you don't want to talk about this. Neither do I. But we have to."

There was nothing but silence as a reply.

"Please, Girl."

More silence.

Bear heaved a sigh, then slowly paced back to the great room and collapsed on the rug, glowering at the fire.

A few minutes later, Bear heard the bedroom door open and Girl's footsteps slowly approaching him. He waited and was rewarded when she slipped down and seated herself, tailor-fashion, in front of him.

"I'm sorry, Bear. But I don't want to go. This is the only time that I have felt free and truly cherished in my adult life. You have no idea how important that is to me." She dropped her head, looking at her hands as she rubbed them together.

Without raising his head, Bear's eyes flicked up to her.

"You are free, Girl. He's dead."

She nodded, then shook her head no. "Yes, he is. But his brothers aren't, and the community around us thought he was just the kindest person and a wonderful dad." She looked up at Bear with tears in her eyes. "They never saw what he did behind closed doors. And the kids never knew – that was the deal. He left them alone. In exchange, I never complained about what he did to me."

She was silent for a long time, staring into the fire. "He hurt me. Over and over and over and over and..."

She fell silent, and her shoulders started shaking. Bear could tell she was sobbing.

He waited for a while. "Your kids are grown and gone?"

She nodded.

"Do they live in the same community?"

She slowly shook her head. "They moved – to get away from me. They think he's the greatest. They both blame me for all the problems between us. They think I was a horrible mother. And I couldn't say a thing in my defence."

She looked up at Bear, her eyes brimming. "They hate me, Bear. My own children *hate* me. I've had broken bones, a concussion, a plate in my ankle, I have only partial vision in one eye because of ..." She took a shaky breath in. "And they hate me."

Bear moved over next to her. He put his paw behind her shoulders and pulled her close. She turned and buried her face in his fur, then wept uncontrollably. Bear gently rubbed her back, listening to her as his heart ached for her.

After a long while, she stopped and sat up. Her face was a wreck. "How can I leave you? You're the only person who has ever helped me. Who has ever cared about me. Who has ever ..." she turned her face down and whispered, "...loved me."

The two friends sat in silence for a long time, breathing together, seeking comfort.

Bear finally exhaled noisily. "And it's because I love you that you have to go, Girl. If you stay, you'll die. The weather gets too cold here. You'll freeze."

She nodded. "I know. I just wish..." she fell silent.

"Believe me, Girl, so do I."

He shook himself. "So, tell me – are there things you've always wanted to do? Things you've wanted to see, places you've wanted to go?"

"Yes."

"What?"

"*Everything.* I've never been anywhere except where I grew up, college, and – well, I won't call it home, where we lived. I want to see everything, Bear. I want to go everywhere."

Bear tried to smile. "Well, it's all just waiting for you out there. Go and get it, Girl."

She nodded. "I know." She wiped her eyes on her sleeves. "The funny thing is that I might be able to afford to."

Bear's head came up. "Oh?"

She attempted to smile, too. "He was never any good at money. I always managed the household finances. And I made more than he did. And I have a pension. My financial advisor told me I have enough, and more, to retire and to travel if I want to."

She looked down again. "But I have no idea how to restart my life – out there," she waved at the door. She smiled a crooked smile. "For one thing, I don't have as much as a penny here, no matter what I might have somewhere else. No ID, no credit cards – nothing."

Bear chuckled. "Don't worry about that. In the first place, there *are* no pennies in Canada. Or so Riley tells me. Do you remember Riley? The human I saved from drowning, and who buys supplies for me?"

Girl nodded.

"Besides," Bear lumbered up and resettled himself on the rug next to her, "I've made some arrangements. I've arranged for Riley to give you a ride into the nearest large town and give you some cash. He tells me about $500 should be a good start. I really have no idea what money is worth nowadays. That sounds like a lot to me, but it probably isn't."

Girl looked up, puzzled. "You – *what?*" Girl shifted and looked worried. "Bear, I can't get into a car with a man I don't know. *I can't!*"

Bear looked at her, puzzled, "It's okay, Girl. I know him."

Girl stared at him. "No, Bear, *no!*"

Bear shook his head, "Why not, Girl? I don't get it."

Girl slowly shook her head, "No – you *don't* get it."

She gulped. "I'll try to explain. When the troll was – hurting me, I tried to tell people – people at work, the police, our neighbours, and no one, I mean *no one* listened to me. For many of them, the image I created was too weird and too different from his public image. Plus, they didn't *want* to believe me because then they would have to *do* something about it, and no one wanted to get involved!

"The police called it a 'domestic' and we would have to sort it out between us – despite the fact that he's almost a foot taller and at least sixty pounds heavier than me! Besides, one of his brothers is a cop – and cops support each other no matter what.

"But the people that hurt the most were some men I thought were friends. I thought they believed me – but the look in their eyes said that they *envied* him, and thought he was *cool* because he was really putting it to me!"

Girl stopped to sniff and wipe the tears from her eyes.

"I, I can't get in a car with a strange man because I don't trust men. *Any* men! For all I know, this Riley guy could sell me out to the troll's brothers. I'm sure they've asked around about me. I know it!"

Bear sat there, stunned. It was an aspect of the whole business he had never considered, but it made sense. He tried to work it out, partly in his head, and partly out loud.

"Oh...kay. Um, well, in the first place, I haven't told him anything about you, not even that you're a woman. All I've said is that I have someone who needs to be transported to where they can get a bus, train, or plane to a major center."

He waited, hoping she would say something to indicate that she was okay with it – but she stayed silent, looking down at her hands.

Bear sat silent for a moment, then asked, "There were no Good Samaritans who got involved?"

Girl shook her head, then looked up and smiled, eyes still glistening with tears, "Well, only one...but he's covered in fur and lives in the Canadian Rockies. He saved my life."

She looked down again, "But aside from you, Bear – no, nobody lifted a finger to help me."

A deep pang went through Bear's heart at the thought of this remarkable woman, beaten and alone – and that no one, *no one* helped her. It made him ashamed to have once been a human. After a while, he cleared his throat.

"Look, I think I understand. The whole idea of – well, doing what the troll did to you is so alien to me that I have a hard time wrapping my head around it."

Girl looked up at him and flashed a fleeting smile at him, nodding.

"But I've been dealing with Riley for years. Not only did I save his life, but I've helped him in the backcountry on several occasions. Plus, I've given him things that he seemed pleased to have. I'll come back to that in a minute.

"My point is, Girl, that Riley doesn't want to lose me as a friend. I think it's a point of pride with him that he knows this magic Bear – and nobody else does. It makes him feel smart to have a secret, to know something that no one else knows. He seemed a little deflated when I told him I had someone staying with me, and, if anything, he tried to be even more helpful."

Bear paused in thought, then shook his ponderous head and said, "Girl, I'm kind of stonkered here. Aside from Riley, I have no idea how to get you out of the mountains. It's not like there's a bus that goes by. If we had the opportunity, we could walk many miles to one of the railway hotels. Then, you could simply walk in without explaining how you got there and arrange transportation. But it's a walk that would take several days from here, and I'd be afraid we might be seen together, especially as we would more or less have to follow the human road. That would *certainly* cause a lot of fuss and bother – and we would both wind up being asked questions we wouldn't want to answer."

Bear shook his head. "At least you would. They'd probably shoot me as a dangerous animal."

Girl looked up, then shook her head. "Not that way, then."

Bear paused, again hoping Girl would say something else. She didn't, and the two friends sat in silence. Finally, Girl sighed and said, "I guess...I guess I'll have to trust this Riley person."

She looked up. "Bear, I trust you. I would trust you with my life. I *do* trust you with my life. If you say he's our best chance, even our only chance, then I'll...I'll do it."

She looked unhappy.

Bear nodded. "Understood." He sighed. "I wish there were another way. Let's try to think of one before the end of the month, okay?"

Girl nodded.

"Oh, and I have something else for you as well." Bear padded into the storeroom, stood up on his hind legs, and reached for a peanut jar from the top shelf. He brought it back to the great room and placed it beside where Girl was seated.

"What's this, Bear?"

"Open it, silly. That's how you find things out, by looking into them."

She felt the jar. It was heavy. She slowly unscrewed the top and peered inside.

"Bear – is that what it looks like?"

Bear shrugged. "Probably. What does it look like?"

"Gold?"

"Well, then, yup – that's what it is."

"But there are little flakes and a number of pebbles – I guess they're nuggets." She looked up at him, "How much is this worth, Bear?"

Bear, who had lain down on the rag rug again, shrugged. "How would I know? What does a loaf of bread cost these days? And how much is gold worth per ounce? I don't worry about it – and Riley seems happy to take whatever I give him and bring me anything I want, so – who needs anything more?"

Girl hefted the jar. "I'd guess this weighs, um, a-a couple of *pounds*. Bear, is this all gold?"

Bear shrugged again, "Probably some dirt and pebbles in there as well. As I said, I really don't worry about it."

Girl looked at him in astonishment. "Um, well – let's say there's just *one* pound of gold in here. That's sixteen ounces. At about – I really don't know, let's say $2,000 an ounce..."

"Really?" Bear looked at her. "Last time I knew anything about it, it was like $35 an ounce." He sighed. "I guess that explains why Riley's happy to bring me anything I want. And why he keeps asking where I get it."

Bear shook his head.

"Bear...if that's even just *one* pound of gold, you're giving me more than $30,000! I can't take this!"

Bear snorted. "And what am *I* going to do with it? Wander into town and buy a fancy car or something?"

He sighed. "Girl, you are the most important person in my life. It's important to me that you have a real chance at a new life. I know this isn't much, but it will get you started. Just be careful where you try to bank it, okay? I've seen humans do weird and terrible things when there's money involved."

"Bear...I can't."

Bear stared at her, "Yes, Girl – you can. And you must."

She stared at him. "Okay, but I'll pay you back..."

Bear chuckled. "Why?"

"Uh..." Girl trailed off, then shook her head. Finally, she put the jar down and moved over and hugged him. "Okay, I'll take it – you big furry rug!"

She leaned back, "But Bear – I still don't want to go." She looked sad.

Bear looked back into the fireplace. "Neither do I want you to go, Girl." He turned to face her, "But wishing won't change things.

"Now, let's talk about how you're going to recreate your life. First, I don't believe you should go back to where you used to live. You said the troll's brothers still live there, and they're going to want some answers – and you don't want to give them anything, not the time of day, and certainly not answers they won't believe.

"Instead, you want to find a place where you can live quietly while you figure things out, arrange for your pension, organize your finances – and the big one! – decide what you want to do with your life. Meanwhile, find a lawyer in your former hometown, and hire her – I'd recommend a woman lawyer; she's more likely to understand the issues involved – and get her to do whatever is necessary to tidy up your affairs there. Do *not* go back!

"Are you with me so far?"

Girl looked stubborn but nodded.

"Okay, Girl. I know that look. What's going on in that little head of yours?"

"Bear – it's too much! I can't manage everything. I can't!"

Bear nodded, thinking. "Yes, I get that it's a lot. You're basically walking away from everything you've known for many years, burning

242

it down, as it were, and starting from scratch. That's a lot for anyone to have to cope with. I get it.

"But Girl – that life is *already gone!* Whether you want to or not, you *can't* go back."

Bear shifted, "Look at it this way: Why did you run away from the troll in the first place?"

Girl looked down, and mumbled.

"I'm sorry. I didn't hear you."

She looked up, angry, and cried, "Because I would have *died* if I'd stayed!" She shifted and looked down. "I'm sorry. I didn't mean to shout at you. You've been nothing but good to me."

She sighed.

"If I had stayed, I would have died. He was getting worse, and I'm not sure I would have survived physically. When he got drunk – which was almost every night – he started talking about breaking both my legs, making me crawl for the rest of my life. That was all I was, he kept telling me: a crawling, simpering nothing, a *nobody* of use to *anyone!*

"But even if I had survived physically, I was dying inside, Bear!" She looked at him, anguish in her face. "I had to leave. I *had* to!"

Bear nodded. "Yes, you did. So now think of it – you're free, he's gone, and you can have the life you always wanted. Why don't we focus on that?"

Girl stared at him, then her shoulders slumped, and she heaved a big sigh. "Yes, alright, I'll try." She looked up again. "It's just a lot."

Bear thought for a moment, "You've probably heard this before, but – do you know how to eat an elephant?"

She stared at him, started to speak, then stopped and shook her head.

"One bite at a time. And that's what we're going to do – invent your future, one bite at a time. Okay?"

She took a deep breath. "I don't know how, but – yeah, okay. Let's make me a real life. How?"

Bear chuckled, "As it happens, strategic planning is something I know a bit about. Let's start by having you tell me what you *don't* want in your life."

And so, the two friends started. Girl eventually went and found an old notebook and a pencil and began taking notes.

When they finished, Girl let out a sigh, focused on the notes, gently laid the pencil down, flipped back through the several pages of notes, then smacked the book closed, got up and hurried to her room, slamming the door.

Bear sighed, started to get up, then collapsed back onto the rug, figuring it would be better to let her settle down before trying to talk with her.

After a long while, Bear heard the door open again as footsteps moved slowly back towards him.

"Bear?"

"Yes, Girl."

"I'm – I'm sorry. I just get overwhelmed by it all. Forgive me?"

Bear raised his head and slowly shook it. "Nothing to forgive. I understand. Planning a life, figuring out what you want, and clawing your way back into living is a *lot*. I get it.

"But Girl – think of the good parts about it. Now that you're free, you can rewrite your life to be anything you want, to have it work any way you want. And if you have money, you can travel and see what you want."

He paused, then asked, "What are some things you've always wanted to see?"

Girl stared at him for a moment. "Paris. I want to see the Eiffel Tower. And the Louvre. And London. And Greece – the Parthenon by moonlight! And San Francisco. And Disneyland. And Tokyo. The Forbidden City in Beijing. Hawaii. Australia...Oh, BEAR! There's so *much* I want to see, and I want to see it all *RIGHT NOW!*"

Bear chuckled, "Well, okay! Then, let's start *right now.* To quote Lao Tzu, 'The journey of a thousand *li* begins with but a single step.' Let's figure out your first, single step."

And so they did.

She had to replace her ID and get new credit cards, preferably under a different name. Girl figured that the troll had traced her through the credit cards she'd used to get to Calgary and into the Rockies. Since one of his brothers was a cop, he'd probably traced her cards illegally. She'd get her lawyer on that. But that meant that she couldn't use her old cards anymore.

They slowly worked through all the steps she'd need to take to establish herself in a new community. They stopped to stretch, chat about other things for a while, eat, or get something to drink, and the day wore on.

By the time they were done, it was fully dark outside, and the fire had burned down. Bear built it up again while Girl rustled up supper for them both and set it on the table. Bear didn't usually sit at the table, but if he sat on the floor by the table, he could lean down and eat.

By this time, Girl seemed happier, as if she could really see her life appearing before her.

They chatted about other things over the meal, laughing and giggling (for her) and chuckling (for him) as they went, talking about Henry and the rabbits, the foolish chipmunks, and everything they'd seen and done over the summer.

Gradually, though, Girl's responses grew shorter, and her face fell, until finally, she ran down and stopped, looking at her hands.

Bear knew what was in her mind. "Yes, I know, Girl. Me, too."

She looked up with tears in her eyes, "I don't want to leave you, Bear. Not just for my sake, but for yours."

Bear turned away to hide his own tears, cleared his throat, and looked back. "And I don't want you to leave. Girl, I lived here for years before you were dropped into my life. I have my forest friends. I – I'll survive."

Girl got up, moved around the table, and hugged Bear hard around his neck. "I know, Bear. I know," she whispered.

But in her heart, she knew he would be terribly lonesome.

And so would she.

"At least we still have some time, Bear."

He didn't speak, merely nodded his head.

They were both unusually quiet that night, lying together on the rag rug, and it was a real question as to whether either of them got much sleep.

But the next morning brought a surprise.

Chapter 44: Girl Says Good-Bye

After a fitful night, the friends woke, bleary-eyed, to a snowstorm. The view outside the windows was almost pure white, with glimpses of flakes blowing by. The cabin was noticeably cooler, and a chilly breeze gusted in under the door.

Girl found that she had burrowed deep into Bear's tummy for warmth and moved into a fetal position under her blanket. Once she was awake, she got up and hurried to her room to put on warmer clothes.

Bear went outside to examine the day, pushing the door closed hard to keep the warmth inside. In the short period he was outdoors, his fur was quickly covered in snow. It was cold, and the wind was vicious.

Lifting his head, he sniffed the air, then looked off to the northwest. The clouds there were dark and menacing and moving quickly towards him.

He shook himself hard to get the snow off, then slipped back indoors, pulling the door behind him. Moving carefully around the rag rug to avoid dripping on it, he built up the fire again. The flames jumped up reassuringly, although they tended to veer and flare as the wind gusted over the top of the chimney.

Girl walked slowly back into the great room, hugging herself, shoulders hunched and head down.

She was wearing slippers for the first time, plus heavy woolen socks, jeans, and a heavy, off-white, cable-knit sweater. "Bear, it's *cold* in here."

Bear nodded, "Yes, and this isn't a patch on what winter's like."

He walked to the window and looked out. "I don't like the way the sky looks. And we shouldn't be having a snowstorm this big this early. Something's wrong."

Just then, there was an irregular tapping at the door, as if someone were rapping a spoon against it.

Bear and Girl looked at each other, then Bear moved and opened the door.

Skrreee! jumped back and flew up to the porch railing, screeching and flapping against the beating wind. Bear stepped out and closed the door, then listened until finally, *Skrreee!* flew off, carried quickly off into the distance.

Bear sighed, then opened the door into the cabin.

"Girl, that was *Skrreee!* She told me that the human I didn't eat – I think she means Riley – is out there with his moving thing and making a lot of noise, calling."

Girl gaped at him. "What?"

Bear looked grim. "There's only one reason why Riley would come here with his truck and make a lot of noise. He's come for you. There must be a problem on the roads."

Girl stood up, arms and legs straight out, "*WHAT?* But... but it's almost two weeks before the end of September, Bear! I can't go now, I *can't!*"

Bear looked down, then up again. "I know – but... Look, let's get you packed, just in case, and see what Riley wants, okay? Maybe it's nothing. And this way, at least I get to introduce you to him."

Girl stood stock still, frozen.

"Girl! We need to pack for you. *Now!*"

"But Bear..."

"Girl, sometimes freak storms come through and they have to close the highways. This is so close to the end of the season that they might just not open them again. Which means that if I'm guessing right, then we HAVE to get you out, *right now!*"

Girl didn't move.

Bear padded quickly into her bedroom, retrieved a suitcase from under the bed and placed it on top. He started taking clothes out of drawers and just piling them in.

Girl entered, pushed him aside, and took over. "You're doing it all *wrong*, Bear!"

She was clearly cross and upset but quickly pulled essential clothes out of the drawers, roughly folded them and placed them in the suitcase.

Bear came in with the peanut butter jar of gold and gave it to her. She glared at him, then shoved it into the suitcase.

After that, there wasn't that much left, and she was done quickly.

"Now get your warmest outdoor clothes on, Girl. Fast! I don't know how long Riley will wait!"

She moved over to the outdoor clothes pegs, pulled on the parka hanging there, then the neck warmer and knitted cap, shoved her feet into her boots, leaned over, laced them up and double-knotted them.

She stood up, stuffing her hands into woolen mittens. "There. Happy?"

Bear just shook his head. "Grab your suitcase and climb onto my back, Girl. And *hold on!*"

She moved over, wrapped one arm around her suitcase, climbed onto Bear's back, and clung to him, her head and one hand over the suitcase, grasping a fistful of his fur, knees clamped against his body. "Ready!" she called.

Bear pushed open the door, moved out, and slammed it behind them. He stepped gingerly down the snow-covered steps, then started moving through the snow, slowly at first, getting a sense of his footing, then quickly moved into a gallop.

Snow and wind whipped at Girl's face as she clung to him, trying desperately to hold onto Bear and her suitcase with her hands and knees as he thudded through the snow. She couldn't see where they were or where they were going, and it seemed like it took forever, but finally, Bear slowed and stopped. She was shivering, despite being close to his body heat.

There was a beat-up pick-up truck in a layby of the human road. Girl squinted through the blowing snow and the glare from the truck's headlights.

"Is this tha fella yuh been tellin' me 'bout?" the man shouted.

"Yes, Riley. This is Girl, Girl, this is Riley."

Riley stared at Girl, as if she was some kind of ghost. "You din' say it was a *girl*, Bear."

Then he shrugged and pushed out his hand.

"Well, pleased to meetcha, I guess. Now we gotta get goin'," Riley called.

Girl hesitantly stuck her mittened hand out and shook Riley's glove.

He turned to Bear. "Bear, they closin' da roads, and probley fer the season, it being so late 'n all. And da weather people says this storm's gonna last for at least two days, mebbe more. Blowed in from th' Arctic an' th' Pacific or sometin'. Bad news!"

He turned back to Girl. "We gotta go, ma'am. Get in!" He hurried around to the driver's side and hauled himself in, slamming the door. "The roads was bad when I come up," he shouted. "They gonna be worse on da way back. We gotta *move!*"

Girl turned to Bear, tears flowing from her eyes. *"BEAR!"*

Bear moved closer to her and grasped her in a hug, hiding his own eyes from her. Finally, he sniffed, "Go now. And go see Paris for me, okay?"

Girl laugh-cried, *"No!* I'm coming back *here* next year. Promise!"

Bear couldn't think of anything to say, so just said, "Go! Or you'll both be stuck here!" He put his head down and used it to butt her towards the truck. She turned to him, grabbed his head in both hands and pressed her forehead against his. "You saved me, Bear. You love me. Nobody's ever done that. I will be back, I *promise!*"

Then, reluctantly, she climbed in, placing her suitcase on the seat beside her, like a barrier between her and Riley.

Bear placed his muzzle on her lap for a moment, then backed away and pushed the door closed with a paw. Girl rolled down the window. "*Bear!*" she sobbed.

"I know Girl. Now GO!"

Riley took off, wheels spinning in the gathering snow. The truck fishtailed, then straightened out and moved quickly away.

Bear watched them drive off, with tears streaming from his eyes.

Chapter 45: The Next Summer

The drive down to Banff was white-knuckle all the way, with Riley grimly silent as he peered through the fogging windshield at the road ahead, wiping it clear with his palm as necessary. At times, the road disappeared in the swirling snow, and Riley slowed to a crawl, yet kept going, not wanting to get trapped.

When they finally saw the streetlights of the town, the road became better defined and had been plowed. Riley sat back and blew out his breath, visibly relieved. Girl could see the sweat on his brow, despite the cold wind that seemed to creep through the floorboards of the old pick-up.

Finally, they came to a stop in front of a bed and breakfast in town. "Bear din' say where he wanted ya to be dropped, but I reckon this is as good as any. Not rilly expensive, like some o' them ritzy places in town, but it should be comferble. And da train station is just up dere, at da end o' Lynx Street. Next train's not 'til tomorrah." Riley pointed straight ahead to the Banff Train Station, then reached into his pants pocket. "Here's da money I promised Bear I'd give ya." He pulled out a wad of bills, and handed it to her.

Taking it gingerly, Girl knew she should get out, but suddenly, it seemed safer in the truck than out in the storm on her own.

Riley sat there for a moment, then rubbed his mouth and said, "'Scuse me, ma'am, but I still got ta get home."

Girl turned and looked at him, then scrambled to get the door open, and clambered down with her suitcase. "Uh, thank you Riley. I don't know how I'll ever repay you."

Riley hung on the steering wheel, looking at her, then looked away. "No 'fence, ma'am, but I wouldn'a done dat drive for hardly nobody. But Bear is prolly de best person I know. Thank *him*. And good luck to ya. You must be rilly important t'him."

Then Riley leaned over, pulled the door closed, put the truck in gear, slithered sideways in the gathering snow, and finally moved off into the distance, leaving her on her own.

Girl took a shuddering breath, then turned, squared her shoulders, and walked up the steps of The Bear's Den Bed and Breakfast.

Her new life had begun.

The next day, she bought a train ticket to Calgary, then found a reasonably priced, if somewhat shabby, hotel near Calgary city center. She went to the American consulate to get a replacement passport, explaining that she had lost hers on a trail in Banff Park. Next, she went to the main branch of a Canadian bank to sell a little of Bear's gold. Once her passport came through, she bought a plane ticket to San Diego as her sister lived not far from there.

She thought the stay with her sister, Joyce, would be a chance to recuperate and get used to being in human company again, but it turned out to be anything but. Her sister naturally enough wanted to know what had happened, and where she had been all these months.

Girl tried to tell Joyce that she had run away from the troll – and was stopped dead there. "Why on Earth would you leave Trevor?" Joyce demanded.

But when Girl tried to explain that she had been abused for many years, Joyce refused to believe her. "I've seen the way you two behave towards each other. You clearly love him, the way you're always glancing at him. And he just loves to take care of you. Why, he hardly ever let you out of his sight the whole time you were here!"

No matter what Girl said, Joyce refused to believe that she had been abused – even when Girl showed her the scars and the plate in her ankle. Joyce always found a way of explaining things away.

"And besides," her sister said, "if you had been really abused like you say you were, you could have just *left*. Why, you could have called me, and I would have bought you a ticket!"

And as far as Joyce was concerned, that settled the matter. Plainly, Girl was at fault for deserting her husband – which was okay, although Joyce, who was single, thought Girl was crazy because the troll was clearly a hunk whom, Joyce said, *she* wouldn't kick out of bed for eating crackers!

Then there was the question of where Girl had been all Summer after leaving the troll. Girl tried to tell her that she had fallen and been rescued by a "guy" called Bear, who lived in a cabin in Banff Park. Joyce seemed doubtful at first, demanding to know if Girl had slept with him. Later, after she had checked online, she pointed out that there were no private cabins in the outback of Banff National Park. She became openly skeptical, and kept digging for answers.

Girl couldn't come up with anything satisfactory, and she knew she couldn't possibly tell Joyce the truth. If Girl so much as mentioned a talking Polar Bear and his animal friends, plus Mother Nature, the North Wind, and the Northern Lights...she was convinced Joyce would try to have her locked up.

But aside from being angry, upset, and hurt by Joyce's refusal to accept Girl's word on anything, Girl began to wonder whether Bear really did exist. Maybe she *had* gone a little crazy. But how could she have survived in the wild if Bear didn't exist?

It worried her.

Girl hurried her preparations to leave. She arranged to have a replacement driver's license sent to her from the Department of Motor Vehicles. She got a new cellphone with lots of data and national coverage. She arranged to open an account with an online bank after making sure she knew how to deposit cash and checks and could transfer funds electronically.

Then she called a former classmate, now a litigation lawyer in New York City, and asked him to find her a good lawyer to help stop her former brothers-in-law from tracking her and to close out her affairs where she had lived. He called back a day later with the name of a top-flight female lawyer, a Eurasian woman named Miko, who specialized in family law, notably abused wives.

Girl called Miko, described her situation was, what she wanted, and formally engaged her, then arranged to e-transfer a retainer. Miko had no trouble believing her tale of abuse. It happened all the time, even though very few people acknowledged it. Girl found it an enormous relief that someone finally believed her.

Next, after some searching, she found a reputable bullion dealer, took a cab to a nearby address, and then walked to the dealer's store. The dealer's security was impressive, but he was baffled when she produced a peanut butter jar containing raw gold. A gift, she explained, from a Canadian friend who lived off the grid and prospected for gold in his spare time.

It turned out to be quite a gift. Even with the dealer's commission, after much humming and hawing, he eventually did an electronic transfer to her online account for $73,485.38. She was stunned by the amount, even as she found the 38¢ to be amusing. The dealer warned her that the IRS would want a cut, as would whatever state she was a resident of, and that he was legally obligated to report it. She figured she'd worry about that later.

Then she caught a plane to Florida to get away from her prying, annoying sister, saying she wanted to lie on the beach now that she was retired – but not a San Diego beach as she had no intention of paying California income taxes. The reality was that she couldn't stand being constantly bombarded with questions when the answers were dismissed out of hand.

Being in the real world turned out to be one hassle after another. Yet, her biggest worry was Bear. Was he all right? Was he *real?*

The winter months passed, yet Girl had very little time to lie on the beach, even though she bought the white bikini she had promised herself.

To start, she was seriously upset when she realized that in her hurry to pack at the cabin, she had left the notebook with all the plans she and Bear had made for reinventing her life. All of the hours of thoughtful planning, discussion, and important details were *gone.*

She felt as if she had failed, not only herself, but Bear, too. She collapsed on the floor and started to weep. She felt overwhelmed, and Bear wasn't there to comfort her this time. She didn't even know where to begin.

But then she had the strangest feeling. It was almost as if Bear *were* there in the room with her, urging her to get up, stand up straight, and get to work. *It's no good crying over spilt Saskatoon berries, Girl,* he would have chuckled, *So get your rear in gear!*

Smiling, she could hear him saying that, and it calmed her.

Wiping her eyes on the back of her sleeve, she pushed herself up, then went out and found a souvenir shop that had blank books bound in faux leather sold as journals. She even found one that looked a little bit like the one she had left in the cabin.

Taking it home, she immediately sat up at the dining room table and started listing everything she could remember about what they had discussed. She started with the main areas that she needed to work on. Along the way, she remembered little bits and pieces of things they'd discussed, so she flipped to separate pages, put a heading at the top of a page, and jotted the things down.

Get your thoughts out of your head, Bear had told her, when they were planning, *and onto the paper. You can organize it and work out the details later, but write it down whenever you think of it! Otherwise, you'll forget and be upset with yourself for not remembering.*

She spent hours that day re-creating the work the two of them had done and jotting down to-dos, large and small, that she needed work on. Along the way, she found that new ideas and insights popped into her head that they hadn't discussed and jotted those down as well.

By the end of the day, she had dozens of pages of notes. She resolved to get another notebook the next day, and use it to organize all of her thoughts, to arrange them in some kind of order. That was what Bear had done – taking the messy piles of seemingly random thoughts, organizing them into groups, dividing them by major tasks, and finally putting the individual steps for each task in something like sequential order.

She felt much better – and proud of herself for not giving up. She felt Bear would approve – and thought that somehow, he was nodding at her with a smile on his face.

Then she looked up and was astonished to see it was dark outside – and realized she was hungry. She hadn't even stopped for lunch!

But it was worth it. It made her feel more in control.

She fixed herself a quick supper, then sat there, munching, as she looked through her notes to decide what needed to be done first.

After getting two more notebooks the next morning, she started on her major task list.

She decided to get the ball rolling for her pension, as the red tape would take time to unravel. She hadn't given proper notice for her civil service job when she escaped from the troll, and even though she had more than enough sick days accumulated to cover the time she had been missing, there was still a fuss about her going AWOL. Her lawyer, Miko eventually settled that by trading sick days for a properly filed notice of retirement, then found out that there were kinks in arranging her pension.

Apparently, the local service board that had employed Girl had somehow managed to undercount her service years through sloppy

258

paperwork. That meant they had been underpaying her for some time, plus her pensionable service years were screwed up. It looked like it would take quite a bit of time and effort to get straightened out, and Miko questioned whether it was worth the hours that she would have to bill Girl in order to do it.

But Girl had had enough of being pushed around and told Miko she wanted every penny she owed – plus interest. She eventually got it – and it turned out to be much more than she had to pay Miko – who, by this time, had become a sympathetic friend as well as her counsellor.

Miko also contacted the troll's brothers, pointing out that they had formed an illegal conspiracy when they traced her credit card purchases by making false declarations. Miko threatened to file criminal charges, but instead accepted a negotiated settlement. The brothers agreed to a restraining order, with a bond from all the brothers, that they would not attempt to contact her, trace her, or in any way interfere with her life. Miko got them to agree to a hefty financial penalty if even one of them violated the order, secured by a mortgage on the oldest one's house.

And, irony of irony, the troll had died without a will, which meant that Girl inherited everything he owned, as well as everything she owned She thought about using his money to have a tombstone engraved and placed in a men's urinal somewhere, so his grave would be pissed on regularly.

Meanwhile, Girl spent her days filing taxes, re-establishing her identity, applying for credit cards under her maiden name, and researching where she might want to retire permanently. Finally, she very timorously started to see if she could find some friends, maybe even a man she could date.

The local library in Dunedin, Florida, where she was renting a small condo on the waterfront, offered various book clubs. She joined one, read the books, and went regularly to the discussions. She developed a number of friendly acquaintances, but so far, no real friends, and especially no datable men.

She found relationships daunting and felt that meeting Bear's friends in the mountains had been easier – then found herself again questioning whether her time in the mountains was real or whether the whole summer had been just some kind of delusion. She kept the stub from her train trip from Banff to Calgary and the empty peanut butter jar that had held the gold Bear had given her as kinds of totems to prove she had been there.

The question of whether she was deluding herself kept coming back to haunt her. To counter it, she began to make plans to go back, once the roads opened again on June 1st – much later than she had expected, to her agonizing dismay. She had to know if Bear was real or not. And, more importantly, that he was all right.

Her sleep became even more fitful as the date for her departure approached. Her fears multiplied when she realized she had no idea how to contact Riley, or even what kind of truck he drove, other than that it was ancient. She decided she would get to Banff in the last week of May and start trying to figure out how to find Bear's cabin again.

Even as she worked on reinventing her life, she worried.

Girl stepped carefully down from the train onto the platform of the Banff station, then looked up at the mountains and inhaled. She was here at last.

The air felt different. The sky looked different. But most importantly, she *felt* different. She felt like a different person – a new one, and suspected that she was beginning to heal inside, as well as the scars outside. She was pleased with all she had accomplished – even though she was frustrated that things all took so long.

She smiled – but knew that she could never be complete until she knew about Bear.

On that subject, she felt as if everything was at stake now, as if everything she had done and hoped for was at risk if she couldn't find him. If he wasn't there, she would doubt her sanity – and that would undermine everything she had accomplished so far in reinventing her life.

Squaring her shoulders – as Bear would have told her to do – she tightened her grip on the straps of her backpack and strode forward, apparently confident but inwardly quivering with a combination of fear and excitement.

She decided to walk to the Bear's Den Bed and Breakfast rather than grab a cab. First, it was only a block or so, as she remembered it. But more importantly, she wanted the time to breathe the mountain air – and hoped Mother Nature was close and could see her resolve.

Girl walked by a tree, glanced up – and saw a chipmunk. Instead of scurrying away, frightened by the human, it sat on the branch and looked back at her. She smiled at it, and it started to move forward, tentatively. Then, a pedestrian passed, going the other way, and it turned and fled. She fancied that it had been coming to greet her – but perhaps she was imagining things.

She checked in quickly at the B&B, unpacked, splashed water on her face, then sought out her host.

"Riley you say? Mmm...no, I can't say that it rings a bell. Who is he? Does he have a first name?"

Girl, swallowed, "It's not important. Just a guy I met last year I'm trying to find. I think he lives somewhere nearby."

The woman smiled at her. "Well then, I hope you find him." She thought for a moment. "If...wait, you say he lives in the mountains?"

Girl shook her head, "No, I don't think so. He just spends a lot of time there."

The woman nodded thoughtfully, "Well...he would have to buy supplies, and the logical place to do that would be the IGA."

Girl looked blank.

The woman smiled, "It's the local supermarket, dear. Everyone goes there sooner or later. If anyone has seen your friend, it's likely to be one of the staff."

Girl thanked her, got directions, and set out for the IGA.

Eventually, she asked almost everyone she could think of in the IGA, as well as some of the local equipment shops, the hardware stores, and, eventually, the car mechanics. She became quite adept at describing this person she had seen for such a short time until difficult conditions and his vintage, rust-brown truck – all to no avail.

Her feet hurt. She was definitely hungry and more than somewhat discouraged. Recognizing the symptoms of low blood sugar, she pushed open the door of a diner on one of the side streets and plopped herself down in a leather-covered booth.

Almost immediately, an older waitress came over with a menu. "Good afternoon, honey. Would you like some water while you decide what you want?"

Girl smiled up at her, "Actually, I think I know what I want."

"All right, then, what can I getcha?"

Girl ordered a bacon, lettuce, and tomato sandwich with plenty of mayonnaise. She flipped open the menu, then asked for a side Caesar salad and a vanilla milkshake. The waitress nodded, wrote on her pad, then moved away, eventually returning with the vanilla shake and a plate with Girl's food.

Placing them carefully on the table, the waitress looked at Girl. "So, what brings you to Banff, honey? You a hiker, a white water rafter, or just love the mountains?" the woman asked.

Girl blinked, "Well, I'm hoping to go hiking for a bit, but first, I want to find someone I met last year who can show me a special spot I visited. He lives somewhere around here, but no one seems to know him."

The waitress, whose name tag said "Susie," cocked an eyebrow. "What's his name?"

Girl looked at her and shrugged. "All I know is that he's called Riley."

"An old coot with a rusted-out Chevy pick-up?"

Girl sat up suddenly, "Yes! Do you know him?"

Susie smiled, "We went to high school together – although he never finished." She chuckled, "I guess that makes me an old coot, too, eh? Yeah, I know him."

"Do you know how I can contact him? A cellphone number perhaps?"

Susie actually laughed. "Riley? With a cellphone? It would probably blow up in his hand, he's so clumsy with anything new. Nah, nobody has a cellphone number for Riley, but he's probably down at the Legion, drinking beer and swapping lies with the other old coots."

Girl looked blank. "What's the Legion? And where is it? And when might he be there?"

Susie looked amused. "Well, the Legion is *supposed* to be a support group for Canadian military veterans, and do good works in the community. And to give them their due, they do that. But they're probably best known as a social club – mostly for old-timers like Riley. The Hall is down by the bridge on Banff Avenue.

"As for when Riley will be there – that may depend on whether he's in funds or not, but this'd be about the right time of day, after lunch."

Girl started to jump up, but Susie made a sitting motion with her hands.

"Whoa! Slow down there. Eat your lunch, dear. If Riley *is* there, he'll be there all afternoon, and if he's not – well, try again another day.

Nobody really knows where he lives – and, like I say, he hasn't got a phone. He's strange, that one. Always has been. Claims he talks to animals and such."

Susie chuckled and moved away, adjusting the pencil behind her ear.

Girl exhaled noisily, then settled back and began to eat.

At least she now knew that Riley existed. And he talked to animals.

She found the Legion Hall without difficulty and walked in, looking around. An older gentleman looked up, then walked over and said, "Can I help you, ma'am?"

Girl looked hard at him, but he wasn't Riley. At least as best she could remember. "I'm looking for a guy named Riley. Susie, down at the diner, told me I might find him here."

The guy straightened up? "Riley? Really? Why would anyone... Well, never mind. None o' my business, I guess." He turned to the hall and shouted, "Hey Riley! There's a good lookin' woman here to see ya! I guess hell is gonna freeze over after all!" He looked at Girl and winked.

Meanwhile, a man who looked as if he'd be left out in the sun too long, looked over at them and frowned, confusion on his face, then stood up and slowly ambled over, hands stuffed in the pockets of his jeans. He ducked his head, "Ma'am? What kin I do fer ya?"

Girl glanced at the first man, who raised his eyebrows, then said, "I'll leave you two kids alone, shall I?" and moved off, chuckling.

Girl looked back at Riley, then dropped her voice. "Riley – it's me. The woman you drove into town in the snowstorm last September. The one Bear asked you to drive here?"

Riley straightened up. "Oh...yeah. I reckon. What 'er ya doing back here? I thought y'ud gone." He looked around, trying to be surreptitious and being anything but managing to look guilty instead.

Girl stared at him, then said, "Could we talk? Outside, perhaps?"

It was Riley's turn to stare, then wiped his face, nodded, and the two of them pushed through the door into the bright sunshine. Girl felt eyes on their backs as they left.

Riley led them off to the left, onto a trail by the river, walked away and then stopped. "That was one wild drive, ma'am. I don' think I'd do that 'gain, if'n I had a choice."

I nodded, "I remember. How is Bear, Riley? Is he okay?"

Riley stood there, looking uncomfortable. "I don' rightly know ma'am. Hain't seen him since then."

Girl stared at him, feeling as if a shock ran through her body, then relaxed. "Of course. The road's closed until tomorrow, isn't it?"

Riley nodded slowly. "Well, yes 'n no. There hain't no services so if'n ya get in trouble, yer shit outta – s'cuse me, ma'am – yer outta luck. I go up there ever oncet in a while. Got some business dere, y'know."

He shifted uncomfortably. "I had 'spected to see him couple, three times, but – nothin'."

Now Girl was concerned, and shook her head. "Would you drive me to where you picked me up? I can pay you for your time."

Riley looked at her and scratched his head. "Um, well, didja want me to wait there fer ya? I'm kinda busy, y'know."

Girl suspected that Riley was anything but busy and wondered if he resented her relationship with Bear. Bear had said something like that. But she couldn't think of another way to find Bear other than through Riley.

"Tell you what, Riley. You take me there and wait for a couple of hours. If I'm not back by then, you can take off. Okay?"

Riley rubbed his hands up and down on his pants. Girl could see he wanted to say no, but couldn't quite bring himself to do so.

"Riley – I know Bear relies on you. He told me so several times when I visited with him. You know, he saved my life, just as he did yours. Please, Riley. It means a lot to me, and I know it will mean a lot to Bear as well."

Riley stared at Girl, then dropped his head. Finally, he said, "Okay, I reckon. When didja wanna go?"

Girl looked at the sky to gauge the time. "It's a bit late today. How about tomorrow morning? Would that work for you?"

Riley stood silent for a while.

"I could pay you $250 for the ride and your time, Riley. Would that be enough?"

He looked up at Girl, rubbed his face with his hand again, then nodded. "Yup. That'd be good. Thank ya ma'am." He stuck his hand out. I took it – it felt dry and hard, as if it, too, had been left out in the sun too long.

They shook once, then let go.

"'Ere ya staying at da Bear Den B&B agin, ma'am?"

Girl nodded.

"Okay. I pick ya up dere tomorrah at ten, right?"

Girl nodded again. "Thank you, Riley. That'll be great."

He ducked his head, turned, and hurried back to the Legion Hall.

Girl hoped he would be there tomorrow.

He was. In fact, he was waiting in his rusted old Chevy pick-up, motor idling, when Girl stepped out of the B&B with her backpack, hat, and water bottle.

He sat in the driver's seat and waited for her to wrestle the door open, then climb up into the truck's cab and lug her backpack up beside her. She groped around for the ends of the lap belt, finally found them buried in the seat, and, with trouble, fastened the ends together. Riley took off, engine spluttering.

The day was fine; the air was warm, and Girl was exhilarated that she was finally going to see Bear.

She hoped.

They drove in silence, Girl listening to the sound of the engine and drinking in the glorious sights of the mountains. The first time she had driven this way, she was barely conscious of them. She had been running away from the troll, and looking for someplace to hide. Now, she could appreciate the view and the sweet freshness of the air – even if she was nervous. She felt her heart beating in her chest.

Eventually, they arrived at the turnout. It didn't look familiar. In fact, nothing about the trip looked familiar, partly because all she had seen was snow when they had driven down to Banff more than eight months earlier. Now the flowers were in bloom, the air was gentle, and it looked like a picture postcard of a tranquil mountain scene.

Girl glanced surreptitiously at Riley, wondering if he had, in fact, brought her to the right turnout. She felt the tension in her fingers where they grasped the handhold on the side of the door, so took a deep breath and consciously relaxed. She had no option but to trust Riley at this point.

"We here, ma'am," was all Riley said, turning off the engine. "I'll wait fer two hours, like we said, right?"

She nodded, smiled at him briefly, then gathered up her backpack, pushed open the door, and clambered down from the cab with her backpack. She stood looking at him for a moment. He was staring straight ahead, with one arm on the sill of the driver's side window. Sighing, she slammed the door closed, shouldered her pack and turned towards the trail.

At first, she wondered if this was the right trail. It didn't look right. Or rather, nothing about it seemed familiar. But as she went, she started to see things that might have looked familiar – she wasn't sure, but sure enough that she kept going.

Then the trail branched. One way looked well-trodden. The other was much fainter. Pausing only briefly, she took the second trail, pushing her way through the brush to follow it.

She still wasn't sure, but it *felt* right.

And then she came to an overhang – and recognized one of the lookouts that she and Bear had sometimes visited. Her heart started beating faster. This was right! She was getting close!

She stopped to take a drink from her water bottle, removed her hat, and wiped sweat off her forehead. Looking up, she saw some kind of large bird circling on the thermals – and wondered if it might be *Skrreee!*, Bear's red-tailed hawk friend. She had no way of telling. It was too far away. But she decided it was and took it as a good sign. She waved to the hawk, hoping it was Bear's friend.

Gripping the straps of her pack, she set off again, excitement beating in her chest. She kept going for what seemed like a long time, allowing her intuition to guide her – and consistently being rewarded with sights of things she and Bear had seen or places they'd gone.

Finally, she saw a break in the woods, and what looked like the meadow. She started to run, an enormous smile on her face. "BEAR!" she cried.

She accelerated into the meadow, bursting through the vegetation, panting both from running and her eagerness to see Bear.

Then skidded to a stop.

The meadow was empty. The cabin was gone. It looked as if nothing man-made had ever been there.

Chapter 46: Always

Girl stood gawking, then turned and looked at the mountains opposite – and recognized the view they had spent so many hours sharing from the cabin's porch. She was *sure* this was the right place. She turned back towards where the cabin should have been – and was jarred again to see nothing, just open space.

She slumped down, legs crossed, and let her backpack slip to the ground. "Oh, Bear!" was all she said, crying.

Was it possible it was all a dream – or a delusion?

NO! She couldn't believe that. She *wouldn't* believe it.

She collapsed on the ground and started sobbing into her arms. All of her hopes, all her expectations – everything she had done, and all of her plans, suddenly seemed like sand, collapsing around her. She was lost, alone, and hurting once again.

She was so absorbed in sobbing that it took a moment until she realized that something was tugging at her hair.

Remembering what Bear had told her about the dangers of the woods, she sat up with a gasp.

And there, sitting smugly in front of her was Henry, the Arctic fox, Bear's trickster friend.

"Henry!" she cried and lunged forward to hug him.

He neatly stepped back, shaking his head, still looking smug.

"Henry?" she sat up, then thought "Where's Bear?"

Henry stood up, turned as if to walk away – then looked back at her over his shoulder, one paw up and waiting.

Girl scrambled up and followed as Henry kept moving forward, always just out of reach – and always moving just a little faster than she was.

After a moment, she realized that Henry was leading her in the direction where she felt the cabin should have been. *Was it possible?* she wondered and hurried after him.

Finally, Henry stopped, turned towards her, and sat down.

"Henry? Where's Bear? Why have you stopped?"

Henry looked behind him, then back at Girl, expectantly.

Girl stood still for a moment, then walked slowly forward, one pace at a time – until her foot struck something – and the cabin gradually appeared, like a fog rolling back. It was real, after all!

Girl quickly ran up the steps to the porch, burst through the door, calling, "Bear! *BEAR!* I'm *HOME!*"

And stopped. The cabin was empty.

It seemed cold and abandoned. She slowly walked over to the fireplace, knelt down, and realized that there had been no fire there for some time.

Where was Bear?

Girl walked back out onto the porch, hoping against hope to see Bear sitting in his usual spot at the end of the porch. Instead, she found Henry sitting on her rocking chair.

Henry nimbly hopped off, then waited expectantly.

Not quite knowing what to do, Girl gingerly lowered herself down onto the chair. Her first thought was to go out looking for Bear, but she remembered that he had specifically told her not to go off into the woods without him as it was dangerous. Plus, Henry was sitting, looking at her, as if wanting to be satisfied that she was going to stay put.

Girl dropped her pack on the porch next to the chair, then sat back, as she had often done during her time here. Almost unbidden, she started rocking, closing her eyes.

She thought of all she had been through. Of the dangers, she had braved to escape the troll. Of how he had caught her and threatened to maim her and make her crawl for the rest of her life. Of how she had escaped again by jumping from the moving truck – and how Bear had saved her.

Which triggered all the memories of the happy times she had spent with Bear. She found tears leaking from her closed eyes. It was almost as if she could hear him...

"GIRL!"

She opened her eyes – and there he was, bounding across the meadow towards her.

"BEAR!"

She leapt down from the porch and ran towards him. Bear slid onto his haunches and opened his arms, and Girl thudded into him, burying her head in his fur as his forepaws closed softly around her. "Oh, BEAR!" was all she managed to say before she started sobbing.

He rocked her gently for what seemed like a long time.

Finally, she pushed back slightly and wiped her eyes on her palms.

"Where were you? I was worried that I had imagined you!" Laugh-crying, she wiped her eyes again, sniffed hard, wiped her nose on her palm, then wiped her palm on her jeans. "Oh, Bear! I...I just can't tell you how much I missed you!"

"And I can't tell you how very, very much I missed you, Girl."

They hugged again, then Bear picked her up and transferred her to his back, ambling towards the cabin, loping up the steps to the porch. Girl jumped nimbly down and plopped herself across the rocking chair.

"So tell me..." Girl started.

"I want to know..." Bear began.

They both laughed. "You first, Bear. Where were you? And why does the cabin feel like you haven't been here?"

Bear just looked at her. "Same, impatient Girl." He chuckled. "Okay, well...

"First, the cabin feels empty because I've been away. I was visiting my human friends."

"Bear! You have *human* friends? People you can talk to? How? Where? Tell me everything! That's wonderful!"

Bear smiled, "Do you remember when you were sick, and I had to find someone to help heal you?"

Girl thought, "Yeah, I think so. That guy came in, very confused and gave me something, um, I dunno, bitter to drink. It actually started to make me feel better right away. Was that him?"

"Hold your horses, Girl. Yes, that was him. He's a member of a local group of First Nations people. They call themselves ..." and Bear made a sound Girl couldn't quite follow, "... which means 'the human beings,' or 'the people.' Remember how he asked if I would come and talk to their Wise Woman at the full moon?"

"I...did he? I'm not sure I remember that part, to be honest."

"Well, he did. I agreed, but only on the condition that no one ever talked about it outside of their group. He agreed.

"Near the next full moon, I went out after you had gone to sleep. He met me outside their settlement and walked me toward their fire circle. I waited outside, away from the circle of light, and Sam – that's the European name he uses – brought the Wise Woman, whose name was Mary – same deal – to meet me, then Sam went back to the fire, leaving us alone.

"The two of us talked for a long time. She wasn't at all surprised that I could talk, and she wasn't surprised that I knew Mother Nature – although she didn't use that name. But she knew who I meant.

"You see, their people never gave up their connection to Mother Nature, but Mary had never known anyone who had actually met Her. I told Mary I hadn't spoken to Her very often and declined to tell her how I became Bear – that came later – but that didn't matter.

"What did matter is that my very existence, and the fact that I had actually met Mother Nature, was complete confirmation of the tribal wisdom that had been handed down from generation to generation. She couldn't stop smiling at me and kept patting my fur, as if to check that I was real.

"She said she wanted to introduce me to the rest of her people – but later. She had concerns about a few of the young men. She was suspicious that they might do the very things that have always worried me about contact with humans – that they might try to trap me and sell me for money. She needed to think about how to manage this.

"When we had chatted for a long time, she sat there, looking at me, eyes shining. At the end, she bowed low, stood up, and hugged me.

"'Thank you, Spirit Bear. Thank you for being you – and for being *here!* You have made an old woman very happy.'

"And that was how it began, Girl. I went to meet her and a select group of their people about once a month, at the full moon. Sometimes, one or two of them come here to visit – but only very occasionally. In turn, they are people I can talk to and provide me with anything human I might want. I've tried to give them something in return, but Mary absolutely refuses to accept anything from me. 'Your presence is enough. It is our honor to help you, as you have helped us, Spirit Bear.'"

Bear looked sheepish. "That's, uh, what they call me – 'Spirit Bear.' Has a nice ring to it, doesn't it?"

Holding her face solemn, Girl stood up and bowed low, "Yes, O Great Spirit Bear, Thou Wise and Holy One!"

Bear stuck his tongue out at her.

Girl giggled, and settled back into her rocking chair again. "Oh, Bear! I am so pleased you're not lonely! I was *worried* about you." She went quiet. "I guess that means you don't really need me anymore, though, doesn't it?"

Bear stared at her, then got up, padded over and placed his muzzle on her lap. Looking up at her, he waggled his eyebrows – and she burst out laughing. "Oh BEAR! I do love you," and leaned down and hugged and kissed him.

"Me, too," said Bear.

After a long and heartfelt hug, during which Girl's eyes started leaking again, Bear got up and moved back to his favorite spot on the end of the porch. "Now, tell me all about you, Girl."

So Girl told him everything that had happened to her since that wild night when she had left so hurriedly in the snowstorm.

"I was cross with you for a long time after that, Bear." She sighed. "I think I blamed you – even though, in my heart, I knew you didn't want it that way. I keep thinking that you can do anything. You truly are magical, Bear."

Bear started chuckling. At first, Girl was confused, then she started to get annoyed. "What? *WHAT?* Why are you chuckling, you nasty Bear, you!"

Bear stopped. "Remember when you first got here and asked how it was that I was a talking Bear?"

Girl looked puzzled for a while, then nodded...and stopped. "Wait! You told me it was magic. And I didn't believe you!" She threw back her head and laughed. "I'm such an idiot! Of *course* it's magic."

She looked fondly at Bear. "And of course you are magic. My magical friend."

She got up, walked over, and hugged Bear.

They talked all through the evening. Bear was concerned that he didn't have anything suitable for her to eat – but Girl had thought of that. In her backpack, she had some better quality freeze-dried beef stew. "It tastes like shit, but at least it's *good* shit," she commented as she made it, chuckling.

Finally, they wound up on the rag rug, Girl lying up against Bear's side, both of them gazing into the fire.

Peaceful.

Content.

Happy in each other's company.

"Bear?"

"Yes, Girl."

"I love you, Bear."

"I love you, too, Girl. Always."

THE END

Afterword

Bear was there to help Girl. If you are being abused and need someone to help, or even just to listen, help is available through the links below.

And if you know someone who you believe is being abused and want to know what to do, the same groups can help.

It can be hard and scary for someone being abused to reach out, so it's important that you let them tell you what they need, and most of all, that you *listen to what they say*. Do not pressure them, but support whatever decisions they make. Changing your life is never easy, particularly when you are under threat of violence or any kind of abuse.

In the United States, contact: thehotline.org
In Canada: sheltersafe.ca
In Great Britain: nationaldahelpline.org.uk
In Australia: 1800respect.org.au
Anywhere else: hotpeachpages.net

Or do an online search for:
"How to escape an abusive relationship."
or
"What to do if someone you know is being abused."

There are many organizations that can help, but these will help you start.

Stay strong and be safe. You are not alone.

Made in United States
Orlando, FL
18 October 2024

52811902R00171